FORGOTTEN REALMS®

the Glass Prison

Monte Cook

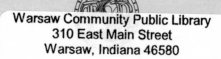

U.S., CANADA,	EUROPEAN HEADQUARTERS
ASIA, PACIFIC, & LATIN AMERICA	Wizards of the Coast, Belgium
Wizards of the Coast, Inc.	P.B. 2031
P.O. Box 707	2600 Berchem
Renton, WA 98057-0707	Belgium
+1-800-324-6496	+32-70-233277

Visit our web site at **www.tsr.com**

Vheod's vision swirled around him. He closed his eyes tightly, hoping to steady himself. When he opened them again, Melann was kneeling over him.

"Vheod, get up," she begged, her voice thin and panicked. "He'll kill us all!"

She was attempting to lift him from the ground by his shoulders, and he allowed her to help him stumble to his feet. The demon's black gaze fell on them both.

"Now, young mortalheart," Chare'en said in a voice like polished obsidian, "I swear by the Abyss that gave birth to us both, you will *die*!"

Coming in 1999

The Dream Spheres
Elaine Cunningham
May

Baldur's Gate
Philip Athans
July

Silverfall:
Stories of the Seven Sisters
Ed Greenwood
August

The Spine of the World
R.A. Salvatore
September

Beyond the High Road
Troy Denning
December

For Sue

Prologue

Run. The mournful baying of the demonic hounds rolled across the landscape from behind Vheod. He couldn't be sure exactly how far behind him they were or when they might catch up to him. All he could do was run. The thorns of the gnarled brier that covered the plain tore at his flesh as he ran, but he did what he could to ignore the pain. The malevolent brier hungrily absorbed Vheod's blood, not allowing a single drop to touch the ground. He didn't worry about the wounds; Vheod was grateful no trail of blood would betray his passage. The thorns drank it all in.

Vheod Runechild's body ached from hours of desperate flight, much of which took him through the Fields of Night Unseen, a meadow filled with vampiric thorns. His limbs grew more and more resistant to each step. Cold sweat ran down his back and clung to his neck. Vheod longed to draw his sword and hack his way through the brier, but he feared leaving an obvious path that his pursuers could trace.

Take the intelligent approach, he kept telling himself. Vheod knew the challenge was to not allow his fear and exhaustion to overwhelm his thoughts. He had to keep a cool head and ignore the deadly forces that marshaled against him. Startling images of the terrible, hungry mouths of the vorrs that chased him came unbidden into his mind. He gritted his teeth and narrowed his eyes, forcing himself onward.

The Taint formed a new, beckoning shape on his arm. The crimson, tattoo-like mark flowed across his flesh like a thing alive. Its changing shape resembled a hand slowly urging him forward. He ignored it.

The field of black thorns flowed over hill after hill. Nowhere offered Vheod relief from their constant clawing at his legs as he ran, the vorrs close behind him. The sky above him bore a reddish-brown hue that recalled either rust or dried blood. Not even the whisper of a breeze came to alleviate the dry, parched heat. The thorns required blood, not water to live. The skies of the nether planes were selfish with their gifts, and usually bestowed moisture only in the form of dangerous storms. Vheod, however, would welcome a storm at this point—it might aid in his escape. Knowing that wishing for help from the environment in this plane of darkness and evil would avail nothing, Vheod pushed himself to keep running.

If I stop, he thought, Nethess's hunters will find me and will offer no mercy.

The rush of air as he fled pulled at his long, brick-red hair. It fluttered along with the tattered, violet cloak that whipped behind him like an extra, frantically flailing limb. It caught on thorns and slowed him, probably even left behind bits for his pursuers to find. Reaching behind him he gathered as much of it as he could and wrapped its length around his arm so it would no longer tangle in the twisted, pointed brier. He wished, too, that he could shed his black steel breastplate. Vheod would do anything for speed now.

For a time the only sounds Vheod could hear were his own labored breaths, the soft footfalls his boots made on the ground, and the tearing of his flesh by the thorns. The vorrs howled again, their baying louder than before. His fear granted speed to his feet, and he ran on faster and faster. He veered to the left, then to the right.

The hounds bayed again, louder still, and from right behind him. Had they caught his scent? He could hear the blood-lusting—no, soul-lusting—glee in their cries. He thought he counted three, if not four, of them from their sounds. He had to think of a plan and quickly.

Let them come to you, he told himself. Fight on your terms, not theirs.

The terrain here rose and fell in rough, jagged little hills amid the thorns. It occurred to Vheod that perhaps he could use that fact to his advantage. Again he veered to one direction, then another, but his mind focused instead on a plan—and on picking his moment carefully.

Leaping into a narrow gully that probably once guided a small brook, Vheod drew his sword and spun even as he struggled to keep his footing. The ravine was deeper than he realized. His foot slipped under him, but somehow he managed to stay standing, though his body twisted around awkwardly. The first hound leaped over the gully, thinking Vheod had done the same. As it flew over the gully, Vheod sprang upward with his blade. It was barely within his reach, and the lunge sent Vheod tumbling off-balance, yet he felt the tip of his sword strike something as he slipped. The yelp from the creature was shrill, its gut torn open. The blow sent it spinning around in midair. The vorr landed to Vheod's side, not to rise again.

The next vorr dived down into the ravine, the bristling, brownish-black hair on its back as rigid as daggers. Vheod pulled himself to his feet and lashed at it with his sword, but the blade cut through only empty air. Abyssal magic had granted these creatures incredible speed. The vorr lunged. Its bite almost caught a bit of Vheod's leg in its jagged, frothing jaws. Vheod's second blow split the gaunt, ragged head of the beast in two.

He turned. The glaring, hungry eyes of the third vorr focused on him and narrowed. Thin legs spread wide, as it thrust its head at him. Savage jaws snapped at him again and again. Vheod pushed the hungry beast back with desperate parries and thrusts.

As he fought to hold the beast back, his ears caught the sounds of a fourth hound on its way. Vheod knew he was in trouble. He had to try something different—and quickly. He reached inward. There were black portions of Vheod's soul that he only rarely allowed himself to see, but now he would try anything. He didn't close his eyes but instead simply looked within rather than without. His body raging with heat and sweat, at the center of the darkness within him he found his own cold, icy heart. It was an empty and motionless place, but he found what he was looking for. In a few short instants, Vheod called on the power innately entwined about the inhuman portion of his soul. Born half tanar'ri, magic flowed within his veins as surely as blood. It came eagerly when he called to it—perhaps too eagerly.

A tingle of chill fingers ran across his skin as he filled himself with the unleashed power. It felt as though the cold would eat away at his skin from the inside, and his muscles all tensed at once. Tapping into that Abyssal energy, he forced the ground away from himself. He pushed down with all his inner might. Beads of sweat ran down his temples and even into his eyes, but he kept them open. Even in the short time it took to call on the power, he was terrified to take his eyes off the demonic hound.

As he concentrated, Vheod rose into the air, levitating out of the reach of the attacking vorr. As he did, the last of the tracking hounds reached the top of the ravine right at his level. Watching its prey float up into the air past it, the beast stood wide-eyed long enough for the swing of Vheod's blade to slash across its face. A second blow brought the creature's life to an end. Vheod looked down at the vorr still in the ravine as it snarled up at him. If the beast had been capable of speech, Vheod knew that snarl would be a curse. Muscles aching, he realized he would have to end this battle soon. The long chase had weakened him too much for a protracted fight.

The beast's hateful gaze unnerved him, and Vheod couldn't stay aloft forever. Rather than wait any longer, he released his grip on the power that held him aloft and let himself drop. As he fell, he pointed his sword down. Blade-first, he crashed into the horrid hound. Vheod's own grunt on impact was drowned out by the vorr's shrill bellow.

As Vheod tried to untangle himself from the beast and get to his feet, his hair covered his face. Seeing nothing, he heard only snarls and whines. By the time he stood, the snarling had stopped. Vheod pushed his hair away from his eyes. His sword remained thrust into the vorr, pinning the now still creature to the ground.

Vheod knew that more would come. He stood for a moment over the bodies of the creatures he'd slain, hoping to catch his breath. Syrupy slime and blood covered his tattered clothes and armor. Panting out tired breaths, his body's aches seemed to beg him to sit or lay—even amid the pricking thorns. He had to push himself onward, however. He couldn't allow himself to think of anything but his goal. He had to escape the Abyss.

Escape presented a great challenge, however, for entrances and exits, often called portals, were hidden and usually guarded. Once the Abyss held something in its fetid grasp, it let go only reluctantly. Vheod had always been within that grasp—he'd lived here his entire life. As horrible as this malevolent plane was, he had little knowledge of anywhere else. A childhood in the deepest, foulest realms of the Abyss had taught him little except how to survive. A half-breed human-tanar'ri could only live among the fiends and horrors spawned in this darkest of otherworldly pits if he could protect himself. The fact that he'd somehow survived against such horrors had to count for something—at least he hoped that to be true. In the Abyss, his fiendish masters and peers had called him a *cambion*—a word that accentuated his half-mortal existence and carried with it all the abuse, oppression, and injustice that had been heaped on him.

While the thorns hungrily absorbed the dead vorrs' spilled blood, Vheod pulled his sword free and set it on the ground. He drew himself up straight and took a deep breath. Gesturing toward the trail he'd left behind him as he ran through the brier, Vheod spoke sorcerous words long ago memorized from an ancient book. He closed his eyes and held forth his battle-scarred hands. Magical power stretched from his fingertips to the thorns trampled in the battle and in his flight. The crushed plants slowly stood upright once again. The savage flora would consume the blood of his foes here, but the scene of battle would still present obvious clues to anyone coming this way. Vheod hoped the spell would keep the thorns from betraying his path from here.

Once he finished with the spell, Vheod picked up his sword and cleaned the blood from it with the end of his cloak. He slowly slid it back into its sheath and slipped away from the scene of the battle with careful, deliberate steps, once again plunging across the violent landscape.

Dark clouds began to obstruct the bloody sky. He wondered if they were actually the visible aspects of spells cast by Nethess to find him. He could almost see the venom of her inhuman eyes glaring down at him through the threatening black clouds. How long could he avoid her reach?

Vheod saw the Taint had moved to the back of his hand from where it had been on his forearm. The indistinct, fluid shape of the mark contrasted with the sharpness of its color, as red and piercing as a babau's eyes.

"What does that mean?" he whispered in frustration at the tattoo as he loped along as fast as his tired legs could carry him. Vheod had never really known what the Taint was, but it had always seemed like some sort of intelligence. It often guided him, though he was never sure to what, or if he interpreted it correctly. All his life, Vheod could find no answers as to its meaning, least of all from the Taint itself.

This time, however, as if in answer to his rhetorical query, the reddish mark twisted and moved like flowing water across his arm, lengthening into a narrow, pointed tower. Or is it an arrow? Vheod thought, shaking his head in confusion.

"Are you trying to tell me something?" he whispered again, his gaze never leaving the mark on his arm. Vheod glanced around, looking for more signs of pursuit. He knew he should be more quiet. He thrust his arm in the direction the narrowest end of the

Taint indicated. When Vheod moved his arm, the pointed scar shifted as he did so that it always oriented in the same direction.

"Yes, you are," Vheod said.

Unknown hours passed since he'd started running, and each time he considered slowing down visions of more vorrs or even worse creatures pushed him onward. Finally, heavy limbs dragged Vheod almost to a halt. No sign of pursuit revealed itself.

As the sky above him continued to darken, taking on the mottled brownish green of a festering sore, a dark tower rose above the uneven horizon and the bloodthirsty brier. At first, all he could do was stare at the distant structure, his mouth slightly open. With his goal finally in sight, he could ignore the fatigue in his body, the sweat coating his flesh, and the stink of the dead vorrs that clung to him like a nagging conscience.

The tower was surrounded by a gray stone wall. Iron supports spaced along the wall spread eons-old rust across the stonework, and Vheod wondered where the moisture to form rust could have come from in this parched wasteland.

Stopping in front of the closed gate, Vheod took a moment to examine the entire place. It was just as he'd heard it described. The thorny plants didn't reach the wall, stopping a few feet away as though even they were wary of the place.

Vheod closed his eyes and breathed a sigh. Opening them again, he knelt to examine his wounds. The thorns had torn numerous and sometimes wide, gaping wounds in the flesh of his lower legs. He'd assumed up until this moment that the pain he felt in his legs came only from his hours of running. Now he realized that a good deal of the fiery torment came from the terrible wounds rent by the thorns. Using the spikes on his breastplate, he tore his cloak into two pieces and wrapped the cloth around his bloody shins and calves. When he finished he stood, stepping closer to the gate. His fist banged against it with what remained of his strength.

The air had grown noticeably colder over the last hour, and the sky continued to grow even darker. Soon it would be so dark that only true natives of the Abyss could see at all—and Vheod knew there were things dwelling in the darkness of the fields behind him that could see much farther in the dark than he could. Vheod pounded on the gate again, harder this time. No sound came from beyond the wall. He pressed on the gate, and it opened with a groan of metal. The walled courtyard around the tower's base lay barren of thorns or any other living thing. The tower itself appeared to have no means of entry.

"Is there anyone here?" Vheod shouted.

Silence.

Vheod stepped through the gateway. A wooden sign with crude lettering hung from a hook on the side of the tower just above eye-level. Written in the tongue of the Lower Planes, the words *"Karreth Edittorn"* were scrawled across it, a name he knew meant "Destiny's Last Hope," in the language of the tower's creators. Vheod had read of the tower once long ago in an otherwise forgotten book, but more recently he'd paid a rutterkin most of his remaining gold and an enchanted cloak for the exact details of the tower's location. He already missed the cloak, and when he looked down at himself he thought again of the Taint. It seemed to have guided him here. Perhaps he'd not needed to pay the rutterkin at all.

As he looked again at the bailey formed by the wall, he noted with suspicion that no one had come to greet him—or fend him off. None of the information he'd gathered said anything about Karreth Edittorn being abandoned.

"Who are you?"

Vheod spun to see who had spoken, but the bailey was still empty. A rustling sound disturbed the air above his head. There three winged creatures hovered like insects. Their flesh was weathered and black, and their small white eyes glistened like pearls. Wings of stretched skin pulled taut over long, spindly bones silently beat with enough power to allow them to float otherwise motionlessly above him.

"Who are you?" one asked again.

"Vheod," he answered, "from the city of Broken Reach."

"And why have you come here, cambion?"

Vheod knew these creatures were varrangoin, the masters of Karreth Edittorn. Sometimes burdened with the misnomer of "Abyssal bats," varrangoin were neither stupid animals nor blind. Instead, these fleshy-winged creatures were powerful and intelligent foes feared even by some of the tanar'ri. It was their role as adversaries that Vheod planned to use to his advantage.

"I've come here to use the portal," he told them.

"And why is that, half-tanar'ri?" the batlike creature asked with a cruel sneer.

"I have angered the marilith Nethess and now seek to avoid her vengeance," he told the varrangoin. Quickly he added, "So that I may do so again." It was a lie, but perhaps it might help him endear himself to these creatures if they thought he was an enemy of their enemy.

The three of them stared down with hard, indecipherable eyes.

"Nethess serves hated Graz'zt," one of them—a different one—finally said. "We would like to see his viper tree orchards uproot themselves to tear his palace down. We would like to see dread Graz'zt and all his minions die slow and painful deaths."

"Then may I use the portal?" Vheod asked. His eyes widened as he stared at the batlike creature.

"We hate your kind, tanar'ri. Why should we help you?"

"Can't you see that if you do, I'll live on to fight against those you hate?"

The varrangoin stared long in silence. Vheod hoped they would buy his bluff.

"Yes," one of them said finally, "we can see that if you live, other tanar'ri will be harmed. If you can reach the portal, you may use it. It should function for you—if Nethess seeks your blood, it is truly your *Last Hope*."

"Where does it lead? Will it take me somewhere safe?"

"Addle-cove! Don't you pay attention? It takes you where it wishes, not where you wish." The creature glared at him then beat its monstrous wings with a powerful motion, swooping even higher, followed immediately by the other two. "It takes you to your *destiny*."

As the varrangoin flew up they pointed to a shimmering hole suddenly forming near the top of the tower that hadn't been there before. A small ledge jutted out underneath it. The window-like hole opened into the side of the structure, as though it might look out from the tower's uppermost room. If that was the portal, how did they expect him to reach it? Vheod circled the tower, but as he suspected, he found no other new means of entry, nor anything resembling stairs or even a ladder. He looked up into

the air above the tower, but the dark sky held only
ever darker clouds.

He was too spent to even think of calling on
tanar'ri power again to lift him to the door. As hard
as it might be to assail the stone wall, it would be
harder to reach into himself for that cold energy, yet
Vheod knew he needed to get to the door right away.

He was still being hunted. He had no time to wait.
Though his tired, bloody legs screamed even as he
considered it, he reached toward the stone wall of the
tower. The old and uneven masonry offered many
easy hand holds on which he pulled himself up. His
feet rested on crumbling stones that threatened to
give way as his hands sought new holds even higher.
Exhaustion and fear slowed his otherwise steady
progress up the side of the tower as tired muscles
began to shake with uncertainty and his mind wandered. Vheod imagined he could hear more vorrs or
other of Nethess's servitors on their way, catching
him at this awkward and defenseless moment. He
imagined horrible vulturelike fiends tearing at him
as he clung to the stones, ripping away his armor and
finally his flesh. He saw huge, bloated demonic toads
making obscene leaps into the air to pull at his
bloody ankles, skeletal babau, with their infernal
gazes, lashing at him with hooks, pulling him down,
and all the fiends feasting on his flesh even while he
still lived.

Reaching the top after a grueling and fearful
ascent, Vheod finally pulled himself up to the ledge.
He eased his tired body down, dangling his weary
legs over the side, but with his body turned so he
could look up and into the large, round opening. It
appeared to lead into the tower, though he actually
saw only darkness. Vheod knew the doorway itself
mattered, not what he could see through it. It was

magical, and it provided a way to leave the Abyss.

The Taint throbbed on his neck. Ignoring it, Vheod reached up, his fingers finding the portal warm to his touch. He sighed and looked into the darkness, wondering where it would lead.

He looked back over the thorn-filled Fields of Night Unseen and hoped it would be the last he ever saw of the Abyss. Each layer held its own mystery and its own terrors. Mortal souls condemned for their evil actions faced torments more terrible than even he could imagine. Eventually, these victims, twisted by aeons of suffering, became tanar'ri themselves. Just such a fiend had fathered Vheod and bestowed on him a wicked, corrupted portion of his essence.

The Abyss was pain, misery, and evil deeds. It spawned from dark, depraved thoughts of murder and revenge, embodied the very essence of wanton destruction, the infliction of suffering, and the chaotic tumult of annihilation. Its layers knew only adversity, calamity, and devastation. Where another world might have rivers of cool water, the Abyss had only acids and poisons. Where another might be wrapped in a cushion of fresh air, the Abyss was home to choking clouds and flesh-eating mists. Where other worlds sported cities, the Abyss held fortresses filled with tortured souls and baleful fiends. It held no safe places and no shelter from the ravages of devastation. The Abyss was all evil, yet it was all Vheod had ever known.

He stood, steadying himself as he stood on the narrow ledge—the long drop to the ground behind him and the unknown darkness before him. A cold, dry wind lifted his long hair and tossed it into his face. Blood still ran from the wounds on his legs. Vheod smiled with bitter disdain.

"I can assume," he said aloud, "that wherever this takes me, it can't be any worse than this."

Vheod leaped through the portal, leaving the Abyss behind him.

Chapter One

"I wonder if the goddess is watching us, right at this moment," Melann said, looking around.

Whitlock's gaze followed hers, and he saw the thick, dark trees surrounding the dusty path on which he and his sister rode. Their horses' hoofbeats metered out the minutes and hours that comprised the otherwise silent days of their travels. Light from the setting sun streaked through the branches around them like streamers on a festival day, and the trees were alive with birds and small animals moving about as late afternoon fell on the Dalelands. As he rode past, Whitlock saw the swirl of leaves overhead as a cascade of water endlessly moving across a sea of green—or at least, what he imagined the sea might look like, as he'd never actually seen the sea.

"Does Chauntea, the Great Mother, watch us every day of our journey or only at certain points?" Melann continued. "Surely a goddess has better things to do in all the Dalelands—all the world—than to continually watch one simple, minor follower like me. Yet how can a mortal begin to put limitations on a goddess?"

Whitlock had heard this from his sister before. While her training taught her that Chauntea was concerned with every aspect of her priests' lives, Melann seemed to find it difficult not to question her own worth in her goddess's eyes. His sister's faith in the greatness and glory of Chauntea, mother of all growing things and the people who tended them, never faltered. Her own importance and self-worth were in question. She voiced these concerns often and aloud. Whitlock's only response was to simply shrug.

"Praise Our Mother," Melann whispered out of habit.

At the sound of his sister's voice, Whitlock turned. A smile came unbidden to his mouth, but his normal, stalwart countenance altered it into a grimace. He wished he could be more like her. The faith that she held in her god, in the completion of their quest, and seemingly in him strengthened Whitlock, even if he was unable to really express such things in words. He saw her as everything that was good in the world, which needed protection by people like him. It was his duty, and he would not shirk it. Duty, steadfastness, and obligation were his gods.

Whitlock wiped sweat from his brow, and readjusted himself in the saddle. He scanned around, always looking for danger.

When they began the trip from Archendale three days earlier, Whitlock had convinced Melann to don a leather jerkin for a modicum of protection. A brown traveling cloak covered most of the armor, but not a wooden amulet bearing Chauntea's symbol—a flower surrounded by a sunburst—displayed prominently at her chest. Melann's faith was her strength, and indeed it allowed her to perform great feats when she called on the power of her patron. That faith, however, also led her to believe that Chauntea would provide her with everything she needed. Whitlock knew that most of the time you had to take care of yourself.

The sound of his glistening chain mail lightly jingling with each step of his mount constantly reminded him of the dangers all around him and the need for protection. He noted each tree, each bend in the road, with careful consideration. Their father had taught him that the spot that appeared safest was actually the best spot for an ambush.

"The people of the Dales," his father used to say, "didn't survive so near dangers like the Zhentarim and Myth Drannor by being trusting. We go through life with our eyes open."

Now, riding into these mysterious elven woods, his sister's safety was his responsibility. Their quest weighed heavily on Whitlock's shoulders.

Melann's long dark hair, tied away from her face in a practical manner, pulled free of the bond a few strands at a time with each rhythmic bounce of the horse. They both had been told that there was a strong familial resemblance between the two of them, but of course Whitlock's hair was much shorter, and for the last few years he'd worn a short-cropped beard. Whitlock had never let himself think much of women and feminine beauty, but he imagined that other men might find his sister attractive. Usually Melann's hands and clothes were covered in fresh dirt, as she spent most of her time helping farmers with their crops or in her own garden. Perhaps if she didn't concern herself with things like that so much, Whitlock thought, she would be married.

Now only the dust of the road covered Melann's hands and clothes. The journey they had been forced into did not allow for the luxury of tending to plants, nor did it take them near too many tilled fields. Only the dust of the road soiled either of them. The two rode in silence, as they had for much of the journey.

Both held their mouths in tight expressions, and their eyes hung heavy and low. Still, Whitlock took Melann's praise to her goddess as a sign of unswerving faith and optimism.

The narrow path cut through the ancient trees in a wilderness neither really fully comprehended. Now, as darkness slowly overcame the light of day, Whitlock grew even more wary. The seriousness of the mission that drove them on made him reluctant to speak, but his silence fostered the cloud of gloom that hung over them as surely as the ancient curse they struggled against hung over their family.

The town of Essembra supposedly lay on this road, and he'd planned on their reaching it by nightfall.

"Did you hear that?" Melann asked softly.

"No," he replied. Her voice broke through Whitlock's silent reverie. He'd heard nothing. Still, caution was always prudent.

"I thought I heard a voice," Melann said, her voice still low. "As though someone called out from far away."

At that moment a deep, resonant voice came from among the trees. Both heard it this time. The man, if it was a man, spoke from what seemed a good distance off to their left. The words were clear but meaningless.

"I think that's Elvish," Melann stated, halting her horse and looking off in the direction from which the voice had come. Whitlock pulled the reins on his own mount and looked back at her.

"Come along, Melann. We've got to get to town before nightfall."

"But—" she began. She was interrupted by another deep voice calling through the trees, this time from the right side of the road. She could find no meaning in the words. Despite the distance from which they seemed to come, the voices were more like whispers than shouts.

"Melann, come along. We have no business in this wood after dark."

"But what if he's in need? His voice seems so mournful—so sad."

Whitlock sighed heavily, even forcefully. "Melann, they call this the Vale of Lost Voices for a reason. People say these woods are filled with ghosts—elven ghosts."

Instinctively, Melann spoke the Chauntean prayer of the dead, looking around the whole time. When she finished the two pressed their heels into the sides of their mounts, urging them onward to the north as the woods around them grew darker and darker with the fading sun.

Neither of them actually noticed just how much they sped their horses until they suddenly had to bring them to a stop. A single figure stood in the road. He fearlessly held his ground even in the face of the galloping horses. Neither his stance nor his expression changed as the two of them struggled to stop their mounts. Once their horses were under control, Melann and Whitlock gazed at the man before them.

Most certainly elven, his lithe form betrayed a deep-seated power. Finely crafted armor seemed to glide over his body and accentuate his features, each line in the armor playing off a similar line in his angular face and body. A sword and bow remained at his back. His eyes were as black as the night that was approaching far too quickly.

Whitlock reached for the hilt of his weapon, but the almost whispering voice of the elf stopped him cold.

Neither sibling could understand his speech, but they watched closely as he raised a graceful, muscular arm and pointed to the west, then again to the northwest. Whitlock followed the elf's long, pointing finger and looked off into the woods but saw nothing. When Whitlock looked back at the elven warrior, he was gone.

"Did you see that?" Melann whispered as though she had no breath within her at all.

"No," Whitlock lied to her and himself, grabbing the bridle of her horse and spurring it and his own to a gallop.

They hardly got more than a hundred yards down the road when a shadowy figured loomed ahead of them. Again they pulled on the reins of their mounts, bringing them to a halt in front of an elven warrior.

"What in the name of . . ." Whitlock didn't finish. Instead, wide-eyed, he stared at the figure.

It was the same warrior they had seen before.

"Wait," the figure whispered, this time in a strangely accented but understandable version of Common. He held forth a stern hand.

"Melann, get back," Whitlock warned.

She didn't heed her brother. "Who are you?" she asked.

The elf did not respond.

"My name is Melann Brandish, and this is my brother, Whitlock," she answered, motioning to her brother.

Whitlock looked at her incredulously. This was no time to hold a conversation, particularly with a ghost!

The features of the elven warrior were more clearly defined now—though Whitlock couldn't reason why. The elf carried a sword and a bow, but he kept the blade sheathed and the bow unstrung. His armor was silver, unlike any Whitlock had ever seen. The apparition's eyes were black like bottomless pits, drawing in light around him.

"Hear me," the warrior said. When he spoke, Whitlock heard voices like his coming from all around them in the woods. "We have buried our dead in these woods for a time longer than you can understand. Warriors fallen from centuries of conflict now lie here. We do not always rest quietly."

Melann shook her head slightly, her mouth agape. Whitlock reached for the reins of her mount, to pull her back. Instead, much to his surprise, she bade her horse ahead a few steps.

"Why are you here?" she asked softly.

Whitlock was stunned by her courage, or carelessness.

"An evil known to us is once again stirring."

Melann recoiled. "What evil? What do you mean?"

Whitlock reached down to where his shield hung on his saddlebag and slowly strapped it to his arm, never taking his eyes off the elven spirit.

"I cannot speak of it."

The warrior shifted his stance. Whitlock wondered if the elf was preparing for something. Perhaps, however, he was just particularly uncomfortable with what he was saying. It was difficult to tell.

"Does it have anything to do with us?" Melann asked the warrior.

"More than you know."

"Melann, we can't trust him," Whitlock whispered quickly. "We should go."

"There is arcane magic born of this wood," the warrior said to Whitlock. "The spirits of elves, ancient when humans first came to the Dales, walk here still. Dragons, elven magic, monstrous creatures, restless dead—the woods are mysterious and deadly."

Was that supposed to be a threat?

Melann ignored Whitlock, her eyes never leaving the stranger.

"We are on a quest," she told him. "Our family has an ancient curse on it, and we think we know how to lift it."

"Melann!" Whitlock spat. Her naivete might spell disaster for them. She was too damned trusting.

The warrior looked at Melann, as if expecting more. The black pits of his eyes widened, but he said nothing. The light breeze stilled, and the forest grew silent.

"The curse strikes down members of my family with no apparent pattern." Only now did Melann's gaze leave the elf, for now it dropped to the ground, and she closed her eyes. "Our . . ." her voice faltered, ". . . our mother and father lay dying in Archenbridge with a horrid disease. It's the only way we can help them."

"What is the only way?" the warrior asked with an ancient, resonant voice.

"That's no business of yours," Whitlock said, reaching slowly for his sword hilt.

"A wizard," Melann explained, "who's now long dead, cursed our family. We've learned that perhaps if we can find his magical staff, we can rid ourselves of the curse."

The warrior paused for a moment, then pointed to the west and said, "*Kirthol Erdel.*"

"What?" Whitlock asked, his hand grasping the hilt of his weapon tightly. His eyes narrowed, and he leaned forward.

Melann answered, but she did not look back at her brother. "That's an ancient elven name for the Thunder Peaks."

The horses shifted nervously, stamping on the ground. Melann and Whitlock pulled back on their reins to keep control. The warrior didn't react.

"Signs and omens show nothing but dark portents for the days ahead," the elf said. "Disturbances in the flow of magic have brought me back here to the corporeal world. Since my return, I have learned of ill tidings from Kirthol Erdel speaking of large and frequent bands of creatures you call gnolls gathering and attacking whatever they come on."

Melann seemed to drink all this information in, but Whitlock was disturbed. "Why are the gnolls gathering?" he asked, reluctant as he was to converse with a ghost.

"I do not know," came the response, "but they seem to be directed by someone."

Again the warrior seemed to shift his position. Whitlock saw his hands twitch and readied himself, but the elf didn't reach for his weapons, so Whitlock still didn't draw his own sword.

"Can't you tell us more than that?" Melann asked, her hands waving toward the warrior. "Does this have anything to do with what we're trying to do?"

The warrior pointed again, toward the east. "Chare'en."

Melann gasped. Whitlock looked at her, to see what she would say next. He hoped it would be nothing—but a part of him was now intrigued at what this long-dead elf had to say.

When Melann said nothing, he whispered again, "We should go."

She paused and drew a breath, still not looking into her brother's disapproving eyes. He did nothing to stop her, though.

"No, Whitlock," Melann said, "we won't learn anything if we don't tell anything." With a quickening pace she continued. "Perhaps Chauntea brought us here—to you—for a reason. Perhaps not. In any case, we do know of someone called Chare'en."

The warrior stared at her in silence.

"Chare'en was the ancient sorcerer who put the curse on our family."

Again, the warrior's hands seemed to twitch.

"He died long ago and was buried in a crypt hidden by an avalanche," Melann said, though it seemed as if she was talking to herself now. "At least, that's what some old family records show. The crypt holds something that can lift the curse. The curse . . . drains their strength until they haven't even the strength to . . . their hearts just stop beating." A tear ran down Melann's face, her lips quivered, but she continued. "We need to find this hidden crypt. We don't know how much longer our parents have left.

"Or how much longer we have left," she added.

The warrior stood silently watching her.

"So, are you saying," Whitlock asked, "that this old sorcerer's crypt is in the Thunder Peaks?"

The elf did not reply.

Melann turned toward Whitlock, wiping away the tear. "I think that's what he's saying. I think Chauntea sent him here to help guide us."

"Tilverton's at the northern edge of the Thunder Peaks," Whitlock told her. "We could make for there from here by staying on the main roads. Rauthauvyr's Road meets up with the Moonsea Ride north of here, then heads west."

"That doesn't seem to be very direct," Melann replied. "I'd like to get there as quickly as we can."

"I'd rather stick to the main roads—particularly while we're here in these damned—" he looked at the elven warrior—"I mean, in these woods."

Whitlock began formulating further plans but was jolted out of his thoughts as the ghostly warrior spoke again. He spoke a single word and pointed to the northwest. As the siblings watched, he faded away into the darkness that surrounded them. The ground where he stood showed no sign of him ever being there at all.

"Vheod?" Whitlock repeated and furrowed his brow. He looked to his sister. "What does that mean?"

Melann shook her head. "That doesn't sound like Elvish at all."

Chapter Two

The portal from the varrangoins' tower opened on this side in a space between the trunks of two oak trees, with their intertwined branches forming the top of the "doorway." A breeze tossed Vheod's long hair, and he shivered in the soft touch of its caress. Here on this world—wherever it was—the air was not abrasive. It didn't tear at his skin as he moved through it as it had all his life in the clutches of the Abyss. The sounds that surrounded him—calling birds, chirping insects, scurrying animals—all seemed so non-threatening. In his home, such an environment always made a wise man suspicious, but here? How could he know?

Vheod looked down at himself as he took a few steps forward. The magical trip had seemed instantaneous, and he looked none the worse for wear. At some point, while he wasn't looking, the Taint had slithered to the underside of his forearm, near his wrist. Its shape resembled a contorted face with narrow eyes and a thin, broad mouth. Tipped points on the sides might have been ears, or they might have been horns. As he examined it, the red mark shifted, the face broadening and the stiff line of the mouth bending into a smile. Vheod couldn't decide whether it was a smile of triumph or a leer of mockery.

In the dim light, trees heavy with leaves reached out in all directions as if searching for the intruder he knew himself to be. The first reaction that came to him was that he didn't belong here. The colors were too calm, the sounds too sweet, and the smells too pure for someone accustomed to the horrors of the Abyss.

Cautiously, Vheod began to explore the immediate area in which he'd arrived. Smooth grass rustled under each step, but he soon found it quite easy to move silently through the wilderness. Ahead the sounds of running, splashing water alerted him, yet drew him onward. A brook cut its way through the landscape, and Vheod, once at its side, suspiciously reached down to touch the water. It was cold, coming down from rocky highlands that rose behind him. Its touch and smell revealed no threat, so he dipped his head down to taste it, for it had been almost a day since his lips had last touched water. The water wasn't only safe and pure but delicious.

This place was as different from the Abyss as he could possibly grasp.

Vheod's imagination could never have conjured a place like this. Surely this was a paradise. What kept all creatures from all worlds from coming here and taking part in the beauty and peace that seemed to come to this place so easily? Was there some guardian he needed to be wary of?

Crouching at the river's bank, Vheod became acutely aware of a horrible smell. A few worried moments passed before he realized the evil odor came from himself. Without another thought, he waded into the cold water, then submerged his entire body. When he could hold his breath no longer he surfaced, then shed his breastplate and all his clothes. He scrubbed each piece of clothing with his palms, then tossed them to the rocks at the water's edge. Once finished, he scrubbed himself with his hands and with sand and pebbles pulled from the bottom. The idea of getting the smell and filth of the Abyss off him consumed Vheod for quite some time. He scrubbed until his body felt raw. His rumbling stomach made him aware of how much time had passed.

Climbing out of the water, he scoured his clothes and armor with the rocks at the side of the river. Finished, he put them back on while still wet.

Now, he thought, it is time to see what paradise has to offer me to eat.

Darkness consumed the forest quickly, but eyes developed in the darkness of the Lower Planes had little trouble finding prey. Vheod's sword was too big and clumsy for hunting, but spells of charming and illusion were powerful, efficient means to provide a night's dinner. By the standards of those sorcerous creatures he was forced to call kin, he was no wizard. Still, he'd learned a few minor spells and possessed some abilities that came naturally to him because of his heritage. That night Vheod even took the time to conjure flame to create a fire in which to roast the tiny, furry animal for which his memory had no name. With a full belly and a weary body, he soon fell asleep next to the fire with his sword next to him. As he drifted into sleep the flames died a slow lingering death of glowing embers.

* * * * *

Bright rays of light woke the cambion from a night of feverish, dark dreams. Vheod's spirits lifted immediately as he remembered where he was—a place far better than any of his dreams. Still, he was surprised and a little annoyed at the amount of light that came from the bright orb high in the sky. Did it have to be so bright? His eyes would need to adjust, and his dark flesh would have to cope with its warmth.

His garments were dry, and his tattered cloak was the cleanest he remembered seeing it. This light revealed more than he was used to seeing. He wondered what it might reveal of himself in the sight of another.

Vheod spent the rest of the day exploring. As the light began to ebb once again, the trees and plants around him grew sharper and more distinct. Objects farther away came into view in the shadowy twilight. His vision improved as the light around him died to levels more like those to which he was accustomed. With keener eyes, Vheod saw figures making their way through the trees. Two men carried a long log through an area of felled trees. He quietly pressed through the foliage to get a better look.

Now he could see more figures in the woods. A dozen men, all wielding axes, shaved the branches from felled trees. A few toted the logs off somewhere else. Each man wore a thick beard, and their thick, sturdy shirts revealed massive, muscular frames. Sweat dripped from brows hung low on weary necks. It looked to Vheod as if these men were ending their day of work, perhaps more hindered by the dying light than he.

"We'll have this area cleared by tomorrow, then we can begin building," Vheod heard one of them say.

"Fine," another replied with a good natured smile, "that's where *my* skills come in."

Vheod's ever-sharpening eyes saw, far beyond the working men, a tiny village of log homes set among the trees, fading into the sea of brown and green around it. Faint wisps of smoke rose from the tiny homes, greeting the first awakening stars of the evening.

These humans were clearing away trees to make space to build, Vheod realized. A simple enough act, he thought, but something far more important occurred to him as a result. The inhabitants of this world master their environment, rather than letting it master them. That wasn't true in the Lower Planes. As powerful as some of the lords of those nether worlds could be, they were always—consciously or unconsciously—servants of the very planes on which they lived. The fact that the Abyss's inhabitants were creatures *of* that plane, where evil and chaos were real, tangible things made them servants. The Abyss *was* chaos and evil, and the tanar'ri and other lower planar creatures that dwelled there, embodiments of those concepts themselves, served the Abyss with a far greater loyalty than any conventional master could ever hope to gain from those under him.

Here, Vheod realized, where the world was a place more than a master, men could make of it what they wanted. Not driven by inborn philosophies or outlooks, they were free to choose their own paths. These weren't people of predetermined destiny but of freedom and choice. Vheod watched these burly, muscular men as they left their work site and was suddenly gripped with sadness—and perhaps envy. He knew that what they had, what he'd never had, was exactly what he wanted.

Vheod fled once again into the darkening forest.

Throughout that night, sounds rose from the village. Laughter and song filled the dark, star-filled sky. At one point, Vheod crept close enough to see six tiny wooden buildings, most glowing cheerfully with interior fires lit probably more for the light than the heat, for it was a warm night. The chirping insects covered the soft sounds of his footfalls as he made his way toward the nearest building. Within, a few people spoke of things the eavesdropping Vheod couldn't understand. As he crouched beneath a window, they talked of someplace called the Dales and of the nearby Desertsmouth Mountains.

As he listened further, he ascertained that this was just a minor settlement to the west of someplace called Shadowdale, at the edge of the Spiderhaunt Woods. The land that rose toward the west evidently led to the aforementioned mountains. Strangely, the people spoke of a fear of the woods. They wouldn't go past the cleared area, telling of dangers much deeper in the forest.

This is the most beautiful place I have ever been, Vheod thought. How could they fear it? Where are they from that this is a place of fear and danger?

Before he could learn anything else, the light in the building dimmed suddenly, and the people grew silent. Vheod waited in the darkness and quiet for a time, lost in his thoughts.

* * * * *

Vheod woke just before dawn to sounds of movement. He kept very still but opened his eyes. Once again, his ability to see in dark conditions served him well. Two bloated humanoid creatures, covered in short, bristling hair lumbered toward him. Without thinking further, the cambion leaped to his feet and drew his sword, which lay beside him while he slept. The dark-furred things jerked back awkwardly but made no sound. Their long arms had dragged along the ground as they moved, but now their clawed hands reached toward their fat bellies. They opened yellow-fanged mouths in an obvious attempt to give him pause.

It didn't work.

Vheod charged, but as he did, he saw what these mysterious creatures were doing. Each pulled a glistening cord from their abdomens. Somehow, these beasts created webs like a spider. What was worse, each seemed to be quickly forming their creations into forbidding nooses or lariats. Vheod reached his foes before they finished. A mighty swing of his sword stopped one of the creatures from its spinning, and it reeled back from the force of the warrior's blow. Black blood mixed with a thin yellow pus ran from the gash the sword made. The creature flung itself toward Vheod in retaliation, but the cambion swung his sword back around, cutting it down before the beast could reach him with its long, clawed arms.

The other hairy creature had finished its spinning by that point. It held a many-stranded loop of spidery silk aloft over its head and grunted, stamping its feet on the ground with rapid thuds. As Vheod prepared to slay the creature before it could use the weapon, he felt something brush against his back. Looking over his shoulder, he saw that a hairy spider, at least a foot across, had dropped down from the trees above on a cord of webbing.

A tug on his arm drew his attention back toward the humanoid foe. With surprising speed, the creature had looped its makeshift weapon around Vheod's free arm. He pulled at the bond, but the hairy, manlike thing tugged back with great strength. It showed a hideous grin, producing more and more web to keep Vheod bound but to stay out of sword's reach. It was waiting for the spider to bite, Vheod thought, and for its venom to bring him down while keeping him off-balance with the web.

The creature was jostling him too much to allow Vheod to use a spell, and he could feel the spider reach his lower back. Vheod reached behind him with his sword, pretending to slash at the spider, but instead flinging the weapon end over end toward the other foe, even as he felt the spider's fangs sink into his flesh.

The sword caught the creature by surprise, slashed its shoulder and knocked it backward off its feet. Vheod didn't waste a moment in running toward his wounded opponent, which was able to right itself by the time he got to it. The important thing to Vheod was that too much slack in the web strand prevented the creature from using it against him now. Snarling, Vheod began pounding at the creature's head with his fists.

At first, the creature attempted to claw and bite Vheod, but the onrush of blow after blow forced it to hold its long, hairy arms in front of it in a hope to block the torrent of attacks. Vheod's furiously pounding fists continued unabated. Blood and pus ran down the creature's face and shoulder, staining its hairy, naked body. The gray-bristled beast fell to its knees, and holding its long-fingered hands over its head, murmured something with a pleading look in its large yellow eyes.

"There is no mercy in the Abyss, creature!" Vheod cried as he lifted his fist, dripping with black blood, down one more time on the beast's face. It fell to the ground with a heavy, wet thud. Reaching behind him, Vheod grabbed the spider and tore it from his back. Holding it in front of him, he shouted, "And tanar'ri cannot be harmed by simple poison!" He crushed the creature in his hand, and a thick, greenish-yellow ooze squirted out and mingled with the black blood running down his arm. The spider stopped squirming. Vheod dropped it to the ground.

He sat on the spot where he'd slept through most of the night and breathed heavily. For a moment, a feeling of satisfaction and triumph welled up inside him, but as the light of this world's day rose over the horizon, he came to a horrible realization.

This isn't the Abyss.

While he held no doubt that these beasts wanted to feed on his blood, the bright light and pure air of this world cried out in disapproval of his savage methods. Perhaps this place offered a different way than wanton destruction. That creature had wanted mercy. Perhaps it expected to get it. Did the warriors of this world, of "the Dales," practice a different sort of philosophy? Perhaps on this world survival wasn't the only goal.

He felt a twinge of kinship with the men he'd seen working the day before. Now, after seeing these hairy, inhuman spider-creatures, Vheod wanted it to be true. He wanted to be a part of this world and its people. It was the best place he'd ever been. Still the attack had taught him an important lesson—there *were* dangers here, just like in the Abyss.

* * * * *

Later on that same day, Vheod took to exploring again. This time he walked in the opposite direction from the settlement he'd visited the night before. Somehow, after his actions that morning, he felt unfit to be around those he was sure were far nobler and more merciful than he.

Gray clouds seeped across and eventually covered the sun after midday, and a few hours before twilight distant flashes of lightning crossed the horizon. Vheod noticed that the deeper he traveled into the woods, the fewer animals he saw or heard. Here and there, spider webs—some of enormous size—clung to the trees, but no other signs of more spiders or spidery humanoids revealed themselves. Perhaps they didn't care for the rain.

When the downpour that Vheod expected finally came, he all but ignored it. Lightning crackled across the sky overhead, and cool winds carried the formerly warm, still air through the trees. The canopy of leaves above him provided shelter from much of the rain, but the water still ran down the branches and gathered in muddy pools at his feet.

Through the haze of the rain, large, dark shapes loomed ahead of him. As he drew closer, Vheod could make out stone structures. Closer still, and he could see that there were two structures, one much larger than the other. Both were ancient and overgrown with climbing plants. The once-cleared area now teemed with brush and tall grass. Rain ran down the moss-covered, crumbling stone walls. It probably, Vheod thought, rained right into the structures themselves, for the wooden slats that once served as roofs for both buildings had collapsed years or even decades ago, leaving only a hint of their passing around the top edges of the walls. Even if he sought shelter—which he didn't—he would find none here. Walking into this seemingly abandoned place Vheod recalled the tower of Destiny's Last Hope. Reflexively he looked at the Taint, wondering if it had led him here as well. The vaguely round shape it presented had no discernible meaning. It lay dead on his arm, looking much like a normal birthmark.

Vheod made note that no wall had ever encircled this place, and that even in their heyday, the buildings offered no defensible positions. What this observation revealed he wasn't sure, other than that in the place he'd grown up, no structure was ever built without defense in mind. Buildings of any sort never lasted long in the Abyss with the horrid conditions, but builders always assumed their work would be attacked. Battle was a way of life there—perhaps not so here.

Closer still to the main building, the rain spattered into a round pool, about fifteen feet across. Its perimeter was girded by mossy stones and had obviously contained a shallow sampling of some brackish, cloudy water, but the storm was quickly replenishing it with clear, pure rain. The door of the larger, two-storied building opened out to the pool and hung partially open. Vheod was surprised the wooden door still hung on its tired, rusted hinges. Peering through the doorway, he'd enough light coming through the open roof to see that only rubble and debris remained within.

The smaller building, with only a single story, possessed a closed wooden door, and Vheod now realized, a more intact roof. As he looked at the structure, the door opened, catching the cambion completely by surprise. Two men stepped slowly out of the doorway, each wearing brown robes with gray stoles bearing no sign or mark.

The rain diminished to a lazy, irritating drizzle, but Vheod hardly noticed.

"Good day to you, traveler," the plumper, shorter of the two said in a soft, kind voice.

"Good day to you," the taller, more broad-shouldered of the pair chimed in with a smile.

Vheod said nothing. This was his first encounter with creatures of this world—not including the battle with those blood-seeking beasts earlier. How to handle it?

"You've come seeking something, my friend?" the round-faced, balding man asked.

"What do you seek?" the bearded, taller man added. Both of them stopped a few paces away from where

Vheod stood. They halted at exactly the same time, exactly the same distance away from him.

Vheod still said nothing.

The rounded, fleshy one said, "My name is Gyrison."

"And I am Arach," the larger, dark-haired man added.

"My name is Vheod," he told them after a long pause.

"Good," Gyrison replied.

"Yes, good," Arach said immediately after.

"We serve here as priests," Gyrison stated with a short bow.

With a sweeping gesture Arach told him, "This is our temple."

As one of them finished a movement or phrase, the other continued it or started another. The two men seemed to Vheod to be more like one.

"Priests of what power?" he asked them, still unsure whether to reach for the hilt of his sword.

"What is it that you seek?" Gyrison asked.

"You're new here, aren't you?" Arach finished.

"I . . . I am," Vheod said slowly, "is that—how do you know that? Is it important? Are outsiders forbidden?"

Both men smiled at Vheod. He noted quickly that the building behind them appeared as empty as the larger.

"You've come to Toril looking for . . . *someone*?" Gyrison asked him.

Toril. The home of my mother.

Vheod answered quickly, if only to keep Arach from asking a different question of him as well. "I have family here. Somewhere."

"Ah," Arach replied. "We can help you find them, traveler."

"Why?"

"Because it's what we do," Gyrison replied. "Because you need us to." He smiled again, in a way Vheod could not interpret.

"Because we can," Arach added.

Vheod looked the two over again. The drizzling precipitation didn't seem to bother them any more than it did him, but the moisture seeped into their brown robes. They seemed to act in perfect concert, but they never looked at each other—only at him. Every instinct within him told him not to trust these two strange men, but he realized that such was the Abyssal way. This was a different world, with different customs, different outlooks, and different approaches. They seemed genuinely generous and hardly a threat. Why not see what they knew?

Vheod pushed the long, wet strands of hair away from his face and asked them, "So what can you tell me?"

"First," Gyrison said, "you must tell us what you seek, exactly."

"Who are your relatives?" Arach asked on his turn.

"My great-grandmother's name was Thean," he said trying to stress the name with the same importance that he remembered it was told to him long ago. That single name was all he knew of his mortal heritage.

"Great-grandparent," Gyrison said thoughtfully.

"Let us take a look," Arach said, motioning toward the pool that Vheod stood beside.

As Vheod turned to look into the water, he realized that the rain had stopped. The pool showed remarkable clarity—no hint of the murkiness that it had just a short time ago. Vheod followed the lead of Gyrison and Arach. He wanted to see, if nothing else, what they would do next.

Still, Vheod paused to think, what joy it might be to find his people here in this world—perhaps they would even accept him as their own. He liked the idea of calling this world home.

Gyrison and Arach stood beside the pool and chanted softly. The strange-sounding words broke Vheod out of his thoughts. He couldn't understand what they said, but it seemed likely they were invoking the magical power of whatever deity they represented. Following his instincts, he kept his gaze on the pool. He was rewarded with a surprising sight.

The water calmed to a smooth plane. In this reflective, shining surface, Vheod saw movement. Two humans—one male, one female—stood before a massive, open doorway leading into darkness. As they looked on, a gigantic shape loomed from the dark portal. The creature that passed through the doorway and into the light was a colossus of dark red flesh pulled taut over a broad, muscular frame. Flames dripped from its body like water. Contracted, draconian wings folded at its back, and muscular, taloned arms gripped a jagged sword and a flaming whip with many tails.

A tanar'ri balor.

"Not great-grandmother," Gyrison said.

The balors were the most powerful of the tanar'ri—they commanded vast legions of lesser fiends and wielded tremendous power. Drenched in flame, their might was rarely questioned.

Further, this balor seemed somehow familiar. It breathed a single word, so low in pitch that Vheod could scarcely comprehend it. "Freedom" was the word he thought it uttered.

"Great-grand*father*," Arach stated with a gesture toward the image.

Great-grandfather.

Chare'en.

Vheod had always heard that Chare'en, the grandfather of the tanar'ri fiend that had cursed his human mother with seed, was imprisoned somewhere, but on this world? Unbelievable—but somehow, it made sense. The tanar'ri side of his family must have had some connection with this world or Vheod's father would never have come in contact with his mother.

Now this vision showed Chare'en free. A balor free in this peaceful and beautiful world could bring only disaster, terror, and death. Further, it would bring Vheod one step closer to the Abyss from which he'd just escaped. A balor would bring more tanar'ri, and Nethess would be sure to learn that he was here. If Chare'en was freed, this place would no longer be safe for him. He had to stop this—but how?

"Tell me," Vheod demanded, "does this sight represent the past, present, or future?"

"Future," Gyrison answered.

"A possible future," Arach added.

"How can I stop it?"

"Stop it?" Gyrison repeated with a look of surprise. Or was it mock surprise? Vheod no longer cared to play these games.

"Where are these two?" Vheod pointed to the humans in the pool's image. They appeared similar in their faces and mannerisms. Perhaps the two were related.

The two priests, for the first time since Vheod had seen them, looked at each other. They said nothing, though it seemed that perhaps their eyes spoke silent words in a language only they shared.

"Where?" Vheod demanded. "You must tell me!"

Gyrison opened his mouth to speak, but Arach held up a hand that silenced the round priest. "There is one, not unlike you, in a place called Tilverton, who can tell you what you need to know."

One like him? What did that mean? Vheod looked at Arach, then Gyrison, and back to Arach. Their plain faces stared at him expressionlessly with their silly, simpleton smiles.

"Very well," Vheod said. Unaccustomed to most niceties, he turned without further word and strode out of the temple. If he was to stop Chare'en, he had to start now. A balor was nothing to underestimate, and he already doubted his own power and skill. The sky, empty of its rain, grew dim as the day drew to a close.

His driven pace took him away from the ruins without so much as a look back, which is why he never saw the enigmatic smiles on the faces of Gyrison and Arach turn more sinister. Nor did he notice that the Taint had formed a wide-mouthed face on the back on his hand, a face that bore the same wicked smile.

Chapter Three

Melann felt much better, having spent some time around those whose faith was so strong and whose devotion was so great. The Abbey of the Golden Sheaf was filled with wonderful growing things and those who truly cared for them. Its stone walls surrounded many plots of ground dedicated to various cultivated fields, gardens and orchards, all larger and more important than the abbey structure itself. She'd never seen such beautiful flowers or such vibrant gardens of vegetables, fruit, and all sorts of wondrous plants. The soil was black with richness and well tended. Even the smell of the abbey gladdened her heart and gave her peace. Despite the importance of the task at hand, she was loathe to leave the abbey and did so only at her brother's repeated urgings.

Her problem, Melann decided while happily joining in the toil of weeding and watering an expansive and robust patch of strawberries, was that she'd been too focused on their quest. While finding the key to ending her family curse and saving her parents was obviously very important, her meager, mortal concerns were nothing compared to the divine nature and endless toil of Chauntea. Melann now believed she had to focus on the teachings and responsibilities of the Mother of All and the duties that fell on her as a servant and representative of that power in the world of men. From now on, she wouldn't let a day go by without nurturing a growing plant. She needed to become her goddess's tool in the world, to help bring forth fruit and abundant life.

Melann had to admit, however, that accomplishing that goal, being true to her beliefs, and being the sort of servant she felt Chauntea wanted her to be might be more of a challenge than she was prepared to face alone. In the abbey, surrounded by the other Watchful Brothers and Sisters of the Earth, staying faithful was simple—she was eager and happy to do nothing but think of Chauntea, and little of herself—but out here on the road, she found herself thinking more and more of her failing parents and the urgent need she felt to accomplish her personal goals.

She couldn't speak of this problem to Whitlock. Melann loved her brother, but she knew he wouldn't understand.

"It's good to be back on the road," he said.

"You didn't care for the time we spent in the Abbey of the Golden Sheaf, did you?" Melann asked.

Whitlock didn't answer. He hadn't cared for the Elven Woods at all.

Traveling westward on a road known as the Moonsea Ride, they kept their backs to the sun throughout the morning. It would probably take them four days to reach Tilver's Gap, and five more to Tilverton. The well-traveled road brought a few other wayfarers past them: merchants with wagons of goods and produce, messengers on swift horses, simple travelers alone or in pairs—even an adventuring company or two. Whitlock, of course, examined each of the people they encountered suspiciously.

He warned her about bandits who posed as travelers to mislead the unwary—but Whitlock was never unwary. Melann, however, couldn't help but think he eyed the approaching adventuring companies with a bit of envy. She knew Whitlock wanted to believe their exciting, adventurous life had been *his* destiny too.

The brothers and sisters at the abbey had been unable to provide any real information regarding their goal other than further news of gathering monstrous humanoids in the direction they rode. Whitlock didn't hide his displeasure over heading directly into such obvious danger.

Melann's mind drifted back to a point ten days earlier, as she and her brother knelt at the bedside of their parents. Cruel fate had struck their mother and father down almost simultaneously, doubling the pain for she and Whitlock. It also doubled the burden, for caring for both parents brought both hardship and radical change to their lives. Whitlock gave up his position among the Ridesmen, the local soldiery, and Melann turned from her duties at the temple known as the Bounty of the Goddess, both to devote their time to tending to their parents. It had been particularly hard on Whitlock to see their father, once a proud warrior, wasting away.

The stench of sickness and strong herbal poultices hung in the still air of the room like a fog. They lay in their single, large bed together, heavily covered in blankets despite the thick layer of fever-sweat that shone on both their faces.

Whitlock entered the room quietly, his movements awkward and overcareful. "I think—we think we've found a means to end the curse, Father."

Too weak to even turn to look on his son, Father whispered, "It takes magic to overcome magic, boy."

Neither of them had ever beheld their father in such an impuissant condition. It was sobering, particularly when it seemed that his mind was still strong.

"You can't lift the curse," Mother said with a weary rasp, "until you discover the nature of the one who cursed us."

Her eyes were sunken and her face was gaunt, with thin, jaundiced flesh pulled tight over softening bones. She was literally wasting away before her daughter's eyes. Melann had no idea how much longer her mother might be able to stave off death.

"But no one's ever told us. . . ." Melann replied.

"My mother told me it was a demon," Mother stated, her voice thick with disease. Melann felt hard-pressed to believe that to be anything more than hyperbole or perhaps the delirium of the disease.

"Father," Whitlock said, "We're going to ride north first to see if we can gather more information. Aunt Marta is going to stay here and look after the two of you. If all goes well, we'll be back in a tenday or two."

A silence filled the air thicker than the sickness. Melann felt as if there should be more to say, but no words came to her.

"Goodbye, children," Mother whispered, pulling Melann down, so her cheek was close to her own. Her breath was strained.

"Ride safely," Father added, his teary eyes closed. "Watch for those who would trick you. It's a cruel world."

Riding off that next day was the most difficult thing Melann had ever done. Neither she nor Whitlock had any idea if they would actually see their parents alive again. Chauntea, she prayed, would watch over them—their care was out of her hands, but their salvation was not.

* * * * *

The Moonsea Ride led the pair along miles and miles of fertile farmland and gentle hills covered with sheep and goats minded carefully by watchful herdsmen. The sky offered few clouds to block the sun. Whitlock's golden brown stallion didn't slow in the heat, but Melann's older mount began to lag as the last few hours of each day did likewise.

At the end of each day, the pair would make their campsite not far from the road in spots that Whitlock deemed defensible. They had brought simple food with them, including bread, cheese, vegetables and some dried meat. Melann supplemented this with wild fruits, leaves, berries, and roots, while Whitlock's skill with a bow occasionally provided some small game.

The night prior to when Whitlock estimated they would arrive in Tilverton, they made their camp in the area known as Tilver's Gap. Stark, knobby peaks rose on either side of them, though in the fading light of day they seemed little more than looming shadows. The pass was a dry, grassy region, notably different than the farmlands they passed through the three previous days.

While Whitlock built a fire, Melann found a small patch of wild berries. She picked a few to accompany their dinner, but he saw she also took some time to pull weeds away from the roots of the plants and provided them with some of the water she carried in a waterskin.

"Waste of time and water," he said softly to himself. "Nature takes care of its own, and what doesn't live wasn't supposed to."

When she was finished, Melann came toward the fire. He was already frying some bread and vegetables. A pale twilight glow came from the west. Melann stared at her brother for a moment. He was content out here. Safe.

"There's always time and water," she said, briskly wiping the dirt from her fingers, "out among the bounties of Our Mother. You need to be more trusting of people."

"What?" Whitlock's brow curved down, and his forehead filled with furrows, but he didn't look up from his cooking.

"We're out here, and not at one of the roadhouses, because you don't trust people. You'd rather be out here alone than have to worry about who presents a threat and who doesn't, or if a thief is going to creep into your room at night. Your instincts are good, and I'll admit you've been keeping us well protected, but Whitlock, not everyone's an orc."

Whitlock looked up at his sister, who still stood at the edge of the firelight. He couldn't hide his irritation.

"Look," he said bitterly, "everything is going just fine the way it is. Let *me* worry about whether there's danger or not. Besides—"

"I can help take some of that responsibility, you know. This journey is just as important to me as it is to you."

"*Besides,*" Whitlock said again, stressing the word and narrowing his gaze, "we will be in Tilverton by tomorrow night. You can sleep in a bed then."

Melann shook her head again. Did he think her so soft?

"This has nothing to do with sleeping in a bed or on the ground," she retorted. "This is about you believing that you have to take care of me and be the sole guardian over the both of us. I can take care of myself. Lifting the curse is my foremost goal too."

Melann rubbed her fingers, working away the soil. She turned, and as if to prove her point to Whitlock she prayed to Chauntea, calling on her power to place a ward around the campsite that would protect them while they slept. When she was finished, she lowered the holy symbol pendant she used to focus the warding and sat beside the fire. Whitlock stared at her in silence, and she stared back.

She dumped the berries out of her pouch and onto the ground.

Whitlock looked down into the meal he was preparing. The truth was, he actually did prefer camping outside to the often more dangerous road-side inns. Tales of diabolical innkeepers who over-came their patrons in the night and murdered them for their possessions or sold them into slav-ery were common in the more unsavory parts of the faraway Moonsea region. Melann just couldn't understand the dangers that reared around them at every turn.

He had not cared much for staying at the Abbey of the Golden Sheaf, either, but that had nothing to do with distrust. Holed up in that walled fortress, tending to their gardens, those people didn't have any idea of what the world was really like. They didn't understand the dangers and the truth behind the evils in the world. Zhentarim, brigands, monsters, undead—one needed to be both strong and aware to survive in a world with such threats. Soldiers, mercenaries, adventurers—they under-stood. They knew the horrors that lurked in dark caverns, evil temples, and dimly lit alleyways, and they were prepared to face them. Like the priests in the Golden Sheaf, his sister was too concerned with lofty religious ideals and not the harsh reali-ties of life.

Neither spoke again as the fire died. Whitlock ate, but Melann waved off any offer of food. Sounds of crickets and buzzing night insects filled the darkness.

* * * * *

The walls of Tilverton rose high above the flat plain on which the city stood. As Whitlock and Melann came just within sight of the city, traffic grew noticeably more congested as smaller paths joined with the road. People slowly traveled to and from the city in heavily laden carts and on fine, tall horses as well as on foot. Situated in the strategic mouth of Tilver's Gap, the city watched over the only easy way between the Thunder Peaks to the south and the Desertsmouth Mountains to the north. Outside of the city, Whitlock and Melann passed a number of homes, most of them herders' and horse ranchers'.

Tilverton had once been an independent frontier town. Now it was under the protection and rule of Cormyr, a powerful kingdom to the south and west. Fortunately, the hand of King Azoun IV was light and beneficent, and Tilverton prospered in the care of the city's Lady Regent, Alasalynn Rowanmantle. The city offered thousands of people a home, safe behind high walls, safe against the dangers of the surrounding mountains.

The road took them past a stockyard that smelled of cattle and other livestock. Eventually the road wound to an open gate offering a means through the protective wall. The noise and smells of thick crowds rose above the wall as they approached. As the sun set, the city's lights guided them easily along their path.

Inside the wall, the streets were alive with humanity. Dancing, colorfully dressed people frolicked in the street to the sounds of melodious horns and stringed instruments. Voices—some beautiful, some not, but all filled with emotion—rose from all quarters of the town, joined in song.

Midsummer had come, and both Melann and Whitlock had completely forgotten it.

This was a festival the siblings had taken part in many times on their own in Archendale. On this day each year, everyone celebrated life with wild festivities, food, wine, and music. Young unwed maidens would hide in the woods, waiting for their suitors to find them and propose marriage. The Long Night, as it was sometimes called, was a time of love and happiness, but it hardly fit into Whitlock and Melann's current plans.

A guard, dressed in surprisingly severe plate armor, brandishing a spear in one hand and a turkey leg in the other, stood by the open gate. His helmet rested at his feet, along with his shield. Juice from his meal ran down his beard. When he looked up, wiping his beard, he saw Melann and Whitlock. The two remained mounted and looked at the festivities with wide-eyed surprise.

"You won't find a room here," he told them. "Inns and rooming houses are full-up. It's the festival." He shooed them off with the turkey leg and looked away.

They could barely hear the guard's words over the music and singing. Whitlock leaned closer to the man, far to one side of his mount and shouted, "Isn't there somewhere we can stay? Anywhere at all?"

The guard paused and stared for a moment. "Well, you could try the Flagon Held High," he said, louder this time. "You can get something to drink there and ask around about a room. Maybe someone will know of someplace." He pointed with his turkey leg. "Follow the Street of the Sorceress until you get to Phorn's Lane. You'll find it." With that, he took a hearty bite from the leg and turned back to watch the dancers in the street.

Melann had little interest in drink, particularly in comparison to her desire to find some information to help them find the Crypt of Chare'en. She looked to Whitlock and simply shrugged rather than attempt to be heard over the noise. He nodded a thank you to the guard. The two rode down the street, carefully avoiding dancers and merrymakers.

The Flagon Held High was a large tavern with new, smooth stone walls and fresh paint on the sign. The drinking, eating, singing, and dancing clientele had spilled out onto Phorn's Lane. Like the rest of the city, the tavern that night bustled with all manner of patrons, rich and poor alike. Tilverton, as a community, apparently wasn't old enough to develop a strict segregation of classes. Melann enjoyed that about the place. Whitlock didn't seem to notice.

The two dismounted and tied their horses to a post a few buildings away from the tavern—as close as they could get. Whitlock pushed his way into the crowd, but Melann slipped through the teeming throng faster than he. He grabbed her arm and held it as they moved. They stuck together as they threaded their way through the wilderness of people.

Inside the tavern, the crowd thickened. The two finally procured some wine as well as a bit of roast pork and vegetables. The meal's flavor almost matched its exorbitant price. While they ate, after actually managing to find a table just then vacated, Melann attempted to ask the barmaid about lodging for the night. The woman just shrugged and moved on, obviously more concerned with serving drinks than chitchat that didn't help her earn her keep.

Whitlock rolled his eyes and motioned to the door. "We'd be better off on the road, I'm afraid."

Melann sighed. She knew he was right, but at the same time, she regretted that duty so consumed her life that they couldn't stop for just one night and take part in this celebration. Instead, it presented them only with another obstacle in their quest.

"Pardon me," a man said, seating himself gingerly on the only empty chair at the small table, "but I couldn't help but overhear that you are in need of lodging." He was tall, with a high forehead and wide cheekbones. His voice carried a slightly annoying nasal quality, accentuated by the fact that he had to almost shout to be overheard in the din. He ran his hand through his thinning black hair and continued, "I know of a place where you can sleep tonight, if you're not too picky."

Whitlock's glare in this newcomer's direction seemed to carry with it all the suspicion and distaste he could muster, which Melann realized was considerable. The man tried not to notice but did anyway. He cleared his throat.

Melann replied, "Where?" Whitlock turned his glare to his sister.

"Well," the man said, turning to Melann, "just outside of town there's an old granary. It's not much of a rooming house, but I can assure you there's room there, plenty of hay and whatnot to sleep on, and it's away from the noise a bit—if that's what you're after. I own the building but no longer use it. You'll find it to the south of the main road, just on the other side of the stockyards. The door bears the name Northrip."

Whitlock shook his head. "Thank you anyway, sir, but . . ."

"Maybe we should look at the place," Melann said to Whitlock. Unfortunately, to be heard, she had to speak loud enough that the stranger heard her as well.

"Yes, by all means, if you wish it. I'm not even going to ask for payment. I just thought someone should benefit from it. It's Midsummer festival, after all."

"You're very generous, sir," Melann said. "Could I ask your name?"

"Oh. Ah, my name is Ferd. Ferd . . . Northrip." He smiled broadly.

"Well then, Ferd, I shall thank Our Mother tonight in my prayers for bringing us to such a generous man."

He smiled nervously as he glanced down at Melann's amulet bearing Chauntea's symbol. "Well, I should be going," he said as he rose from the table.

"You don't actually trust him, do you?" Whitlock demanded as Ferd disappeared into the crowd.

"Well, we've little reason to trust or distrust him, but I suppose we could just make our camp outside of town as we have been, at least for tonight." She sighed.

"I'm glad to hear that," Whitlock said, and Melann realized he didn't notice her exasperation.

When they finally left the Flagon Held High the singing had stopped, but that didn't reduce the overall commotion. The dark night was riven by innumerable torches throughout the city, almost resembling daylight. Most of the people outside seemed to be looking off to the north. Melann and Whitlock followed along and did the same. In the north, flashes of lightning tore up the dark sky. Soon, the thunder that the lightning brought with it would be heard even over the noises of the crowd, Melann observed, and rain would pour down, bringing a quick end to the festivities. The approaching storm had the appearance of an invading army bent on destruction.

Melann's attention drew toward the crowd around her. "A storm," someone cried. "But that never happens!" another declared. "A storm on Midsummer's Eve!" ". . . a terrible sign." "A bad omen!" ". . . poor portents for the future . . ."

Melann herself knew their words rang true. The gods usually blessed Midsummer with a clear night in which all could celebrate until dawn, or so she'd been taught. A storm—a terrible storm such as this—was said to presage terrible events. Something horrible threatened this city and beyond. Her flesh grew cold.

A chilling, harsh wind blew in from the north, causing the torchlight to flicker, and tugged at the party clothes of the dancers and celebrants.

Whitlock looked at her and said, "We're going to need shelter."

"We've no choice, then," she replied, her mind more focused on the ominous, thundering harbinger roaring down from the north than on her brother's statement of the obvious.

"You're right," Whitlock said. She knew he hated not having a choice.

* * * * *

The grain house sat just where Ferd said it would. The door bore a wooden sign with a crude scrawl on it: Northrip. Gray, bare boards made up the building, and there was a single window. Through the rain, which had started just a few minutes before they found the building, they could see dim light slipping through spaces between some of the boards.

Melann pointed at the light and whispered, "Perhaps Ferd offered the grain house to some other traveler needing shelter." Whitlock's hand went to his sword hilt.

The door opened easily. Melann paused, speaking the words of a minor blessing. Whitlock stepped forward, his ready hand still clutching his sheathed sword's hilt. He continually adjusted his grip, nervous but ready to draw it if he must. Dust covered the bare floor inside, and Whitlock's boots stirred up small clouds as he entered. A closed door on the far wall probably led into the grain bin. A rust-encrusted pitchfork hung on an equally rusty nail next to the door. The light they had seen evidently came from within the grain bin.

"Who's there?" a rough voice called from beyond the door.

Whitlock shot a glance at Melann. She spoke, raising her voice to be heard over the rain. "Ferd Northrip gave us his permission to stay the night here."

"Wha—" the voice began, then the speaker paused. "Oh, *Ferd* sent you." Sudden sounds coming from beyond followed these last words.

The door opened and out stepped a man. He was at least six feet tall with a great girth. Hairy bare arms hung at his sides, his roughly woven clothes marking him as a man of little means. His broad face suggested more beast than man. His upturned nose showed too much nostril, and his eyes were small, like dark animal holes. He glared at the pair, looking each up and down.

"My name is Melann, and this is my brother Whitlock."

The man just grunted, looking at them as though taking inventory.

Whitlock said, "And who are you, sir?"

He grunted again. "Name's Orrag Grinmash," he said with a voice coarser than his clothing. He rubbed his unshaven face with a massive hand.

Whitlock's mind held little doubt that Orrag was some sort of thief or brigand. In fact, he thought, "Ferd" was probably his accomplice. Now Orrag prepared to attack them while they slept and take their belongings. The whole scheme was a well-rehearsed plot. Generosity indeed! Whitlock would show him that he wasn't so easily tricked and robbed. He knew that a circumspect eye is a Dalesman's greatest asset.

"Orrag, Our Mother Chauntea has brought us here to this shelter. She is a great provider and takes care of her servants well," Melann said.

From outside, a howling cry grew in intensity, then whistled all around them. The light flickered in the wind, from which this old building offered only meager shelter. A steady drumming began against the roof and walls.

Orrag seemed a little surprised by her words. "Hmm. Yes, I suppose so."

Orrag stepped into the small room with Melann and Whitlock. He smelled of alcohol and old sweat. Whitlock looked carefully on the large man for weapons but couldn't see any obvious signs.

"So, here for the festival?" Orrag asked casually, moving around the other two, as if making for the door.

"No, actually," Melann answered.

Orrag stopped and seemed surprised. "No?"

"No. We're just passing through," Whitlock stated flatly, turning slowly to follow Orrag, watching his every move. Something about the way he walked, and the scars on his hairy arms and face told Whitlock that combat and strife had traveled Orrag's way before.

"We're on an important quest," Melann solemnly told him, her words slow and weighty.

"Quest?" She suddenly had Orrag's full attention. He spoke quickly. "What sort of quest?"

"We're looking for the tomb of an old wizard in the Thunder Peaks," she replied.

"Melann, that's enough!" Whitlock hissed, his hand ready to draw his blade at any moment. His taut wrist ached from the position, and his fingers rebelled at the tension, but he held firm. Wind rattled the entire structure, but the old building had probably weathered many such storms in its time.

"Really?" Orrag seemed intrigued—or perhaps afraid. He ignored Whitlock. "What wizard?"

Whitlock heard Melann's voice in his ear: "Maybe he can help us. We're seeking information. Who's to say where it might come from?"

Before Whitlock could reply, Orrag asked her again, "What's the wizard's name?"

Melann turned to him. "Chare'en."

Orrag reacted as if struck. He stepped backward and leaned heavily against the wall behind him. He rubbed his rough jowls again and closed his eyes. Melann and Whitlock both watched him, bewildered and wary. Finally, he spoke. "Wizard . . . Chare'en . . ." He paused.

"Do you know of him?" Whitlock demanded.

"Why?" Orrag asked. Lightning flashed in the small window, followed immediately by a sharp slap of thunder.

"We seek something that lies within his tomb," Melann said. "It will help us remove an ancient curse." She added with a whisper, "We hope."

Again Orrag paused, deep in thought. Eventually he pushed himself away from the wall and regained a bit of his former, gruff composure. He circled around the siblings again. As before, Whitlock turned slowly to continue to face the bestial man, hand ready to draw his sword. Orrag stopped at the doorway from which he'd emerged.

"I can tell you where to find the crypt that you seek. How about that? Is that helpful?" Orrag told them, an unknowable smile coming to his gap-filled mouth. The only teeth that remained were slightly pointed.

"This . . . man doesn't know anything," Whitlock told Melann, pointing an accusing finger at Orrag's wide chest. "We should leave. The rain would be better than this." Thunder rumbled outside.

"Oh, I know how to find it. I know a fair bit about those peaks and the valleys in between. I know some of the goblins and orcs that live there."

"No more proof do we need that this man's a liar. Goblins and orcs—vermin!"

"Whitlock," Melann said softly, "I felt that Chauntea brought us here, and now we're seeing her plans for us come to fruition. This man can tell us how to get to the object of our quest. This is it, can't you feel it?" She clapped her hands together and took a step closer to Orrag, her blue eyes peering into his misshapen face.

" 'Course, it'll cost you." Orrag said quietly, seeming to hide a smile behind those cruel lips.

"What?" Whitlock turned back to the man who now leaned in the door frame. The light beyond revealed a simple bed made of hay illuminated by a lantern. Miscellaneous equipment, books, and what appeared to be maps lay scattered around the floor.

"The information will cost you," Orrag stated.

"How much?" Whitlock asked suspiciously. Still convinced the man was a thief, the warrior planted his feet squarely on the dirt floor, as if a battle-ready stance might grant him greater resolve or awareness. He could use either.

"Well, let's see," Orrag said slowly, over-dramatically, mocking a ponderous, thoughtful look. "This is obviously important knowledge, you understand. Hard to come by. I'd wager you couldn't find it anywhere else."

Orrag fanned the flames of Whitlock's fears masterfully.

"I would say about a hundred gold pieces ought to cover it," he stated finally.

Melann looked to Whitlock. He carried their money and knew that was approximately all that they had, but if Orrag actually knew the location of the crypt, could any price be too great? Melann seemed to have no doubt that Orrag spoke the truth.

"Whitlock?" Her eyes were wide and moist. "It seems so clear that Chauntea has brought us here. A *grain house*, no less! That's got to be a sure sign of Chauntea's involvement."

Of course, Whitlock thought, Melann would always optimistically believe anything that sounded like what she wanted to hear. But, he had to admit, this could be their only chance. She seemed to have been right about the elven ghost. He looked into his sister's eyes and saw only confidence. Perhaps her goddess had brought them here. Who knew?

"All right," Whitlock told Orrag through clenched teeth. "We'll pay your price."

"Good. Let's see it," Orrag rubbed his cheek and opened his eyes wide.

"No," Melann said suddenly. "You talk, then we pay."

She knew they would be better to provide a united front, and so backed up her brother's tendency for suspicion. Whitlock turned back to her and nodded with a slight smile.

Orrag didn't flinch. "All right, fine," he said. "You seem like trustworthy folks." He cleared his throat. "Ride east away from town for a full day until you come to a small lake, then head south into the Thunder Peaks. You'll pass through wooded hills, but it's the easiest way through that portion of the mountains. After another three days' ride, you'll come on a narrow vale that'll lead you to a high cliff face. You'll find what you're looking for there." During his explanation, Melann produced a piece of parchment and took some notes so they wouldn't forget.

"The entrance to the Crypt of Chare'en," Orrag told them, "was built into the side of that tall, smooth cliff, but it was covered in a landslide long ago. If you have to get in," Orrag grinned, "you'll have to dig."

Whitlock and Melann conferred for a moment, determining whether or not they had all the details they needed. Orrag claimed ignorance regarding anything but the actual location of the place. When Whitlock felt assured they could find the crypt on their own, he handed Orrag a leather bag with its strap pulled tight. "Here's your money, half-orc."

Orrag raised his eyebrow and looked at Whitlock. He took the bag and opening it, peering within to eye the coins.

Whitlock turned to the rough wood door leading outside. The wind still rattled the boards of the granary's roof, but he had no intention of spending the night in the same structure as a brigand with orc blood. The storm had been fierce but mercifully short. Opening the door, he looked at Melann. She came with him, but glanced back at Orrag.

"Thank you, sir," she told him, "and may Chauntea be with you." Orrag didn't speak as they left, but his face contorted as if the priest's parting words were a curse and not a blessing.

Chapter Four

Ravens are liars. Though most people don't believe animals to be part of the struggle between good and evil, no one, including the Ravenwitch, ever asked the ravens. Of course, even if she did ask, she probably wouldn't get a truthful answer. The Ravenwitch knew her creatures enjoyed falsehood for its own sake and maliciously sought to trick and fool other creatures—and each other—whenever they could. They laughed at the misery and confusion of others and relished the infliction of pain and the letting of blood.

The Ravenwitch spoke to her feathered servants at length, in their own language, asking them the location of Yrrin. She quickly tired of their silly half-truths and used her power over them—master to familiar. Yrrin had been gone for at least half the day, and she needed him.

"Yrrin is gone," one raven said.

"Yes, my dear," the Ravenwitch replied, "I know that. I need to know where he has gone."

"Away," another raven cawed.

Her hair, as smooth and dark as a moonless night, reached to her waist and almost seemed like part of her long black dress. A cape covered in black feathers trailed behind her along the wooden floor of her tree home. All around her were dozens of ravens.

The birds perched on every nook and ledge they could find, hopped across the floor, and flew about her head. She enjoyed, as always, their grace and beauty as they flew, but today she needed information, and she needed it quickly. The Ravenwitch didn't smile at her servants' antics this day. Dark eyes slowly began to smolder like kindling at the beginning of a dangerous fire. Her thin, graceful lips drew tight as she raised a graceful, milky white hand. A raven lit there and looked at her with eyes almost as black as her own.

"Where is Yrrin, my friend?" she asked the raven coolly.

"Flown away," the raven replied, "gone to join King Azoun for tea!"

Without warning, yellow, soundless flames surrounded the raven and the witch's hand. The bird's wings rose up in surprise and pain, but it couldn't leave her hand. The other ravens in the room took to the air, agitated and excited. Each black, round eye focused on its pain-wracked comrade. Raven thought held little room for compassion but a good deal for intimidation by example. Observe the misfortunes of others closely, lest they befall you—that was the way of the raven.

"I am sorry, friend, but I have no interest in your little games this day," she whispered to the raven.

"He went outside," the raven said with a quivering beak. "He never returned from fetching water from the river!"

The flame stopped. Neither the raven nor her hand showed any sign of burns. The raven flew off, its flight wobbly and erratic, but it was unharmed. The ravens echoed choruses of apologies and pleas of forgiveness from the Ravenwitch, but she dismissed them with a gesture.

"I know you cannot help your natures, my friends," she said, crossing to the staircase. "It is a terrible thing for a creature to deny its true nature."

The Ravenwitch lived in a tree. This particular tree, however, stretched its branches much higher than those around it—more than almost any natural tree. The massive trunk stood like a tower in the middle of the forest, yet as big as it was, the hollow space within, where the witch lived with her familiars, was even larger than one might expect. Despite the room inside, the tree lived and in fact flourished with the presence and care of the witch and her familiars. The Ravenwitch flowed down wooden stairs that had never known a nail, saw, or even a chisel, her long hair and dress trailing behind her like a wake. The ancient grandfather of trees had formed the stairs, the various levels, and all the other portions of the interior structure, coaxed and encouraged by the arcane spells of its mistress. The tree was as much a familiar as the hundreds of ravens that called its inner chambers and high branches home.

The tree provided a narrow crack in its outer surface as an exit. The Ravenwitch passed through the curtain of black roses that entwined the tree's bark and branches, avoiding each of the prickling thorns with a smooth fluidity. The dark rose vines gave the entire tree a somber, sinister look as it rose up far too high, blotting out the sun. One might have even thought it dead and blackened from far off. The grass around the base of the tree stood tall and thick, but the witch's passing betrayed no presence. Ravens in the branches of the monstrous tree flitted and called, but she paid them little attention. She passed a number of normal trees in the forest descending a gentle slope. The Thunder Peaks rose around her in all directions, circling her hidden valley.

The Ravenwitch's attention focused on finding her servant, Yrrin. For years he'd served her faithfully, and now she suddenly felt something amiss. The winds greeted her with scents she couldn't immediately identify, but that somehow struck her as wrong. When Yrrin had come to her he was nothing more than a man. She rewarded him with power and ability. Her gift: Yrrin could transform himself into a raven the size of a bear, and he need not fear simple blades—only magic and silver could harm him. The Ravenwitch remade Yrrin into a creature of magic, blessed with the ability to change his shape. In return he performed chores, carried messages, and gathered information for her, though her ravens and divinations also provided her important knowledge and secrets.

But where was Yrrin now?

The edge of the river waited at the bottom of the valley's slope. Tall grass grew even into the water. Beyond the river the land sloped upward toward yet another hill and eventually another peak. Insects buzzed at the river's bank, and tiny animals and birds cavorted around her. The slow-moving stream smelled of loam and decaying plants as the summer sun beat down on it. What drew the Ravenwitch's interest, however, were the trampled areas of grass she saw in the distance. She followed the river to where the grass lay matted to the ground. It appeared that a number of creatures had passed through this area. The odors she did not care for grew stronger.

The Ravenwitch heard the sounds. Grunting, cackling, and even howling rose in the distance, accompanying the sounds of movement. She moved closer, slipping down into the tall grass and deftly, softly passing through it, allowing it to cover her approach.

A number of creatures with canine features—shaggy, dirty, grayish-red hair covering their bodies, long snouts, and tall, pointed ears—milled about across the river. Yellowish-green manes ran down their backs, with tufts of long hair the same color spotting their muscular, massive bodies. The creatures were taller than a man, some reaching almost eight feet in height. Their faces resembled jackals or perhaps hyenas, and they wore scraps of armor and brandished large, mannish weapons.

Gnolls.

Usually such stupid, magic-poor creatures hardly presented enough reason to cause her worry. None of them appeared to see her, and her magic could ensure they wouldn't. A chill ran down her spine with clammy, ghostly fingers. Her eyes darted back and forth across the group of gnolls. Why was she so disturbed by them? And where was Yrrin?

The answers to both questions came to her after she moved just a few steps more along the bank. A body lay among the grass and reeds on the river's opposite side. Bloody and tattered, the body of Yrrin remained utterly still, just a few steps away from the laughing, snorting beast-men. The Ravenwitch stared at her fallen companion for a while, realizing her magic could do nothing to bring him back. He was gone.

Without another thought, the Ravenwitch stood. A few of the creatures on the opposite bank turned toward her with wide eyes and growls of surprise, but she ignored them. Uttering just a few magic syllables, she raised both hands high above her head. By this time, all the gnolls were looking at her, a few grabbing spears or other weapons. They were just in time to watch black lightning arc from her open palms. The spell screamed like a soul afire, and the air around the bolt of power sizzled and roiled as if it abhorred its presence. Black fingers stretched out across the river in less than an instant, striking the first gnoll in the chest. The creature exploded, spraying tiny bits of flesh and blood in a small radius of pain around it. The bolt continued, lancing into a nearby gnoll. Its life ended in grisly death as did the first's. The third gnoll, directly behind the second, seemed to actually evaporate when caught in the spell's grasp, and the bolt likewise rendered the creature struck next into a reddish-brown vapor. Again and again the black lightning arced from target to target, until fully a dozen gnolls lay virtually disintegrated in a horrible display of sorcery.

"Damn you!" the Ravenwitch spat at their smoldering remains.

More gnolls were here earlier, she could tell by the amount of traffic that had passed through, but why? How had they slain her wereraven servant? They must have possessed some sort of magic. That disturbed her. The Ravenwitch would never have given the creatures such credit, but the truth of it lay obvious on the opposite bank.

The Ravenwitch cursed again and turned back toward her tree home. Yrrin would remain where he fell, for such was the way of the raven, and thus her way as well. The living always required more tending to than the dead, and this day two things burned within her: fear of the unknown and a need for vengeance.

* * * * *

Back inside the tree, the Ravenwitch sat swallowed in a large, padded, well-worn chair. Before her, a circular basin held clear water as unmoving as the iris of a huge eye. She wiped her brow and attempted to calm herself, preparing to cast her divinations. Ravens of various sizes flitted about the room, cawing softly—almost cooing. Dark eyes focused on the glassy water that reflected her round, smooth cheeks and ever-so-slightly pointed chin.

Finally ready, she held a tightly clenched fist aloft over the basin as she had many times in the past. The Ravenwitch slowly unclenched her hand, and black rose petals drifted down onto the water's surface where they bobbed and floated. More and more of the petals fell, until the basin was black with swirling, floating cusps of velvet. As she stared, the petals formed patterns on the water's surface. Patterns only she could perceive, revealing secrets only she could interpret, showed themselves as the divination that magic tore from the ether.

The Ravenwitch saw in the pattern a large form, domineering and powerful, rising from a place where it had long been imprisoned: a tanar'ri noble. Power such as it held was just the sort of power the Ravenwitch could understand, respect, and rightfully fear. This tanar'ri, she saw, would quickly gather power around it as it amassed strength. The being would threaten the entire area—the Thunder Peaks, the Dalelands, and perhaps even beyond, if given the chance. Already, she saw with vision beyond vision, the gnolls gathered instinctively to serve the tanar'ri.

A tanar'ri named Chare'en.

She recognized him from old tales she'd read in the ancient tomes that filled the high shelves of her own library. The Ravenwitch felt that cold chill return to run down her spine once again. She shivered and tried to ignore it. The pool fluttered to life yet again.

She watched the swirling patterns and peculiar symbols of the magic waters reveal the actions of others. The Ravenwitch's inner vision conjured forth a number of different forces currently coming together. Each of these forces, she saw, possessed different motives. Each was bent on helping to free the creature—some inadvertently, but some after years and years of careful, meticulous planning.

Chapter Five

It was good to have a purpose. Vheod's footsteps no longer fell gingerly on the ground with the tentativeness of an explorer, but instead his stride betrayed the resolute determination of a man with a mission.

The village he'd observed earlier lay on the outskirts of the forest. Two days previous, Vheod watched laborers work to clear more of the land. As the sun rose into the morning sky this day, those same workers returned to their tasks. Sounds of axes against wood and falling trees filled the rapidly warming air.

Vheod hoped that someone here could direct him in which way to go. He needed to find the two people shown to him who would free Chare'en. Were they servants of the balor? Somehow he doubted that. More likely, he thought, they would inadvertently loose the tanar'ri lord through some other action. Stopping them, then, would be as simple as finding them in time and warning them.

He had no idea where this place, Tilverton, might lie. He was unsure even of its nature, though he assumed it must be a city or a fortress of some kind, since people obviously lived there.

In his previous visit, Vheod had slipped into the village after the descent of night. In the Abyss, he learned to approach others with either subtlety and guile or domineering aggression. The stealthy approach had served its purpose so far—now it was time for a change of pace.

Leaving the cover of the woods, Vheod entered the tiny settlement, walking amid the small buildings constructed of felled logs fitted crudely together. Smoke rose from a number of them, carrying with it good, wholesome smells that tugged at Vheod's nose, making him suddenly aware of his own hunger. Trying to ignore the feeling, he walked toward a central area from which all the other buildings seemed to radiate and the largest building in town stood. He never reached it.

A man dressed in rough, sturdy clothes stepped through an open doorway. As he walked he pulled thick leather work gloves onto his hands, despite the growing heat of the day. His face concealed with a thick beard, the man looked up at Vheod with surprise.

"Who in the name of Helm are you?" the man asked.

"Silence," Vheod said, attempting to sound as powerful and confident as he could, despite his smoky, scratched voice. "I am Vheod Runechild, and I must know where the place called Tilverton lies."

The man backed slowly into the open doorway. "Feshik! Get out here," he yelled, still staring at Vheod.

"And bring my sword," he added over his shoulder.

Vheod was confused. He looked around, even behind him, but saw nothing. By the time he returned his gaze to the man, a young boy had appeared in the doorway, attempting to peer around the large man. The child's black hair was tousled, and his eyes opened almost as wide as his mouth as he stared at Vheod.

"Who is that, Papa?" the child asked.

"I said to bring my sword!" the man replied, pushing the child backward into the house with a wide, gloved hand.

"You don't need your sword," Vheod said, extending an empty hand in the man's direction. "I have need of knowledge. Aid me and no one will be harmed."

"What you'll get is a taste of steel, demon."

Demon? Was it so obvious? "As I said, there's no need for that."

"What's going on here, Tallin?" a voice came from behind Vheod, causing him to whirl in surprise, his hand instinctively going for his sword hilt—an action he immediately regretted. He just was not accustomed to this sort of peaceful approach. His instincts were too versed in danger.

Behind him stood another man, larger but older than the first. His yellow hair receded from his forehead, and his face was clean shaven. He hefted a wood axe at the ready as Vheod turned. The cambion pulled his hand away from his hilt, holding his hands open and high in front of him.

"I don't want to have to hurt you," he said.

"Who is he, Tallin?" The axeman asked. His eyes narrowed as he examined Vheod.

"I figure he's a servant of the Spider Lord," the man in the door replied.

Vheod looked behind him now to see the child bring a broadsword to the man. The boy lifted the heavy sword with both hands, handing it to the man carefully. The child's wide eyes remained focused on Vheod.

"Get back inside now, Feshik," Tallin told him. The boy complied, eyes still wide with fear.

"Looks a little like a dark elf to me," the man with the axe stated.

A dark elf? A drow? Servant of Lolth? Vheod knew of the drow and their Abyssal mistress, the spider queen Lolth.

"I assure you, I'm no drow," he told them, hands still help open in front of him. "And I'm no one's servant."

"Mallach! Chorrad!" the older man cried out in the direction of the woods. "Get over here, we've got a . . . we've got something."

Vheod saw doors to the buildings around him begin to open, and frightened eyes peered out.

"I've come here," Vheod explained again, "just to get some informa—"

"Be quiet!" Tallin spat out, stepping forward, his bared sword upraised.

Vheod turned back fully to face him. How long could he keep from drawing his own blade? Vheod thought they would respect his powerful demeanor and help him. Why wouldn't they even listen?

"Whatever it is, it ain't human," the man behind him now said, "and it ain't, well . . . anything good. You can tell that just by looking."

"Look, demon—or whatever you are—leave us or die," Tallin said, staring Vheod in the eye.

"You don't need to be afraid," Vheod said, pleading with his open hands.

Looking down, he could see that the Taint was no longer on either arm. *Where was it?* He sometimes suspected that it altered when others looked at him, perhaps communicating something to them. Perhaps others saw something in the mark that he didn't, which might suggest that his own body conspired with others against him—a paranoiac's nightmare.

"He's a drow," a female voice called from an open door across the way.

Another, a male, replied, "Drow don't have red hair."

"I'll bet he was conjured up in that storm yesterday," still another voice called out. "Manchal says storms like that are a sign that a doorway between worlds is opening."

Footfalls grew louder behind him, coming from the direction of the woods.

"I just need to know how to find a place called—"

Tallin watched something over Vheod's shoulder and suddenly drew himself up taller, as if more confident. The footsteps behind Vheod were louder still. He lunged at Vheod with his sword, shouting, "I said, get away from here!"

Vheod dodged to one side to avoid the sword blow and could hear the man behind him moving closer, probably with that axe ready to cleave his skull.

"I don't want to fight you!" Vheod finally cried. He couldn't keep his rising anger and frustration from showing in his voice.

"You'll not find us to be defenseless prey," Tallin said, again raising his blade.

Vheod drew his sword, the Abyssal steel ringing in the morning air.

Just then, two more men ran up the bare earthen road. One carried an axe, the other a long knife. They cried out in surprise and ran at Vheod.

Vheod shot his blade straight out at the one called Tallin, catching him right where he wanted—the wrist of his sword arm. Tallin's blade flung end over end through the air as his fingers splayed wide. His other hand reached up to grasp at the painful but minor wound. Tallin cursed, but Vheod had no time to listen. Two more men approached, and there was still someone behind him with a—

Pain flared in Vheod's armored shoulder as metal clanged against metal next to Vheod's ear. The man had struck his shoulder but fortunately hadn't penetrated the pauldron. Vheod turned and brought his sword up to block the man's second blow. The two other men charged toward him, and he could hear more humans stirring all around, probably grabbing weapons to help.

"Go back where you came from!" the axe wielder shouted.

Vheod now knew he would have to kill all these insufferable, intolerant, misbegotten fools who—

No.

Something within him bade him to fight that urge. Perhaps because of the growing distance from the baleful Abyss, other forces were able to work within him, despite the fact that he still felt the evil in his nature as strongly as ever. Years of swordplay beckoned his arm to raise the weapon and cut down these men. Vheod forced his arm to remain still. He was suddenly forced to remember days earlier when Nethess had hired him to kill an enemy of hers. Living by his wits and fighting skills, Vheod took the job. To his surprise, Vheod discovered that his target was a human mortal—not a tanar'ri. Further surprising him, Vheod found he could not kill the man. At the last moment, the mortal portion of Vheod's soul had conjured forth his conscience, which stayed his hand. He couldn't kill a man as easily or thoughtlessly as he might slay a fiend.

This discovery may have surprised Vheod, but it only enraged Nethess. Now he found the same strange reluctance. He had to think of another way.

There was no time for a spell. If he fought these men, he would end up killing them. Vheod reached deep within himself, thrusting a mental hand deep into the dark well of fiendish power. He called to it, like a master calls an attack dog. Dark energy welled up inside him, climbing up his throat from his gut. Vheod choked back the bile that it brought with it and thrust the energy out from him into the world. A magical darkness exuded from every pore, enveloping him and hiding him from sight. It spread impenetrable darkness as well. Though he'd called for such darkness before—it was a common enough trick among the tanar'ri—he never noticed that the darkness seemed oily and smelled of spoiled food. It had never occurred to him to pay attention before now.

Vheod tried to comfort himself in the fact that the darkness would eventually fade. He couldn't spare the time to think about it any further. The darkness kept the men from attacking him. Their shouts of surprise and terror only helped create further confusion. Vheod knew from experience that once oncoming foes were thrust into such darkness, they were likely to begin swinging their weapons wildly. He immediately dived to the ground and began to crawl a few feet away.

Still within the mass of inky blackness, Vheod muttered sorcerous words long-practiced, forming a short incantation. He couldn't see, but he could feel the power unleashed by his spell spreading over him. Starting at his fingers, a prickling sensation spread down his arms, across his chest, down his body and back up until it covered his head. He had used this particular incantation many times, so he didn't need to see to know what the spell accomplished. In fact, sight wouldn't allow him to see the effect at all—that was the point. This spell rendered him beyond the vision of those who sought him. He held his breath as the magical effect finished clothing him in invisibility. Then, and only then, he slipped out of the darkness altogether.

By that time, as he blinked away the sudden light of day outside his dark creation, he saw his assailants drawing away from the oily cloud, recoiling from the frightening and surprising magic.

"I told you he was some creature of evil!" the axeman shouted to anyone who might listen.

A young woman ran up with a strung hunting bow pulled taut with a nocked arrow. She pointed it at the roiling blackness, but one of the men who had run in from the forest grasped the bow before she could loose her missile.

"No!" he told her. "It might fly through the darkness and strike someone on the other side. Everyone, wait. We've got to find him. I've seen this spell before."

"But Chorrad," a man's voice called out, "we've got to do something before he attacks us—or the children!" It was Tallin. He still grasped his wrist, but he'd regained his blade. A woman in a simple dress stood behind him with a bloody cloth that she tried to apply to his arm, but he pushed her back with a determined scowl.

Vheod determined then that his only recourse was to slip out of the village before a real fight started. A voice in his head nagged him, telling him: these simpletons deserve whatever harsh treatment you deal out. You tried to approach in peace, and they attacked you. Shaking his head, he tried to think about something else. How was he going to find Tilverton now?

Using soft, slow movements, he slipped out of the village's center and the crowd of people gathering there, despite the fact that all of them were looking for him. His spell proved more than capable of hiding him. He escaped with ease, but he wasn't glad. He knew no more than he had before, except that help was going to be harder to obtain than he'd thought.

Perhaps this world had no place for him after all.

At the edge of the settlement, Vheod found a small stable and corral with a handful of creatures he knew to be horses. He'd seen the animals before, though he'd seen creatures used as mounts in the Abyss that seemed as different from these noble beasts as one could possibly get.

Vheod approached the wooden fence around the beasts' corral. They snorted at his presence, probably catching a whiff of his odor since his magic made it impossible for them to see him. The horses grew more uneasy as he climbed over the fence. They stamped and nervously walked around in their confines. Vheod had no charms prepared that might tame one. Still, his determination to leave the village with speed gripped him. He approached one of the horses as quietly as he was able.

Reassuring himself that his actions were justified, he leaped atop the creature in a single, swift motion. He'd ridden a few different creatures in his life and knew a little about such beasts.

Unfortunately, it was only a very little. Worse, his smell—or perhaps his general otherworldly nature—spooked the animal. The horse reared up. He'd not yet completely steadied himself on the horse's back to begin with, so Vheod's fingers clutched at the creature's mane and neck. It reared again and jumped forward. Vheod slipped and landed on the side opposite the one from which he'd approached the horse.

"There he is! By the horses!"

An older man stood ten yards away from the edge of the fence. He held a staff before himself and used it to point right at Vheod as he lay in the dust.

The man could see him?

Then Vheod noticed the symbol that hung from the tip of the man's staff. While he didn't recognize it specifically, he knew it for what it was—the holy symbol of a priest. Some divine-granted sight must allow him to see that which was otherwise invisible.

Curse all gods!

Vheod could already hear people running toward them. The words and gestures to a spell of fire and destruction came to his mind, seemingly unbidden.

No!

Still invisible, he didn't need to resort to attack yet, and hopefully not at all. Vheod wished he'd been taught more potent magic—particularly something that might counter the priest's ability to detect him. Studies of that degree, however, had been beyond him. He had only the simplest spells at his command.

A deep snort came from directly above him. He rolled to one side, still lying on the ground. A horse's hoof crashed down to the ground where he'd lain. The horses stomped around and snorted, shaking their manes and whinnying. Looking back at the priest, Vheod saw the gray-bearded, bald man stretch his neck one way then the other. Perhaps, Vheod thought, it was difficult for the priest to keep an eye on him with the confusing movements of the horses all around him. Behind the man, more of the villagers came running. Most carried weapons, shaking them in tight fists.

Vheod grabbed a small stone from within his reach and hurled it at the nearest building behind the cleric. He hoped the horses shielded his action. The old man quickly turned toward the sound of it striking the wood. As he did, the others behind him also turned.

Vheod once again hurled himself over the back of one of the mounts, this time prepared for its violent reaction. It did indeed rear, but Vheod gripped at the horse's neck tightly, his strong legs wrapping around its midsection as best he could. Utilizing the beast's fear and anger, he coaxed it toward the fence. It bolted in that direction. When the horse reached the fence, it leaped over it without slowing. Vheod dug his boot heels into its sides and yanked at the mane, hoping to make it even angrier. The horse carried him far and fast away from the village. He didn't look back.

* * * * *

Vheod didn't know what direction to ride other than *away*. He left the forest, the thick clumping of trees giving way abruptly to a grassland of gently rolling hills. A warm breeze brushed across the landscape against the direction in which he rode. The miles passed by him, Vheod using the horse's anger and fear as best he could. Eventually the horse slowed. Apparently its anger could only last so long. Vheod grew tired of aggravating it, anyway. The two moved slowly through the tall grasses, the sun—the very existence of which Vheod was only now growing accustomed to—washing light and heat over them. The sun had been easier to ignore in the dense forest. Now he felt its heat and experienced its blinding light without protection. Both Vheod and the horse glistened with perspiration.

Miles of open grassland around him, the forest now a thin dark line on the horizon, Vheod became more aware of the fact that he had no idea where he was or where he was going. Why was he here at all?

The horse carried him slowly down the side of a gentle hill. The tall grass brushed against the bottoms of his feet. His mount seemed tired, reluctant, and quite irritated. Even if he knew where he was going, Vheod was unsure that he could force this horse to actually take him there. It seemed unlikely that he could spur the beast on only by continuing to aggravate it. Unfortunately, he knew no other way.

Glancing down, he saw the Taint had once again returned to his hand. Further, it resumed the appearance of a guiding arrow, pointing toward what Vheod believed to be south. Could he trust it? The Taint could be some intelligent, malevolent ally of his dark half. It could be a manifestation of the tanar'ri part of him.

Perhaps the best thing he could do would be to stop right where he was. Surely he could insure that no action beyond his control could be wrought by his dark half here in the middle of nowhere, but that could be exactly what it wanted. How could he know for sure?

Another rider through the grassland approached over a nearby hill. From this distance, Vheod could see that it was a woman on a horse, but little more. She veered her horse toward him.

As she approached, Vheod considered flight, or at least keeping a good distance away. He didn't want another situation like the one at the village. Before he could get control of his unwilling mount, however, she rode up within just a few yards.

"Good day," she said, her voice as smooth as the seductive succubi of the Abyss. When her horse moved, she moved as well, as though she and her mount were a single creature with a single mind. Her movements were slow and sure, betraying an unfailing grace. Her petite features included delightfully smooth skin and delicate, pointed ears. Long, silver hair nestled around her thin neck like waves carefully caressing a shoreline. She wore a heavy green cloak the very color of the grass around them draped over her shoulders despite the heat, yet Vheod couldn't see a hint of perspiration on her face or neck.

Most surprisingly, she didn't seem at all fazed by his appearance, unlike the villagers earlier that morning.

"Hello," Vheod returned tentatively.

"Your horse doesn't like you," she told him with a hint of a smile.

"Um, no, I think not," Vheod replied, still watching her with scrutiny.

"Well, I hope you are not traveling a great distance then," she said.

"Actually, lady, I have no idea how far I must ride."

"Really?" Her clear, gray eyes betrayed a hint of skepticism, and nothing more.

"I am not from . . . from around here. My destination is known to me in name only."

"I see," she said. "Well, my name is Tianna. I am riding to the mountains to the west. Do you believe your travels will take you there, or elsewhere?"

"I go to a place called Tilverton, and my name, fair lady, is Vheod Runechild."

"Ah. Tilverton is a human city that lies almost straight south of here, in a place called Tilver's Gap. The Gap itself lies between the Desertsmouth Mountains," she said, pointing to the west with a long, elegant finger, "and the Thunder Peaks to the south."

Vheod followed her hand and looked about carefully, attempting to fully establish his bearings. "Then I am afraid our paths cross only here," he told her. His voice conveyed his regret.

Vheod wished he could ride with Tianna for a while. Only now did he realize the loneliness he'd felt since his arrival here. He had so many questions about the nature of this world, and it seemed as though she would be willing to answer them. He knew that haste was important and thus allowed himself only one question.

"Tell me, Tianna, before we part company—for I must be on my way—why are you not alarmed at my appearance, as others have been?"

She gave him a cautious smile, but one not without some warmth. "Vheod, we of the elves are not strangers to cambions, or to those traveling from other planes."

Vheod was taken aback. "Is it that obvious—my tanar'ri heritage?"

Tianna looked at Vheod, studying his features for a moment. "No," she replied, "not to one without any experience with beings from other planes. However, there is a certain, well, quality to you, an indefinable characteristic that gives you a sense of . . . *otherness*." She paused to look at him, watching his eyes. Perhaps she was attempting to determine the effect her words had on him.

"Many of those you encounter here may be able to sense that you are different in some way," she said.

"That will certainly make any time I spend here harder," he said, looking at the ground, struck as severely as if he'd been in battle. His voice was edged with sudden bitterness, but he didn't have the time to consider if its target was his own nature, or the people who were prejudiced against him.

"Perhaps it will fade over time," she said. "Or perhaps your own nobility will be enough to override anyone's antagonistic first impression."

He looked up at Tianna again and smiled as though she'd just healed a bleeding wound. Her hair shone in a way that made him believe that a special place existed for it in the moonlight, and that its proper place didn't lie in the sun. She was beautiful.

"But you must be on your way," she finally added with some regret, "as you said."

Vheod hated to hear it, but the truth couldn't be denied. Duty and responsibility called to him with voices filled with fear. "Yes, I suppose so."

"Before you go, however," she said, reaching into a saddlebag, "I think that you should have this." She produced a small charm on a silver chain, holding it up to let it glint in the sunlight.

"What is it?"

"A magical trinket," she said with a delicate shrug, "with a single use. It grants the wearer a power called *longstepping*. Essentially, it will allow you to travel to a destination in almost no time. You can use it to reach Tilverton today, rather than the three days' ride it might take from here. It will also allow you to bypass a dangerous area known as Shadow Gap."

Vheod stared in surprise, taking in everything she said. "But, why?"

She smiled slyly. "If you use this, then I can take back this horse to where you got it."

"What? How did you—"

"I'm sorry, Vheod, but it's obvious that you just arrived here at the edge of the Dales, let alone Faerûn and even Toril. Judging by your ride, the steed's demeanor, and the fact that you have no riding tackle, it becomes fairly obvious how you came on your mount.

"Further, I am a bit of a seer when it comes to people. You—at least a part of you—didn't want to take the horse. I can return him, if you'll tell me where he comes from."

Vheod's mouth hung agape as wide as the young boy in the doorway earlier that morning. He quickly closed it, feeling quite the fool, but remained entranced by Tianna and her kindness. Without a word, he slid down off the horse's back and stepped toward her. Tianna urged her mount ahead a few steps until she reached him. She held out the silver charm.

"It only works once," she reminded him.

"Thank you," Vheod said as he grasped the tiny charm in his weathered hand. "How can I repay you?"

"You cannot, to tell the truth," Tianna said, "but that's not the point. I want to help you."

She looked deeply into his dark eyes and leaned down close to his face. "I just thought that you probably needed to see a little of the good in the world. You needed some kindness. My gift is really a minor one."

"But there you are wrong," Vheod returned her look with a slow shake of his head. "This is a great gift, one I will remember for all my years."

"May there be many of them," she said, straightening in her ornate saddle.

Tianna rode over to Vheod's grazing horse, and drew an extra bridle from her saddlebag. The horse looked at her with calm, welcoming eyes. It nuzzled her thigh with its nose. She placed the bridle on the beast and readied to lead it away, then turned back to Vheod.

"The village lies almost directly in your path, at the edge of the woods to the west." Vheod gripped the charm even tighter in his sweaty palm. "They may have unkind things to say of me," he told her. "They may not welcome you if you claim to be my friend."

"Do not concern yourself with such things. I can take care of everything. Safe journey, Vheod, and be well."

"Yes, ah . . . safe journey to you as well, Tianna." Vheod was unused to pleasantries. Tianna turned to leave.

"Wait," Vheod called out.

Tianna turned to look back at him. She kept her smile.

"You said you are a seer when it comes to people. Can you tell me—is it possible for a place to change a person? Can this world be changing me?"

Tianna shook her head gently. "No, Vheod, only you can change yourself." She turned again, whispered something to her horse that Vheod couldn't hear, then rode off in the direction Vheod had come.

He turned southward, in the direction he understood Tilverton to be. He opened his hand to look at the silver, arrow-shaped charm in his palm. Its shape beckoned him to look back at the Taint, still on the other side of his hand. It remained in its arrow shape, and still pointed, as if directing him where *it* wanted him to go.

It pointed south, toward Tilverton.

Chapter Six

No wind blew through the hot summer air. The stillness made for a stiflingly hot ride through the grass-covered hills. Whitlock and Melann could see the Thunder Peaks rise higher and higher before them as they approached, yet no pace they kept could satisfy their desire to reach their intended destination. Melann was quiet, but she gave Whitlock the impression she was very pleased with all that had happened. Obviously she was still confident that her god was guiding them.

Whitlock, however, grew ever more pensive as he rode. The mountains ahead would be dangerous—he remembered clearly what they had heard about an amassing of gnolls. Further, who could guess what other sorts of dangers might lie there? He knew he was up to the challenge, but he also knew that the coming days might require him to use every bit of his skill and experience to insure that both he and his sister survived.

The sea of green and brown grasses occasionally broke on rocky islands that seemed to grow in frequency as they approached the mountains. Birds occasionally flew across the virtually cloudless blue sky. By midday on their first day out from Tilverton, they were covered in sweat as they stopped for a noon meal. They ate dry bread and even drier venison purchased way back in Essembra. The harsh sun would soon scorch their skins, so Melann took the time to mash some herbs she brought, mixing them with water to create a thin paste to spread over their exposed flesh.

"We should have remained in Tilverton, at least long enough to obtain more information about where we're headed," Whitlock said between careful swallows from his waterskin to wash down the dry lunch.

"And waste valuable time?" Melann countered, finishing her herbal mixture.

"We could have at least confirmed what he told us," Whitlock said. "Further, we could have restocked our supplies a bit." He tore at the dry bread with his teeth like a dog, shaking his head back and forth before gaining a crusty mouthful. "Not that we have much in the way of gold left."

"Once we get into the mountains, there will be wild game, and Our Mother will provide berries, roots, and other things to collect. I'm not worried."

"Of course you're not worried!" Whitlock suddenly exploded. "I have to worry for the both of us. You're so busy praying and thinking about your god that I have to work twice as hard to keep us safe, provide food, and find our way. Don't you realize the responsibility that is placed on me? The burdens I must face?"

Melann sat in stunned silence, staring at her brother, which made him feel guilty and self-conscious. He brushed bread crumbs out of his beard and took a drink of water—anything to divert his gaze from his sister's wide-eyed stare.

"Is that really what you think?" Melann asked quietly.

Whitlock said nothing.

"You think I don't worry?" Melann asked. "All I do is worry. I worry that when I spend all my time focused on my religious duties I neglect you, and Mother, and Father, and even myself. I worry that when I do what I personally feel compelled to do that I am not truly as devoted as I should be to Chauntea. I worry that I'm not worthy to be a priestess, or that as a priestess, I make a poor daughter—or sister. Don't tell me I don't worry. If it seems I let you take care of things like navigation or keeping watch at night, it's because I trust you and know how capable you are."

She added, after a moment's thought, "Besides, if we need food, the Mother of All can grant me the power to create it. You know that."

Whitlock wasn't an eloquent man. So many things jumped to his mind to say, but the words to explain them escaped him. Instead, he stood and began to gather up what they had unpacked for their meal.

"I'm sorry," he said finally, glancing only momentarily at his sister.

Melann sighed softly. She smiled a little and helped him pack their things into saddlebags so they could continue their journey.

By nightfall, Whitlock and Melann were well into the rocky, mountainous region known as the Thunder Peaks. Night in the mountains came quickly once the sun disappeared over the mountains, and it came with an utter darkness for which neither Whitlock nor Melann was really prepared. Tall peaks to all sides blocked out even most of the starlight, which encouraged them both to huddle even closer to their campfire. The darkness carried a chill with it, as well as an utter silence.

Neither sibling spoke. Instead they simply ate their small meal absorbed in their own thoughts. Whitlock's heavy eyelids bade him to lay back on his bedroll as he ate. His sister stood, mumbling softly something about checking on the horses before going to sleep.

Thunderous sounds rent the silence of the cool evening, and Whitlock sat up only to see two large shapes looming out of the darkness toward him. He grabbed his broadsword and held it in front of him as the two figures—massive, hairy creatures standing upright like men—lunged at him. One carried a short spear and a shield. The other wielded a huge flail in both of its hispid claws. The musky, animal scent that clung to these intruders brought visions of kennels and caged animals to Whitlock's mind.

The first creature lunged with its spear at Whitlock, who blocked the blow with his blade. Following its initial attack, the canine-faced assailant jabbed at him. It forced him back and off-balance. Whitlock attempted to regain his footing just as the second beast charged at him, howling, with the flail held high over its head. Whitlock held his sword up to counter the blow, but his feet failed him, and he tumbled backward over his bedroll. The flail barely missed his head as he fell, his fortune owing more to luck than skill. The second creature stabbed with its iron-tipped spear, but it glanced off the mail on Whitlock's chest making a resounding ringing noise. Whitlock would probably show a bruise there later, but if he'd not been too tired to yet remove his armor, he would probably be dead.

Knocked off his feet, Whitlock only managed to yell out briefly to Melann as he fought off his attackers.

Where was she? If he was attacked, certainly she was too.

The growling, bestial figure with the flail brought it down at Whitlock, but he managed to roll out of the way. The flail struck the ground next to him with a dull thud. The warrior rolled again and half regained his feet, keeping out of reach of the spear-wielder. Still unsteady, he realized that he stood next to where he'd placed his shield by the fire and grabbed it. The gnolls charged at him as he pushed his left arm through the shield's straps. Brandishing the metal shield with his family crest emblazoned on it, Whitlock threw himself at the advancing foes.

With his shield to parry the spearman's jabs, Whitlock thrust his blade at the other gnoll. The blow slid along the creature's leather-armored side, but he drew blood. The monster howled in pain. Sidestepping the campfire, Whitlock positioned himself where the wounded gnoll couldn't get at him without first going around the fire. With that in mind, he broke the other creature's spear with two mighty hacks on its haft and slashed at the creature's arm, driving it back so that it cowered behind its own shield. Unfortunately, his attacks had taken too long. The flail-wielder had already gone around the fire and came up behind him. All Whitlock could do was bring his shield around as he turned to face the flanking foe and even that came too late. The flail crashed into his side, sending him sprawling toward the fire.

Fortunately, Whitlock hadn't lost his wits, despite the terrific blow. He drew the shield underneath himself, so that it not only protected him from most of the flames but gave him an instant leverage point to fling himself out of the fire. Unfortunately, he inhaled a lungful of smoke and lay hacking and coughing on the ground as both gnolls rushed toward him. Through teary eyes, Whitlock saw his foes advance and raised his singed shield arm to protect his battered body.

"Melann!"

He still heard no answer. Gods help him if anything had happened to her. He realized then that while he fought these gnolls, he had no idea how many might actually be out in the darkness around the camp.

Whitlock slashed at the approaching gnoll. His blow sent the creature toppling to the ground. The other beast-man, still weaponless, paused just long enough for Whitlock to stand again. It bared yellow, pointed teeth as it stepped forward. It raised its clawed hand like a weapon. The gnoll blocked Whitlock's sword blow with its wooden shield and lashed at him with its claws. Again Whitlock caught a good whiff of its animalistic scent, but it actually helped clear his senses. His second thrust caught the creature on its exposed, shieldless side, and it crumpled as the blade slid into its flesh.

The other hirsute gnoll regained its feet, but its crooked stance betrayed that it was obviously quite hurt. It dropped its heavy flail and backed away, but Whitlock charged. He bashed into the creature with his shield, knocking it down again. A sudden chop from his sword made sure it wouldn't rise again. A small, greenish stone rolled from its dead hand as it fell to the ground.

Whitlock breathed deeply, trying to expel the last bit of smoke and soot from his lungs and mouth. His shoulder ached from the heavy blow he'd suffered from the gnoll's flail, but he pushed that from his attention.

"Melann!" he called into the inky, black night.

Whitlock stumbled to where they'd put the horses. They were gone. He found no sign of Melann either. The dark night kept its secrets well hidden.

Whitlock saw a dark shape near or on the ground, farther into the darkness.

"Melann?"

No answer. Whitlock ran back to the fire. His scuffle through it had scattered the wood, and the separated flames were dying quickly. He grabbed a flaming brand, its end unburned but painfully hot. Whitlock returned to where he'd seen the shape. It was a body. A gnoll. Further, the beast-man still lived, though the sounds of its breathing were heavy and thick, as though it had suffered a wound against its chest. Sure enough, a closer look revealed that its crude leather armor was stained with dark blood.

"Where is my sister?" Whitlock demanded.

The creature turned over to face the warrior. Its large, brown eyes showed only incomprehension and pain. A snarl escaped its bristling, bloody snout.

Whitlock placed his booted foot over the creature's chest and pressed down. "Where . . . is . . . my . . . sister?" he said, each word forced through clenched, bile-coated teeth. The creature didn't reply.

Perhaps, he thought, Melann managed to run into the woods. Maybe when the gnolls appeared, she saw them coming and slipped away. It seemed too much to hope for, but Whitlock looked around him, wishing to see her come out of the darkness unscathed.

How was this gnoll injured? Whitlock looked down at it and saw that its wound might have been inflicted with a blunt object, like a club. Melann carried a small baton to use in self defense. She must have fought them. Perhaps she drove them off, as he had done, but then where was she?

His mind searched for an answer when, just a few feet off to the gnoll's side, Whitlock saw a bit of cloth lying on the ground. It was a small piece torn from Melann's traveling cloak.

"No!"

He brought his sword down on the neck of the dying gnoll.

Chapter Seven

Tianna's charm of longstepping proved to be as potent as she had claimed.

Once he activated the charm, Vheod was transported—not instantaneously, but with incredible speed—across the barren landscape. As he watched, trees, rivers, hills, mountains, and even miles of open space passed before his eyes so quickly he could scarcely recognize them as anything but colored blurs. Rather than feeling the wind whip across his body, Vheod felt instead that he stretched his body the entire distance, as though, just for a moment, he existed in his starting and ending points at the same time, as well as all the points in between.

The sensation ended, and Vheod dizzily lurched to keep his feet under him. Disoriented and reeling, he could tell that a city lay in the distance. Regaining his balance, his vision clearing, Vheod saw that the city was surrounded by a high wall, with a few buildings outside. Most of the outbuildings looked like animal pens or barns—perhaps a stockyard or something similar.

The process of traveling so quickly made it very difficult for him to get his bearings. It was as though a part of his mind was left behind when he activated the magical charm and still believed that he remained, or at least he should have remained, back where he started. The disorientation made even walking difficult at first, but he adapted and accommodated eventually.

This must be Tilverton, Vheod reasoned. Or at least he hoped it was. After taking a breath or two to recover and alleviate the pain in his aching head, he walked toward the wall and what appeared to be an open gate.

Tilverton bustled noisily. Herders brought their flocks in for market, and farmers hauled produce through the gate on carts and wagons. People moved into and out of the city watched only casually by guards. Vheod wondered if he, too, would be allowed entrance to the city, or if the guards would stop him for the same reasons the villagers had driven him out of their community only hours before.

Vheod ran his hands through his long hair, smoothing his red tresses and pulling them behind his head. He dusted off his dark brown pants and tattered violet cape. His long sword clattered in its sheath against his leg. He stopped suddenly. Something made him think of the Taint. He looked quickly but carefully over his exposed skin for it. It was nowhere he could find. That meant it had either moved to a spot under his clothing or armor, or it was somewhere he couldn't see it, like his face.

The thought that other people might be able to see the Taint while he couldn't gave Vheod great concern. Who knew what shape it might take without his knowledge? Not more than a hundred yards away from the city gate, he drew forth his sword. Taking his cloak with his other hand, he tried to polish a bit of the sword's blade as best he could hoping to shine it to a reflective sheen. His efforts were partially successful, and he gazed into the spot, angling the blade back and forth to look at different parts of his face and neck. Though it was far from a thorough search, he saw no trace of the tattoo anywhere on his face. With a sigh, he sheathed his sword and continued on to the gate.

Vheod passed through without the guards so much as raising an eyebrow. No one in the street paid him any particular attention, in fact.

From at least one point of view, a city is just a city, no matter where in this or any other world it might sit. It seemed to Vheod that only one city actually existed, and all the others were merely extensions of this metaphysical, ubiquitous city. Vheod looked about Tilverton and realized that at its heart it differed only slightly from any of the other cities he'd ever wandered through.

Vheod had spent most of his time in the Abyss in cities made of dark bricks and bone. He resided longest in Broken Reach, a vast catacomb of intrigue and betrayal ruled by a succubus named Red Shroud. There he worked for a guild of assassins called the Bloody Dagger. Those of the Dagger killed for money, usually hired by some minor tanar'ri noble to kill an opponent or a superior. Even in the lawless, amoral plane of the Abyss, however, Vheod had occasionally thought his profession was less than ethical. Normally he'd been able to push such thoughts from his conscience, glad to see each and every fiendish victim die by his hand. The teeming streets of Tilverton, and his almost instinctual ability to blend into the crowd and avoid the eyes of those who passed by him, brought back those thoughts. The city—the ubiquitous city—was a symbol of shame to him now.

Vheod entered the town from the north and wandered through the streets of Tilverton for quite some time. A melancholy washed over him, and he walked through the streets in a fog. Shaking his head, he brought himself back to the task at hand. He found Tilverton; now he needed to find someone whom Gyrison and Arach had described as being like him. Vheod needed information.

A city, as an entity, thrives with a life of its own, serving the needs of those who live in it, yet feeding off them as they move through its streets. A city always contained major arteries and paths through which its life flowed, but also held darker, less-frequented areas where few inhabitants and fewer outsiders visited. A city always held some sort of authority or organization, even if it hid its presence very well in the cacophony and mayhem that teemed within its walls—such was often the way of Abyssal cities. Even in the Abyss, however, cities held gathering places, like taverns, alehouses, or festhalls. Even in the Abyss, when one sought information, it was just such a gathering place that offered the best chance to obtain what one needed.

Using an urban instinct fostered by a life on the streets, Vheod looked for an appropriate tavern. In the Abyss, a wise cambion clung to back alleyways and the streets less frequented—better to keep hidden, to avoid drawing attention. These places provided peace from the bustle and din that always came to the life flow areas of the city.

In one such forgotten, forsaken corner, wandering down a street that might not even have a name, he came on a door. The door lay under a sign that rocked back and forth on the breeze on rusty iron rings suspended from a pole. The sign read only, "Drink."

Vheod pushed the old, warped wooden door open and stepped into the smoky room. Three high-placed windows provided a little light, though a few oil lamps burned on tables. The place smelled of ale and humanity, both stale. Three or four patrons drank quietly, all of them alone. He stood in the doorway, looking at each individual and all the establishment held.

He must have remained there too long, for finally a man sitting up against the wooden bar turned to him and said with a hoarse voice, "The Flagon Held High is on the other side of town," as if that would mean something to Vheod. The speaker was short, with stout arms and legs, a thick brown beard, and a round face.

Vheod ignored his words, but approached. Still watching the rest of the room, he peered into the man's tight eyes, which reminded Vheod of nail heads. "Have you seen anyone . . . like me around here?"

"My friend," the man said with a narrow, sidelong gaze and an ever-so-slight slur, "I've never seen anyone like you in my life. What's wrong with you?"

Vheod studied him silently, then said, "There is nothing wrong with me, 'friend.' Begone." Vheod dismissed the man with a gesture and stepped up to the stained wooden bar.

"Same to you, beautiful," the man muttered, walking away.

"Watch out," a woman said, carrying a tray of empty flagons and almost bumping into Vheod. She smiled without really looking at him and moved to the bar.

"Excuse me," Vheod said, following her. She was stout and short, with her mahogany hair pulled back into a round knob, though hours of work had coaxed some rogue strands down to lie by the sides of her face.

"Yes?" She turned. "You need something to drink?" Her face was careworn, Vheod thought, but her eyes were friendly.

"Ah, no." Vheod shook his head. "What I'd like is for you to tell me something. It might seem odd, but, well—I'm new around here."

"What do you need to know?" The woman set down her tray and nodded toward him.

Vheod chewed his lip a moment. "I need to know what you see when you look at me."

"What?"

"What do I look like to you? Do I look like everyone else?" Vheod stroked his rough jaw. He glanced down to see the Taint once again on the back of his right hand. He covered it quickly with his left. His eyes darted.

"No," she said, raising her brow thoughtfully, "not like everyone else. That's for sure."

What did that mean? "Have you ever seen anyone like me before?"

She moved her mouth to one side, as if considering what to say. "Are you a half-elf?"

"Half-elf?" Then people are familiar with half-blooded humans here, he thought.

"Yes, you know," she asked, "was only one of your parents human?"

"As a matter of fact, yes."

"He ain't pretty enough to be a half-elf," the man with the thick beard said from behind them. Vheod turned back to him and scowled.

"I thought I told you to leave," Vheod clipped.

"Don't listen to him," the woman said to Vheod. "He's a drunk."

"More like half-*orc*," the bearded man continued, pointing a thick finger at Vheod.

"Do not make me speak to you again," Vheod hissed at him through clenched teeth, then turned back to the serving woman. She was already moving the empty flagons from her tray into a water-filled barrel burgeoning with other dirty dishes floating amid fading soap bubbles.

A tall man with gray hair moved up from behind the bar. Though he'd just come into the room through the door behind the bar, he joined in the conversation as though he'd been there all the time.

Looking at Vheod for a moment, he said, "Nah. The only half-orc I've ever seen 'round here is Orrag, and he don't have no pointed ears like this here fella."

"Hush now, Ponter," the woman said to him with a slight push of her hand against his shoulder.

"Orrag? Who is Orrag?" Vheod asked.

Orcs, Vheod knew, were an evil and bestial race that populated many prime worlds as well as other planes. Half-orcs? A human-orc crossbreed might not be all that dissimilar to a cambion, from a certain point of view. Is that who Gyrison and Arach meant?

"Believe me, you don't want to know," the woman said.

"But I do," Vheod replied.

"Orrag'd put a knife in your ribs, fella," the tall barman said with a nod of his head.

"Ponter, hush." The woman finished emptying her tray and used it to lightly shove the tall man.

"Look, I need to know more about this half-orc. I wish to meet him. I may have . . . business with him."

"Business with Orrag?" the bearded man said quietly, into his flagon. "I knew I didn't like you."

Before Vheod could respond, the tall man, Ponter, reached across the bar and placed his hand on Vheod's arm. Leaning in close, he whispered, "Listen, if you really want to meet up with Orrag, stay right where you are. He usually comes into the place on mid-tenday nights—he steers clear of The Flagon Held High and other more . . . visible places.

My place ain't on any maps, if you see what I mean."

"I think perhaps I do," Vheod replied quietly. "I thank you, sir. I will remain."

"Why don't you have something to drink in the meanwhile?" Ponter asked him in his normal, loud voice, straightening up and away from Vheod.

"Good enough," Vheod replied, digging into a pouch and wondering what they used for money here.

Vheod fortunately had a few coins in his pouch that he could convince Ponter to accept, though none of them were minted on this world. The day in the tavern stretched on for what seemed like many. By the time the darkness of night consumed what little light managed to seep in through the small windows, Vheod had drunk his fill. More than once he wished that the establishment served food. The annoying short man left finally, and Vheod claimed a tottering, ale-slick table near one wall.

With the advent of darkness, the tavern attracted more activity, but the patrons generally kept quiet and to themselves, content simply to drink. Vheod found it difficult to believe the inhabitants of a beautiful world like this, untainted by real evil, might spend their evenings in this vapid locale. Boredom began clawing at him, and he soon found himself growing drowsy. He leaned back in his chair against the stone wall, telling himself he would close his eyes just for a moment—

"You got business with me?"

Vheod snapped his eyes open. A large, wide-shouldered man with a fleshy face and a stomach that hung liberally over his belt stood over Vheod. His breath stank, and his narrow eyes hid little of the malice that lay within them. His porcine face and jowls, along with his pointed, yellow teeth made him the least appealing creature Vheod had seen since his encounter with the hairy spider-beasts in the woods.

When Vheod didn't reply immediately, the man spoke again. "I'm pretty sure I don't know you, do I? I think I'd remember you."

"Are you Orrag?" Vheod asked him, pushing himself away from the wall and righting his chair.

"Maybe. Depends on who's asking." He took a long draught from his flagon.

"I see," Vheod said. "I understand. My name is Vheod, and I was instructed to speak with you."

"You been talking to Ferd?" Orrag said, ale running down his flabby chin and running into one of the folds of flesh in his neck.

"Ah, no, not that I'm aware of, in any event."

Orrag pulled another chair away from the table and thrust his bulk into it with such force that Vheod almost expected it would break. "Something about you interests me," Orrag said, with a hint of a crooked smile. "What is it?"

Vheod had seen smiles on fiends that seemed more pleasant. Still, this creature might have some information, and he'd certainly dealt with fouler beasts in the past. He would have to choose his words carefully, however. He suspected that Orrag was sharper than he appeared.

Again annoyed at Vheod's unresponsiveness, Orrag asked, "What's your story, Vheod?"

"It's a long one," Vheod retorted, "but perhaps some of it might be of interest to you."

"I doubt it," Orrag lied, "but I must admit there's something intriguing about you. You're not from around here, are you?" Before Vheod could answer, the half-orc continued. "I'll tell you what. Let's make this interesting. You tell me a tale, and if I find it interesting, I'll listen to whatever business you're supposed to have with me. Sound fair?"

Vheod had expected Orrag to be less than reputable from Ponter's brief comments earlier that day. His disgusting appearance and mannerisms were almost unnoticeable to someone who had spent his entire life among the fiends of the Lower Planes. However, something about Orrag puzzled him. The half-orc's manner suggested an unspoken agenda— almost as if he recognized who Vheod was, or *what* he was.

"Perhaps I can come up with something that might pique your curiosity," Vheod said slowly. "I can tell you of the place from which I hail. My homeland holds many tales, let me tell you."

Orrag simply nodded and took a small, noisy sip from his flagon.

Vheod cleared his throat and began his tale. "Many centuries ago, so I was told, the Abyssal Lord Demogorgon commissioned a ship to be built."

"A ship?" Orrag asked.

Vheod scowled. "Yes."

Orrag said nothing, but sipped his drink once again.

"This ship wasn't just a normal craft, meant to sail the seas. No, wind and oarsmen were not to propel this craft. This was a ship that would sail the River Styx itself. On the Styx, a craft can travel between any of the Lower Planes—the Abyss, Gehenna, Pandemonium, even Baator. Furthermore, this ship would ply the waters between all the planes and travel to any world that its captain might choose to visit. Its enchanted rudder would direct the ship on a sorcerous journey anywhere in the multiverse."

Orrag raised his brow and took another sip, his eyes never leaving Vheod.

"A tanar'ri shipwright by the name of Reyniss had garnered a reputation among important circles deep within the Abyss. His skills were well known." Vheod paused for a moment, considering his words. "There are more malignant seas and fetid rivers flowing through the Abyss than you might think."

Orrag continued to stare silently.

"Demogorgon contacted Reyniss," Vheod continued, "by means of a mephit, a tiny, dark servitor of the Lower Planar lords. It flitted through the brooding caverns and dismal swamps of the Abyss to bring him this message: 'I, Demogorgon, Tanar'ri Prince and Lord of All that Swims in Darkness, wish to commission you to undertake your greatest achievement,' it said. 'Come to me, and I will tell you of the glories and riches that will be yours should you craft the ship that I desire.'

"Reyniss knew better than to trust Demogorgon, for even the greatest of fiends can know treachery at the hands of an Abyssal Lord. Thus the shipwright gathered together all of the sorcerous protections he could muster and filled his own dark lair with defenses and traps to ward away intruders. Cautiously, he made his way to Ungorth Reddik, Demogorgon's fortress.

"Ungorth Reddik rose from a grotesque bog deep in the Abyss. Swarming about it were Demogorgon's fiendish servants and all sorts of scaly monstrosities that worshiped him. Reyniss ignored them, and entered the fortress through gargoyle-protected gates.

"Demogorgon greeted the shipwright with caliginous smiles across both his houndlike faces. Within dark Ungorth Reddik, the two fiends forged their agreement. Reyniss agreed to build the ship that would sail the Styx and throughout the planes of existence. Demogorgon agreed to pay him in gold, jewels and the lorn currency common to the Lower Planes."

Vheod paused to see if Orrag understood his reference. The fat man widened his bulging eyes ever so slightly and shook his face just enough to make his jowls wobble.

"Souls, my friend. The spirits of evil mortals. On the dire planes, these souls are traded among the powerful fiends the way mortals might exchange a gem or a trinket." Vheod wondered if these statements would have any effect on Orrag. Did the man worry about his own eternal fate? Orrag, however, showed no sign that Vheod's words had any meaning for him. Vheod wasn't surprised. He smiled inwardly. The fate of evil souls wasn't something he relished dwelling on himself. Vheod had no idea if he truly had a mortal soul, and if so, what fate awaited it. Was damnation a foregone conclusion for a cambion? Was he already so damned? Was he, because of the tanar'ri blood in his veins, not a true mortal at all? He didn't know, and most of the time, he kept himself too busy to contemplate it. Purpose.

Of course, it might be that Orrag was too dim to understand the implications of this portion of the tale, but Vheod perceived a good deal of cunning— quite likely malicious cunning—in Orrag's dark, small, bulging eyes. Orrag wasn't stupid. In any event, the half-orc grew visibly anxious for the tale to continue. Vheod obliged.

"So Reyniss returned to his own lair near the strange, arcane shipyards in which he plied his craft. Utilizing more sorcery than mundane labor, Reyniss began building the ship, which he'd already in his designs named *Demonwing*. He employed tanar'ri of all types to help in the construction of the huge craft.

To hold the correct enchantments, Reyniss's plans called for the ship's hull to be made of stone rather than wood. This strange stone would still allow the ship to float on the waves, but it would also withstand the journey between the planes.

"Sails of flesh and a rudder of bone completed the grisly, fiendish *Demonwing*. When construction was complete, Reyniss sent a mephit to relate the news to Demogorgon. When the demon prince heard the news, he appeared almost immediately in the ship-yards, standing before Reyniss's creation. The fiendish prince was well pleased. Reyniss felt sure that his reward would put him in a position to advance in the tanar'ri ranks, making him a ruler over many lesser fiends.

"Demogorgon instead made Reyniss a further offer. He told the shipwright he would grant him twice the agreed-upon payment. Reyniss eyed the monstrous Demogorgon, with his two heads, tall, narrow reptilian body, and tentacles rather than arms, with suspicion . . . as I'm sure you can understand."

Vheod paused and looked at Orrag, who said nothing.

"Reyniss," he continued, "heart full of suspicion, asked Demogorgon what he would need to do to gain this double reward.

" 'Think of it as a wager,' Demogorgon said with a voice like wet velvet.

" 'What sort of wager, oh prince?' Reyniss asked.

" 'Just this,' Demogorgon replied. 'If you can use this ship to travel to the plane of ultimate chaos, Limbo, and back again in less than three days' time, I shall grant you the increased reward.'

" 'And if I cannot?' Reyniss asked.

" 'Then you get nothing, and I get the ship.'

"Now Reyniss knew full well that he could get the ship to the chaotic morass of Limbo and back in three

107

days. The question was, did Demogorgon have some trick or treachery here? Did the fiendish prince plan on sending minions out to attack Reyniss as he sailed to stop him on his journey? Why would Demogorgon risk damaging or destroying the ship in that way? Surely he wouldn't do such a thing.

"Perhaps, Reyniss thought to himself, Demogorgon merely wanted Reyniss to show him he was actually getting all he'd asked for.

"So Reyniss agreed. He gathered together a crew of tanar'ri and they left immediately. Reyniss set sail for Limbo, steering the craft along the River Styx and through the howling caverns of Pandemonium. He made his way across the Sea of Madness and through the Straits of Insanity, plunging headlong in the miasma of churning matter and energy in the plane of Limbo. Gathering some of the chaos-stuff that fills that plane as proof, he turned the craft around and sailed back toward the Abyss.

"Nothing attacked *Demonwing*. Demogorgon played no tricks and cast no betrayals. Reyniss arrived back in his own shipyards sooner than even he thought possible. His toothy tanar'ri smile was almost as broad as his pride-filled chest.

"When Reyniss disembarked, Prince Demogorgon waited for him, stony-faced. Reyniss expected his reward would come to him at any moment, and he leered at the Abyssal Lord in anticipation and greed. 'You took me up on my wager,' Demogorgon said. 'Did you not expect treachery?'

"Reyniss, his mind still filled with the thoughts of his riches, replied, 'Oh, I thought about it, but then I realized you would never endanger the ship you wanted so badly just to get out of your obligation. And I was right!'

"Demogorgon spoke, his voice like iron against stone, 'You were wrong. Oh, I took no action against your journey—that is true enough—but the fact that you believed I might not shows your utter stupidity. I had thought to make you my personal lieutenant and chief builder, but anyone who so completely fails to comprehend the ways of the Abyss shouldn't be suffered to live. Of course I would have endangered the ship if I thought it might keep me from paying. However, when you accepted the wager, I knew I didn't have to.' And with that, Demogorgon strangled the fiendish life out of Reyniss with his own tendrils of rotting death."

Orrag remained silent for a moment. Vheod watched him closely, waiting for a reaction.

A smile came to the half-orc's dark lips like a snake rearing up from its coils. "An excellent tale, my friend. Demogorgon! The Abyss! A magical ship!" Orrag exclaimed. "Excellent." He downed the rest of his drink in a single gulp.

"Well then," Vheod said slowly, "I believe you agreed to listen to what I had to say."

"Yes, my friend," Orrag said, yellow teeth showing. "What is this all about?"

"First, I must ask a little more about you, Orrag. What is it that you do? I must know if you are the right man to whom to pose my questions."

Orrag's face showed an evil pride. He leaned back away from the table and looked around the tavern. The patrons were still few in number, and no one paid them any attention. He swooped in close, leaning across the table.

"Well," he began, "here in Tilverton, we have a group called the Rogues. They operate out of the ancient sewer system and take what they want from locals or travelers."

"Thieves." Vheod stated.

"A guild," said Orrag. Vheod knew a little something about guilds. His thoughts raced back to his days among the Bloody Daggers.

"I, on the other hand," Orrag continued, "run a small group of . . . businessmen who live by their wits and procure what they require—while keeping out of the reach of the Rogues."

Vheod was hardly surprised. Orrag ran a gang of thieves that even the other local thieves didn't care for. How could Orrag help him? Why had Gyrison and Arach sent him here?

"So, Vheod, what am I supposed to do for you?"

"I'm looking for someone," Vheod said quietly. "Two people, actually."

"Why should I know anything about that?"

"Call it a hunch," Vheod said, standing. "Wait here."

Vheod walked to the bar and asked for another ale. While the serving woman poured his drink into a wooden flagon, he asked her quietly, "Tell me what you can about Orrag." He added a moment later an unfamiliar, "Please."

"A thief and a murderer," she said quietly, looking over Vheod's shoulder at the half-orc. "What else is there to know?"

"I see," Vheod said. Those things he'd already guessed. "What I mean is, is there anything *else* he's known for?"

"Anything else?" she replied, shaking her head. "Not that I know of. Isn't that enough?"

"I'm not sure," Vheod said, laying down a few coins he received as change from his previous purchase. Something about Orrag bothered him. The half-orc was more than just a thief. He took the ale back to the table and set it down in front of Orrag.

"So who are you looking for?" Orrag asked with a furrowed brow narrowing his eyes.

"Like I said: two people, a man and woman—they look similar enough to be related, probably siblings."

Orrag grunted and worked his jaw. "And do I know them or something?"

Vheod ran his fingers through his long, snarled hair. "I think, somehow, you might."

"Why?"

"Would you be someone people might come to, looking for information?"

"What sort of information?" Orrag grasped the flagon, but didn't drink.

"The location of something, perhaps outside of town."

Orrag's silence worried Vheod. The cambion considered a few spells that might be appropriate should his questions provoke an attack from Orrag. Vheod had seen better attempts at deception—he was, after all, from the Abyss. He didn't have time to play Orrag's little games. He just needed the information.

Finally the half-orc spoke, obviously choosing his words carefully. "I have a contact or two in the wilderness . . . among those who dwell in caves rather than cities."

"I think I understand," Vheod said. "So has anyone come to you recently? A brother and sister, perhaps?"

"As a matter of fact, yes, storyteller," Orrag stated with a strange smile.

Vheod grasped at Orrag's words like a falling man to a ledge. "And what did you tell them? Where did they go?"

"So, you're interested too?" Orrag's smile broadened. "This is starting to make sense."

"What? Do you need payment?" Vheod's words were quick and harsh.

"Oh, not from you. I like you. I think I understand you."

Before Vheod could speak, Orrag continued. "I sent them to find the Crypt of Chare'en. Do you know about the crypt?"

"Crypt?"

Crypt? Chare'en was dead? Of course not.

"Yes," Orrag said, with a serpentine smile widening his fat cheeks. "These two youngsters came to me looking for directions to the crypt of the ancient wizard Chare'en." Orrag seemed to watch Vheod very closely as he spoke the last words.

"So what did you tell them?"

"I told you, I've got some contacts up in the mountains. I knew where they needed to go. I sent them on their way."

"That was very kind of you," Vheod said, still careful.

"They were sent to me by my friend, Ferd," Orrag told him with an exhalation that Vheod thought was supposed to be a laugh.

Vheod said nothing.

"Ferd sent them to me so that I could, ah, procure some of their wealth," Orrag said with a smile and a wave of his hand.

"But?"

"But as it turns out, they sought information I had, and they were willing to pay very well for it." He took a draught from the flagon

Vheod let him wipe away the ale from his mouth before speaking again. "But if you were going to rob them anyway, why did you care to give them the location?"

Orrag stared, caught in the obvious lie.

"Call it a change of heart," he said after a moment. Vheod didn't have time to figure out Orrag's real motivations.

"Then you'll tell me how to get there as well?"

"Certainly," Orrag said. He repeated the same instructions he'd given to Whitlock and Melann the previous night.

Vheod listened carefully, committing the directions and each landmark to memory. He would need to get a horse. This time he would pay for it.

"Here's a warning as well, storyteller," Orrag added at the end. "There's a dangerous sorceress out near there called the Ravenwitch. Be careful you don't run afoul of her."

"I'm not worried. I don't have time to be worried," Vheod said as he stood.

Orrag smirked but then asked, "So why are you so interested? Are you really after those two, or is it what they're looking for you're concerned with?"

Vheod already started toward the door. He turned back to say, "If I find them quickly enough, I won't need to worry about what they're looking for."

A worried look crossed Orrag's face, which in turn worried Vheod. Neither spoke. Vheod's hand flexed, ready to go to his sword hilt. Orrag's hand slid under the table.

Another moment passed.

Finally, determined, Vheod turned and went for the door and exited into the dark, ill-used street.

Chapter Eight

After he made a more usable torch from some cloth wrapped around a small piece of wood, Whitlock examined the area near the camp. He'd been able to determine that there were at least a dozen gnolls here, even though he'd only seen a few. Broken branches, trampled grass, and footprints scattered about led him to the conclusion that these gnolls had taken the horses. Worst of all, however, they had taken Melann. He had no idea if she was alive or dead—only that she was gone and that they had carried her away.

The gnolls would be difficult to track, Whitlock figured, particularly in the darkness of the night. The horses, however, might be easier to follow. Obviously, the beasts weren't happily led away. Signs of struggle here and there provided a path of sorts for Whitlock to follow even in the darkness. He pushed into the woods. The torch was in one hand and his sword in the other. His shield rested on his back, but he'd left the rest of their equipment back at the camp. There was no time to worry about that now.

Whitlock could think of nothing other than finding his sister. She was out in the forest, helpless, in the hands of monsters. It was his fault—it had to be. It was his responsibility to watch over her.

Wet grass made for slippery footing as he ran through the darkness. Whitlock's eyes never stopped scanning around him, looking for signs of the horses' reluctant passage through the brush. His makeshift torch began to die as he reached a narrow creek babbling against rounded stones through the tumbled terrain. He could hear insects chirping around the water but still found no sign of his quarry.

Whitlock allowed himself to think only that Melann was still alive. She obviously put up a struggle. The dying gnoll he finished off lay in grisly testament to that. Yet there hadn't been enough blood to suggest that they had killed her. He found no trace of her at all but for the torn bit of cloth.

Whitlock followed the creek for a short distance, then splashed across it in his heavy leather boots. His brand flared, then died. Whitlock glanced around, hoping his eyes would adjust to the absolute darkness around him. The chill of the night bit into his wet legs, but he ignored the feeling and walked onward, into the pitch darkness.

Unsure how long he'd been searching, Whitlock heard low growls and snarls and a slight rustling through the undergrowth. The noise seemed to come from one direction, then another. He tried frantically to follow the sound, but no matter which direction he started, it faded.

Whitlock stood in the darkness, alone and confused. He couldn't determine which way he heard what he thought to be the gnolls. He wasn't sure how to get back to his campsite. His body ached from the blows he'd taken, and he was exhausted.

Like a granted wish, a cry cut through the night. A snarling bellow of pain rose up, passing through the trees to Whitlock's eager ears. As the warrior followed the sound, more bestial shouts joined the first. Whitlock himself yelled out, "Melann!"

This time, an answer came.

"Whitlock?" Melann's voice came through the darkness. "Whitlock, I'm here!"

"Melann, I'm coming! Hang on!"

With renewed fervor, Whitlock charged up the darkened, forested hillside away from the creek and the previous path of his search. Melann had to be at the top of this hill, as did a number of gnolls, by the sound of it. Branches and growth from the forest floor lurched at him as he ran through them, tearing at his clothes and flesh. Leaves battered his face and eyes. He held his free arm in front of his face as he ran. He pushed himself through it all, wishing for a path up the hill. Dark trees loomed at him from all sides, their branches waving at him, clawing like barely seen monsters. Still he drove himself onward. The trees seemed to thin as he worked his way through them, but as the hill grew bald, the surface sprouted rocks and bare stones that he would have to clamber over or move around, slowing him down even more without light to help him.

But then, as if by an act of a god, light came.

Ahead of him, higher on the hill, a brilliant display of light appeared suddenly, shining down toward him. It cut through the night, dispelling the dark and allowing Whitlock to see, at least a little. The sudden flare of illumination caught him off guard and even made him stumble, but he was apparently not the only one, for with the light's flaring came more bestial cries of surprise.

Guided by that beacon, he moved faster and more determined than ever.

Climbing over a large, irregular boulder, he reached what seemed to be the top of the large, bald hill. In a nimbus of light without source, he saw a number of tall, massive shapes moving about a smaller one.

Melann!

Screaming a hoarse, incoherent wail, Whitlock charged into the scene, his sword raised high above his head. He'd slung his shield over one shoulder by its strap, but now he brought it down to use in battle.

Melann held a small, crude mace with a wooden haft and a lead-covered head. Her free arm hung limp and bloody at her side. Near her, at least nine gnolls bared their teeth and lunged at her with spears and clubs and maces of their own. Whitlock noticed as he drew closer that three of the creatures didn't move at all—they seemed to be held utterly frozen in place. Further, one gnoll held no weapon but instead clamped his hands over his eyes. That one stood within the center of the globe of light, and Whitlock realized that he'd been the focus of Melann's spell, or rather his eyes had been.

As Whitlock approached, the remaining five gnolls turned toward him, as did his sister.

"Praise to the Great Mother!" Melann said.

Whitlock said nothing as he threw himself into battle. Three of the musky gnolls met his charge and engaged him. Another continued his attack on Melann, which she fended off with the mace. A fifth attempted in vain to shake free his companions held motionless by Melann's priestly powers. The blinded gnoll fell to his knees and howled skyward like a wolf.

Long, houndish snouts snapped at Whitlock, and spears lanced in, seeking his blood. His shield turned away the first few attacks long enough for him to bring his already bloodied broadsword down on the head of the foe to his right. As the gnoll fell, he turned to see how Melann fared.

Whitlock saw Melann pound her foe with the mace, but her well-placed blows only made the brute cringe. It stabbed at her with its spear, forcing her to step back. Whitlock knew that if the gnoll kept her at a distance, the longer spear would always win out against the short mace. Two gnolls rushed him, and Whitlock threw his weight into a swinging blow with his sword that broke both spears as they jabbed at him. He snarled with rage, shaking both his sword and shield above his head. Whitlock stared into the eyes of the pair of gnolls, baring his teeth, his eyes wild with rage.

With roars that sounded almost like shrieks, the gnolls turned and fled. Whitlock ignored them and stepped over the felled creature to get to Melann's side. Her foe, seeing him chase off the others, also ran into the darkness.

"Are you all right?" he asked, looking down at her bloody arm.

"I will be," she said in a half whisper, obviously exhausted. "I was lucky in that I got the opportunity to call on Chauntea. Her power allowed me to hold a few and blind one. That gave me time to grab a weapon and free myself."

"I feared you were . . ." Whitlock couldn't finish, perhaps because of her, but more likely because of himself.

"I'm fine, really," she said more forcefully, more reassuringly. "I feared for you, too."

Whitlock turned, his sword held in front of him. His wounded shoulder could no longer support the weight of the shield on his arm, so he let it drop. The light began to fade. The blinded creature ran down the hill, its hands still clutched over its magically bedazzled eyes. The gnoll took the light with him as it fled. The thought of giving chase burned in Whitlock's heart, but his body begged him not to go. Every muscle screamed with exhaustion.

He turned toward the unmoving gnolls, standing like statues in the quickly fading light. Each was captured in a pose of savagery and fierce attack. He raised his sword, but Melann put a hand on his shoulder.

"No. Let's just go," she told him. "Let's just get out of here. We're alive and we're free. They left the horses tied up at the bottom of the hill. I think they were trying to decide whether to use them or eat them. I think that they were definitely planning on eating me. Luckily, they thought they'd hurt me more than they actually did. By the time they carried me here, I was able to call on Chauntea for aid. Praise Our Mother."

Whitlock noticed for the first time that a thin trickle of almost dried blood marked the side of his sister's face. They must have clubbed her in the camp and dragged her off, thinking she was dead or dying.

"All right," he said, clasping his hand around hers. The light was completely gone again. "Let's go."

The unmoving gnolls, with their outstretched claws and snarling mouths, remained like standing stones at the top of the hill as Melann and Whitlock made their way slowly down the slope. They found their horses tied to a tree just as Melann had said.

Whitlock didn't even try to lead the horses or Melann back to their original camp. It would be difficult to find it now, but in the morning they could retrace their steps and gather up the equipment and food they'd left behind.

The two pushed themselves to move at least a mile away from the gnolls' camp on the bald hill, following the stream. At that point, Melann once again called on Chauntea's granted magic and healed her brother's wounded shoulder with a cool, soothing touch. He smiled in appreciation. When she finished with Whitlock she mended her own injured arm with magic, then her head wound, which still bled slightly.

Now that his head had cleared slightly, Whitlock realized he'd left his shield on the hill. "Damn," he said softly. No way were they going back. Always keep your wits about you, his father used to tell him. Damn.

"The gnolls had a small bag of green stones with them," she told him, still rubbing her arm. The leather armor had been cut away by a gnoll's weapon. "They seemed to really value them. The one next to the brute that carried me away from our camp kept checking the bag."

"What were they, gems?" Whitlock asked, distracted with thoughts of what to do next.

"No, I don't think so, but I'm not sure what they were."

"Well," he said after a moment, looking her in the eye, "I hope we never find out."

Melann smiled and nodded.

Whitlock was more concerned with the practical matters at hand. It seemed that the gnolls would return. It was only a hunch, but somehow he felt they still watched from the darkness surrounding them. Behind every boulder or tree, in any hole or cranny, they might wait. They now knew he and Melann could defend themselves, but did that mean they would only return next time in greater numbers?

The fact that his shoulder now felt both pleasantly warm and cool at the same time, rather than stiff with an aching pain, renewed Whitlock. Something within him begged for sleep, but he knew it would be better if they put even more distance between them and the gnolls. Once Melann had exhausted her power by healing the worst of her wounds, he put his arm around her for support and grabbed the reins of both horses. He led all of them even farther away into the night. Less than four hours before dawn, they foundered into a dry gully near the stream. They lay down close to the horses, without a fire. Both collapsed into sleep almost immediately.

Chapter Nine

The horse was as swift as Vheod had hoped it would be. He sped through the wilderness and into the mountains. The horse's hooves and Vheod's heartbeat were the only sounds either heard for hours on end. Vheod focused only on speed, and it seemed his mount took this as a sign to do likewise. He learned from his earlier experience with a horse that he should treat it well if he was to expect it to do as he wished. Here, unlike in the Abyss, it seemed that kindness could accomplish as much as cruelty or threats—perhaps more.

He followed Orrag's directions carefully, riding into the mountains toward the end of the first day. Even with the steeper, rougher terrain, Vheod attempted to keep a steady, rapid pace. The horse didn't fight him, and they made good time. The Thunder Peaks rose high and jagged into the blue sky thick with a heatborn haze. Most of the time, no path offered itself to the rider and mount, and he charged headlong into thick, green brush full of flowering plants that had just passed their full bloom. Discarded, wilted petals scattered as they rode through the growth.

As the horse crested the top of a tall hill, Vheod brought it to a stop to give it a short rest and survey the landscape ahead of him. Orrag, it seemed so far, hadn't lied to him. Nevertheless, he couldn't help but feel as though something was wrong. It seemed as though he was being led rather than following his own path. Vheod spat on the ground and attempted to turn his attentions elsewhere.

The horse breathed heavily but already seemed ready to continue. Vheod leaned forward and patted his mount on its neck. The horse, it seemed, was strong as well as swift. Moreover, after only one day, he and it had already seemed to form a bond.

"I'll call you Stonesong," Vheod whispered in its ear, "because you are both solid and graceful." He looked around at the wide open sky and the vast green and brown terrain stretching in all directions. "You do your world proud," he added before straightening again on Stonesong's back.

He inhaled deeply of the warm, dry air and smiled. His eyes glistened in the sun.

Just for a moment, Vheod considered that keeping Chare'en from wreaking havoc on this world might be a good thing all by itself, even if it didn't benefit him directly. What an odd thought. He tried to think of something else.

That night Vheod camped in the moonlight, enjoying a gentle, cool night breeze that rid him of the perspiration of the long day's ride in the summer heat. The truth was Vheod really hadn't noticed the heat much. In the Abyss, conditions varied from intolerably hot to deadly cold, and thus he developed a fair bit of immunity to such variances. His tanar'ri heritage helped in that regard as well. Vheod's flesh was thick and tough, resistant to things that would bother or even actually harm a mortal man.

Greater than human endurance had its limits, however, and sleep eventually claimed Vheod. He dreamed of shadowy, winged shapes, tumbling rocks, and storms underground. Even with his body on this mortal world, his mind dragged him back into the Abyss. Or was it some baleful future he saw in his dream? His sleep fitful, he awoke before the sun fully rose above the horizon.

Another day of hard riding took Vheod deeper into the Thunder Peaks. The terrain had grown steadily rockier and rougher. Stonesong's path likewise became steadily more circuitous as Vheod was forced to guide him around steep hills and jagged rocks. The cool breeze of the previous night had become a hot wind blowing through the afternoon. Vheod ignored it, but his horse didn't. By late afternoon, he could see that Stonesong probably couldn't take this speed in this heat for much longer. Rather than run the horse to its death, he slowed down.

The slowing pace was a stroke of good luck in Vheod's search, for now he moved slowly enough to grow more aware of his surroundings. A few hours before sunset, Vheod heard the sound of metal against metal. A moment later came a cry of pain or rage.

Battle!

Alerted and wary, Vheod followed the sounds. A narrow path led up a short but steep ridge, and he passed through some leafy green trees and underbrush quickly but cautiously.

Over a hundred yards ahead of him, Vheod saw what appeared to be a battle. Only after a moment's consideration could he determine that actually a large force was attacking a small one. Huge, hirsute footmen surged around a pair of mounted combatants, attempting to bring them down.

The mounted warriors were a man and a woman.

Vheod drew forth his long sword and galloped into the fray bellowing out *ti'teriinn akinni!* a tanar'ri battle-cry meaning "blood of my enemies, seek my blade."

Some of the hairy brutes were clad in leather armor; some wore the hides of creatures Vheod couldn't begin to guess at. Many wielded long spears, but a significant number brandished large, heavy weapons like morning stars, flails, axes, and gargantuan blades. He knew these creatures were gnolls, bestial humanoids familiar to him because some of them served—even worshiped—tanar'ri masters.

As Vheod crossed the distance he saw the two humans at the center of the melee—almost certainly the pair he'd come looking for. Each had the dark hair and high cheekbones of the people he'd seen in Arach and Gyrison's pool. The woman swung a mace, warding away attackers hoping to dismount her with their long weapons. The man wore chain mail and hacked at his foes with a broadsword in one hand and a flail that appeared to have come from one of his assailants in the other. Both fought well, the man particularly impressive in his skill.

Vheod slowed his horse. It occurred to him that if the gnolls slew this pair, his troubles might indeed be over. If they were to free Chare'en, their deaths would insure Vheod's victory. Watching the brutes tear into the two mounted figures caused the hair on Vheod's neck to bristle. His hands flexed around the hilt of his blade. No. He couldn't. Vheod spurred the horse into the battle.

The attacking creatures noticed Vheod's charge when he was halfway to them. The gnolls were at least two dozen in number. Most of the terrifying swarm were unable to get at their prey—only so many could reach the two defenders at once. Many of them turned, attempting to set themselves for Vheod's charge, but they weren't quick enough.

Vheod crashed into them, his horse knocking two over before he could even reach an opponent with his blade. Vheod's sword bit into one that had fallen, forcing him to reach down farther than he would have liked. He wasn't accustomed to fighting on horseback. Spears lashed and stabbed at him, but his breastplate served him well, turning away those points he couldn't dodge.

Though Vheod could spare little time to notice, the woman used the distraction he caused to take the time to cast a spell. A large hammer of magical energy appeared near her, wielded by no hand. This shimmering blue weapon lashed out into the crowd of humanoids, striking even as she defended herself with her own weapon. She shouted something, but the only word he really heard held no meaning for him.

"Chauntea!"

Inspired by her actions, Vheod uttered the words of a spell of his own. He learned this minor spell from a spellbook he'd stolen from a foul and disgusting human wizard who lived among the tanar'ri for a time in the city of Broken Reach. With a gesture, a handful of knives—created from a reddish, magical light—flew from his hand and unerringly struck a pair of the bestial foes as they approached. Both gnolls fell under the sorcerous onslaught, not to rise again.

Even as he cast his spell, a terrific blow struck him from behind, and Vheod found himself hurtling toward the ground. He managed to roll as he landed, to soften the impact. The uncoordinated attack of the gnolls even allowed him time to get to his knees before any of the creatures could react. They charged at him, but his blade stabbed into one advancing gnoll's heart before the creature could ever swing its

126

own weapon. He fended away two other gnolls' spear jabs before a particularly large specimen circled behind his horse hefting a large axe-mace.

Still on his knees, he could no longer see the pair he'd charged into the fight to aid over the heads of the gnolls that surrounded him. The large gnoll obviously wanted to fight him, but Vheod had other plans. He reached out with his free left hand and grabbed one of the nearby gnolls' spear. As he hoped, the creature clung to its weapon with all its might. Rather than attempt to disarm it, Vheod used the leverage to gain his feet, then flung the gnoll with all his might toward the large oncoming foe. As they crashed together, roaring in protest, Vheod parried away two other attacks and dived between the slow-moving, hyena-faced humanoids to reach the pair defending themselves in the middle of the fray.

Already, dead or injured gnolls piled around their rearing horses, felled by the warrior's blows or the woman's spells. Vheod sliced into a gnoll from behind as he charged toward them.

"I must talk to you," Vheod shouted earnestly up at the two of them.

The chainmail-clad man ignored him, too preoccupied with at least four foes all around him to notice. The woman only stared at him incredulously—as if he were a madman.

"Talk?" She shouted. Her assailants drew her attention away from him so she couldn't finish whatever she was going to say.

Vheod ran between them, using them and the fact that the gnolls were focusing on them to gain himself a free moment. He called forth a power he used very infrequently, one that drew on the dark, fiendish portion of his soul. As he felt the chill energy run from the pit of his stomach to his hands, he dashed out and laid his hand on the shoulder of the nearest gnoll. The creature howled as if struck and ran off, out of the battle and toward the nearby hills.

Vheod touched another, then another, each suddenly gripped by terror with his merest touch. They fled the battle in terror, as if the cambion's touch called up their greatest and most horrific fear. After the first three or four so affected, some of those gnolls not touched by Vheod's terrifying power retreated of their own free will, seeing their fellows running from what appeared to be something more dreadful than they wanted to face. Soon the pair on horseback simply watched as one by one their foes retreated into the wilderness.

The gnolls eventually all fled, but not before more than ten of them lay scattered about, dead or dying. The man's leg bled from a terrible wound. As Vheod looked around for surviving gnolls, he saw that his horse lay on the ground, a spear protruding from its side.

Putting the horse out of his mind, Vheod turned his attention to the two humans. This was a moment he'd both been looking forward to and yet dreaded. What were the right words to say? Vheod wondered if these two knew what they were doing, and if so, if he'd done the right thing in helping them against the gnolls.

The woman stared at him. "Thank . . . thank you," she said, clearly out of breath.

"What's going on?" Vheod asked. "Why were the gnolls attacking you?" He wiped the blood away from his sword.

"There seem to be a lot of them around here," the warrior said, pained, though it was no answer to Vheod's question. Besides his chain mail, the human wore simple clothes covered with the dust of extensive travels. His face was covered in a dark beard and mustache, and his dark hair was short.

"They came out of nowhere," the woman answered. "That's the second time we've been attacked. Just last night they came into our camp. They're everywhere around here. We've heard they're gathering for some reason."

Vheod found the young woman compelling. Her long dark hair was tousled from the battle, and even though her clothes and cloak were covered in dirt and blood, her eyes were soft and gentle. She guided her horse nearer her companion and bent over in her saddle to look at his wound. He motioned her away.

"We've got to get moving," the man told her. "They might return at any moment." He spoke through gritted teeth and swallowed heavily. His face was clenched in obvious pain, but the woman left him alone.

She turned to Vheod, who was preparing to see to his horse. Stonesong shook his head, whinnying in short bursts. The horse's body twitched and convulsed, his stiff legs now and again flailing against nothing. Vheod almost couldn't bring himself to look at the animal. I brought you to this, he thought, and I am sorry.

As eager as he was to speak with these others, he couldn't focus on anything until he did all that he could for Stonesong. It appeared that all he could do was end the animal's misery. The mercy of death was a concept that came easily to him. In his lifetime he'd seen many who were in such pain that death brought only relief. Stonesong was in as much pain as anything he'd seen in the Abyss. The sight seemed particularly offensive here away from the hellish Lower Planes.

"You served me only a short time, but you did so admirably."

Vheod cut the horse's throat. It was a swift, clean gesture. Stonesong's painful sounds ended immediately.

The woman seemed compelled to stay until the deed was done. Arms folded in front of her, she kept silent on her own horse while Vheod did what he felt he had to do. When he'd wiped Stonesong's blood from his blade he turned and looked at her. She returned the long look, gazing right into his eyes, but still said nothing. Somehow, Vheod could sense her concern and compassion. It seemed remarkable to him that someone—a stranger—might care that much about him or his mount.

Vheod tried to smile but only managed a nod in her direction. She smiled back.

"Thank you," he whispered.

"My brother is eager to go," she said softly, "and he won't allow me to tend to his wound until we leave the area. Will you come with us?"

Vheod nodded. She helped him onto the back of her own horse.

* * * * *

Whitlock found a small copse of trees for them to rest in, well out of sight of the surrounding area. The three dismounted, and Melann immediately made Whitlock sit down so she could treat his wound. Whitlock, barely able to stand, found it easy to oblige.

"Look, now that we're safely away, I've got to speak with you," the stranger said.

Whitlock gritted his teeth through the pain as Melann lifted the lower portion of his hauberk and pulled the blood-stained cloth away from his leg. "Who are you?" she asked the stranger as she worked.

"My name is Vheod Runechild," he replied.

"I am Melann Brandish, and this is my brother Whitlock."

"What are you doing out here?" Whitlock asked through teeth clenched in pain.

"Looking for you," Vheod stated.

"What?" Whitlock started in surprise, then again in pain as his movements put his leg in a bad position.

"What do you mean?" Melann asked Vheod, turning away from Whitlock for the moment.

"I came here looking for you, to warn you that you are about to do something . . . terrible." Vheod stood over the two of them, a few steps away.

"What thing?" Whitlock asked, his voice raising in volume, his brow furrowed. "What are you talking about? How do you know anything about us?"

"You intend to free the tanar'ri Chare'en from his prison." Vheod said.

"What?" Whitlock said. "What are you talking about?"

"Just as I've said; you're about to release a terrible evil into the world."

"No, we're not," Whitlock said quickly. "Our business is our own. Besides, isn't tanar'ri just another word for demon? If anyone's going to have anything to do with a demon, it's probably you. You look like you're probably a demon yourself. Come to think of it, what did you do back there to frighten all the gnolls away?" Whitlock grimaced from the pain.

"Just a moment," Melann implored, and called on Chauntea to grant her the ability to heal her brother's wound. When she was finished, she urged Whitlock to lean back and rest easy for a moment. "I'll talk to him," she whispered to her brother.

Whitlock grimaced. He was worried that the gnolls might come back. In fact, he really didn't understand why they ran away in the first place. The twosome—or rather, the threesome—had slain a fair number, but the gnolls had seemed certain of victory. Somehow, the dark-skinned stranger forced them to flee. The thought didn't comfort Whitlock, it fueled his suspicions.

Melann got up and moved to Vheod, motioning with her hand that they should walk a few steps away. "Please, sir—" she began.

"Vheod," he corrected.

Whitlock strained to hear them as he lay on the ground and watched. He could feel the divine energy knitting his wounds together, but he ignored it in favor of the conversation being held.

"All right," she said with a gentle smile, "Vheod, could you please tell me what all this is about?"

"I've told you what I know—what you need to know." Vheod shook his head. "Are you or are you not going to free Chare'en?"

"Free him?" Melann asked, her face showing confusion. "He's dead."

Vheod paused. He cocked his head and stared into the sky through narrow eyes. Whitlock studied this strange man. His breastplate was forged from some black metal covered in bizarre barbs and spikes. It was like nothing he'd ever seen before. The stranger had surprisingly long, reddish hair and a dark, weathered look to his skin. His features were gaunt and pointed—his appearance didn't suggest the kind of warrior Whitlock had seen in the fight earlier. Something about him, Whitlock thought, made him appear *different*—almost detached from the world around him.

Vheod said, "When I spoke to Orrag—"

"Oh, you know that misbegotten half-orc?" Whitlock called out from behind them. "Well, that at least explains something." It confirmed his suspicions that Vheod wasn't to be trusted after all.

Vheod turned to look at Whitlock and said, "I spoke to him briefly while I was looking for you. He indicated you might think Chare'en is a long dead wizard. I can tell you you're wrong about that. I don't know why you believe it, but you're wrong. He's an imprisoned tanar'ri, and if you go to where he waits you'll risk freeing him."

"How did you know to look for *us*?" Melann asked.

Vheod turned back to her. "I spoke to these two men—priests, I believe. They showed me your image in a magical pool and revealed to me that you were going to free Chare'en."

"Vheod," she asked him, "where are you from? Do you have something to do with the elves?" She glanced at Whitlock with a look that was supposed to carry with it some meaning—Whitlock was sure of that, but he didn't know what he was supposed to gain from it. The pain kept him from being able to concentrate.

Vheod paused, his eyes widening slightly, as if he was caught in a trap. "I'm not an elf."

"But that's not what I asked," she said gently.

"I come from another plane, if you must know." Vheod said sullenly. "I came here seeking my heritage—my family—and instead I met a pair of priests who warned me that the two of you are going to do something awful. I've searched for you ever since."

"You're a cambion, aren't you?" Melann asked, taking a step backward.

Vheod stared at her flatly. Before he could answer, Whitlock asked from behind them, "What's a cambion?"

Vheod looked at Melann. "Yes," he said. "Does it make a difference?"

"Shouldn't it?" She shook her head, mouth slightly open.

"What's a cambion?" Whitlock demanded, standing up. The wound was almost entirely healed by the spell, and he felt much stronger.

"My father was a tanar'ri, but my mother was a human—from this world. Don't judge me by that, though. I am my own man."

All three stood in silence, a gentle breeze blowing through the trees, providing relief to an otherwise sweltering day. A few insects flew around their faces, Melann brushing away the buzzing from her ear. She turned to Whitlock.

"He helped us fight off the gnolls. He might have saved our lives. We owe him our thanks and respect for that." She knew just what to say to him. Those were words she knew he would take to heart, and she was right. Whitlock couldn't argue with that.

"Well, I suppose that's true enough," he said to Vheod. "We thank you for that, sir."

Vheod looked back and forth between the two of them, his long hair tossed about in the breeze. He seemed confused.

Melann's church spoke of tanar'ri distantly—as only something to be feared and destroyed. That had been easy enough for Whitlock to accept. Until this moment, Whitlock hadn't even been certain they were real. Demons were just something that didn't come up in everyday life. Now one stood before him, and he owed the demon a debt. Whitlock still didn't understand why Vheod sought them and what it was he was trying to accomplish. It might be best, Whitlock thought, to never find out.

"We must be on our way," Whitlock said.

"Wait," Vheod implored. "Haven't you been listening to anything I've said? Chare'en is a *balor*! If you go to him you'll loose a terrible evil into this world."

"First of all," Whitlock said, "there's already evil in this world—plenty of it. Second, Chare'en's not a demon, he's a long-dead wizard. And third, why, by the name of all that's holy, should we listen to you? Just because you helped us against those gnolls? Now we're supposed to believe everything you say? Does everyone in the world think I'm a complete idiot? I'll have no more of this. Melann, come, we're leaving."

"Wait," Vheod said again.

A long silence passed as the siblings both looked at the mysterious newcomer. Vheod stood very still, his arms hanging down at his sides. Melann seemed uncomfortable and shifted her weight from one foot to the other. Whitlock glanced between the two of them, wanting nothing more than to leave. Damn the debt.

"If what you are saying is true," Melann said, "then our family is doomed . . . and so are we."

* * * * *

Now it was Vheod's turn to be confused. He looked deeply into Melann's brown eyes and saw sincerity and sadness. Her long, dark hair had fallen out of the tie that had held it behind her head, and now it cascaded around her smooth, slightly sunburned face. As tears welled in her eyes, Vheod took a step forward and placed his hand on her arm.

"Perhaps you could tell me what it is you're doing here, and why you seek Chare'en," he said, attempting to keep his voice at a gentle level.

"Our family, long ago, had a curse placed on it. We don't know all the details, but we've been told it happened in the days of Chare'en, a powerful wizard. In his tomb we believe we'll find a magical staff that can remove the curse from our family." Melann wiped her eyes before continuing. "It's most important that we find the tomb now. Both our parents have fallen ill—struck down by the curse."

"I see," Vheod replied, already deep in thought and filled with doubts.

His own motives seemed shallow and selfish now. If Melann and Whitlock were correct, it would be wrong to stop them. But no, he *knew* Chare'en was his great-grandfather, a tanar'ri balor, not some mortal sorcerer. Vheod had been telling them about the great wrong that would be inflicted on the world if Chare'en were freed—now he was beginning to realize how true his words were. He wondered if it was his responsibility to make sure that the balor stayed imprisoned. He wondered too at the circumstances in which the balor was imprisoned. Was there any truth at all about this magical staff? Melann certainly seemed to honestly believe in the curse.

The fact that Melann didn't immediately assume he was lying or even attack him on learning of his true nature gave Vheod hope that perhaps he could convince her he was right. She obviously was reasonable. Her brother, on the other hand, appeared otherwise.

"Look, Melann," Whitlock said to his sister, "there's no need to tell this . . . man about our business." He turned to Vheod. "As I said before, thanks for your help, and thank you for your warning. Now we must be going."

"I can't let you do that."

"You can't *let* us?" Whitlock spat. "Are you going to attack us? Come on, demon—I'll have at you." Whitlock drew his broadsword.

Vheod's hand flexed, seeking the hilt of his own blade. He stopped. Instead, he simply held his ground. "I would not fight you, sir. I don't seek further bloodshed. I've already seen a surprising amount of that on such a beautiful, peaceful-seeming world."

"You *must* be from somewhere else," Whitlock sneered, his sword still pointed at Vheod. "Beautiful, perhaps, but peaceful? Experience has taught me something else."

Vheod said nothing.

"You won't stop us from doing what we've set out to do," Whitlock continued. "We'll do what we think is best.

Melann spoke up. "You must understand, Vheod, we can't possibly turn back after all we've been through." She raised her hands in an emphatic gesture. "We can't just give up on the only hope we have for our family—not just on the words of a stranger. I mean, no offense but . . . I'm sure you understand."

The worst part of it for Vheod was that he did understand. He would do the same thing in their place. He couldn't possibly expect them to simply do as he said when so much was at stake for them. Yet he was certain that if left alone, they would take actions that would spell disaster for both him and them—and probably the whole world. He certainly had no desire to see Melann hurt, especially when he could do something to stop it. He didn't even wish ill on hot-tempered, untrusting Whitlock. In reversed positions, Vheod would probably react much as the human warrior did.

"Well, perhaps we can reach a compromise. What if I accompany you to Chare'en's 'crypt'? Then we can see which one of us is correct." And, he thought to himself, I can make sure that if I'm right, Chare'en is not freed—no matter what. The real question burning in Vheod's heart was whether or not he himself could be trusted going to Chare'en.

"I don't like this," Whitlock said quietly to his sister, though Vheod could hear him.

Before Melann could answer, Vheod said to Whitlock, "Isn't this the best way to keep an eye on me? If I'm trying to do something wrong, would I not be better within sword's reach? The best way to watch your enemies is to keep them close enough to kill, the saying goes. It's a saying where I come from, in any event. Besides, those gnolls will probably come back—just as you said."

Perhaps, Vheod thought, it would be good that Whitlock and Melann watched him very closely. Whitlock may very well be right not to trust him. He looked, almost reflexively, for the Taint. It resided on his forearm, as though it wanted him to see it. The tattoo had taken on the form of a laughing, leering face.

Whitlock didn't say anything. Instead he folded his arms in front of him defiantly.

Melann approached Vheod, extending her hand. "We would appreciate your company, Vheod Runechild."

Chapter Ten

"So, are you a wizard?"

"Me?" Melann asked in surprise.

The summer sun would soon set, and the shadows around them grew long. The looming shadows of the mountains already swathed much of the surrounding area in a blanket of darkness. She looked down at Vheod, who had asked the question, and apparently had asked it with sincerity. His eyes told her that he indeed sought an answer. Vheod walked alongside their horses while she and her brother rode. Melann was amazed that he could keep up the pace over the hours of the journey. A full day had passed since their paths joined, and he never once showed signs of tiring—though he slept the night before like any mortal man.

Whitlock never ceased his constant vigil, convinced the gnolls would attack again. His caution probably slowed their pace a little, but no one commented on it.

"In the battle with the gnolls," Vheod said, "you cast a spell that struck down a number of them."

Melann laughed for a moment, more out of the joy of actually laughing than the humor of what Vheod really said. He didn't seem to take offense at her laughing at him—instead, it seemed to bring a smile to his own face. She was fascinated with his long hair and dark, rough skin—but mostly she enjoyed looking into his face. She saw a sort of nobility in his eyes. She believed that a tanar'ri, raised in the Abyss no less, trying to overcome its inherent evil was perhaps the noblest thing she'd ever heard of.

"I'm not a wizard, but a Watchful Sister of the Earth. A follower and servant of Chauntea, Our Mother," she said with a smile.

Vheod looked puzzled. "Our Mother?"

"Yes. Chauntea nurtures and provides for our world. She loves and cares for all growing things." It felt strange to be talking about her faith with a tanar'ri—or half tanar'ri, anyway. According to all she'd ever read or been taught about creatures such as he, Vheod was an abomination. Of course, she really hadn't read that much. Demonology was hardly a requirement for a priest of Chauntea. She'd heard a few stories about creatures summoned by wizards or great monstrosities that walked the land in earlier, more arcane ages, but she honestly never thought she might ever, or could ever, simply talk with one.

"I see. There are few priests where I come from, and they all worship, well . . . things better left unworshiped and names better left unspoken. I am more familiar with wizardry than priestcraft. Forgive me."

Melann kept her smile. "You don't need to be sorry."

What must it have been like to have lived in—well, wherever he came from? A place of evil and darkness, certainly, but now he was here, and he'd seen beauty and freedom. Could anyone in the world appreciate the Mother of All's goodness and bounty more than he?

Melann turned away from him, looking at the green, rolling hills that led up in every direction to high, rocky peaks. Birds sang in the trees that dotted the hills, and the nurturing sun blazed down in all its glory, as if to spread its energy on the world for one last moment as it prepared to rest for the night. It was so easy to trust utterly in the goodness and might of Chauntea gazing on such a scene. It was easy to see that she guided all things with her divine hands.

But what if Vheod was right? What if Melann and Whitlock couldn't find the cure for the wasting disease that drained away their parents' lives? Worse yet, what if in so trying they freed some horrible evil? Surely Chauntea wouldn't lead her down such a path. Melann decided that Vheod must be mistaken. He must.

"What's it like to believe in something so wholeheartedly?" Vheod asked her, staring straight ahead as he walked, "How can you trust in what you believe? And if the god you serve is truly worthy of service, how can you know that you are worthy to serve?" Vheod looked up at her. "I'm sorry. I have no business asking such—"

"No, that's quite all right." Melann swallowed. How did this man—if man he was—see her so clearly? His questions cut right to the heart of what troubled her, and why she was plagued with self-doubt.

"Proof that Our Mother is worthy of worship is all around you. Didn't you say yesterday that you found our world beautiful? That's the work of Chauntea." She forced herself to smile, hoping it would cover for the fact that she left his last question unanswered.

Vheod just nodded, and didn't press any further.

Whitlock remained closed mouthed. He obviously didn't trust Vheod. His every mannerism made this clear to Melann, and maybe to Vheod. Melann wasn't so certain. She wasn't willing to dismiss Vheod as quickly as her brother had. The elf spirit in the Vale of Lost Voices had spoken Vheod's name. That had to mean something.

* * * * *

When darkness overcame the vale through which they traveled, the three of them stopped to sleep for the night. Vheod helped Whitlock gather wood for a fire. Neither of them spoke, but both kept a sharp eye out for more gnolls.

Melann had gathered some wild berries when they stopped earlier that day for a short rest. When they returned, she offered these to both men to supplement their rations. As he was the previous night, Vheod was grateful that they shared their food with him, for he had brought nothing to eat himself. Fortunately, his inhuman nature usually allowed him to go for long periods without needing to eat. Usually, Vheod didn't think of food until the pangs of hunger allowed him to think of nothing else.

He happily accepted the berries, as well as leftover meat from some game birds Whitlock had killed the previous morning. While they ate, Whitlock muttered quietly about needing to hunt again the next day. Vheod planned to help him but kept quiet for now.

Removing his breastplate, Vheod stretched out near the fire. The heat didn't bother him. Night birds, insects, and the crackling fire made the only noise for quite some time. To Vheod it seemed there were a great many birds in the area, but he realized it was probably normal and thought nothing more of it. Like the previous night, the three of them didn't really know what to say to each other. Unlike the last night, however, they weren't so exhausted that they collapsed into almost immediate sleep. Melann finally broke the silence.

"Do you know anything about these green stones?"

She held up a small glassy stone she'd pulled from her pouch, rolling it between her thumb and forefinger. It was lustrous and sparkled in the firelight. Vheod reached toward her with his hand open. She dropped the stone into his palm, and he felt the stone's smooth surface between his fingers.

He shook his head and said, "No, I've no idea. Does it have meaning?"

"I'm beginning to think so," she told him. "I took this from one of the gnolls that attacked us the first time. I noticed the second group also had some of them. They're collecting them, I think. The stones have meaning to the gnolls. It's a piece of the puzzle as to why they're gathering, I think."

Vheod nodded and looked again at the stone. "Do you think," he asked her slowly, "it has anything to do with us, or with Chare'en?"

"I'm not sure, but I have a feeling it does."

Vheod just nodded again. He kept the stone.

Melann did not object. In fact, she changed the subject entirely. "Vheod, if you don't feel I'm prying too much, could you tell us a little more about yourself? I mean, we're traveling together, and yet I still feel as if I hardly know anything about you."

Vheod should have been prepared for this, he realized, but he wasn't. Surely these two, particularly Melann, wouldn't want to hear about the horrors of the Abyss. Whitlock would probably trust him less than he already did. Melann, on the other hand, seemed sincerely friendly and welcoming, though Vheod found that hard to believe. Why should one such as she be so accepting of one such as him?

Perhaps she didn't truly understand what he was. All the more reason not to tell them.

Vheod swallowed his food and lied, "There's really very little to tell."

"Oh, I find that remarkably hard to believe," she replied. Her eyes widened. "I mean, you don't even come from this world. That alone is the most incredible thing I've ever heard."

"Well, as I said yesterday, my family—my mother's side—came from this world. I understand they were great sorcerers."

"That figures," Whitlock added with his mouth full.

Melann shot a glare at him but quickly looked back to Vheod. If that was meant to be an insult, Vheod didn't understand it, so he chose to ignore it.

Vheod put his food down, no longer in a mood to eat. "I, unfortunately, never knew my mother. She died when I was born. I've been told that's typical when humans give birth to nonhuman offspring. I also never knew my father. Most likely, he doesn't even know I exist. Born in the bowels of the Abyss, I was raised by creatures some call alu-fiends. They're sort of half human like me. Anyway, there were three of them, and they took me after my mother died, deciding to care for me so that I would grow and serve them as a protector. Unfortunately, they died long before I was old enough to protect them. That's the way of things in the Abyss.

"I grew up on the streets of a city called Broken Reach. I met many . . . unique individuals there." Vheod chortled humorlessly. "It's more cosmopolitan than you might think. Creatures from hundreds of worlds and planes walked those streets. That's where I first heard of Toril. In Broken Reach I learned to be a thief first, a warrior second, and a wizard last. Each type of skill was helpful in my survival. You see, they don't care for my kind in the Abyss. I was looked down on because I was a half-breed."

"I imagine they didn't like the other differences you displayed as well," Melann said.

"What do you mean?" Vheod asked.

"The tanar'ri," she answered, matter-of-factly. "They're completely evil. They embody all that is chaos and evil in the multiverse. You're not like that, right? I don't know if most tanar'ri have the free will to choose to be what they are, but you're different in at least that one way."

Vheod thought for a moment. Tanar'ri live in dark, tortuous places and think only of death and rage. Life in this world was more than that.

"I hated them," he answered finally. "I hated what they did to me, and I hated to think of myself as one of them. I never really gave it much more thought than that. I rarely had time to think about whether what I was doing was evil or not."

Before he could stop to think, he found himself continuing on. "Don't get me wrong. In the Abyss I learned to steal, to kill, and to do as I wanted. I worked as a professional assassin." Vheod sighed deeply and looked at the ground. "Just before I left I was hired by a tanar'ri named Nethess to kill a man, and I found I couldn't do it. I'd killed tanar'ri before—and other monstrous things—but I couldn't kill this mortal man. Something stayed my hand. I'm really not sure what it was. For my troubles, I was hounded until I fled. I wound up here."

He looked at Melann with a darting glance. Vheod realized he'd said much more than he'd intended to say, and with much more emotion. He breathed heavily and drew his knees up to his chest. He wished he still had his armor on. He looked away.

"What a sad, sad tale," Melann whispered.

"So you really are what you say you are," Whitlock said. It was a statement rather than a question.

"Why would I lie about that?" Vheod retorted, a little more edge to his voice than he wished.

Whitlock just nodded and gave him a stern smile—or perhaps it was a grimace, Vheod couldn't tell. A few more moments of silence passed. Whitlock finished eating. Melann had finished a few minutes before. He took to gathering the remaining food and utensils and packed them into the saddle bags that lay by his bedroll.

"What does your tattoo mean?" Melann asked Vheod quietly.

Again, Vheod's mind reeled. His eyes grew wide. Lords of the Abyss! The Taint! Who knows what shapes it had taken, or where it had placed itself, making his companions believe him to be even more strange. He glanced down at his arms, but it wasn't there.

"The tattoo—on your chest, just below your neck," Melann nodded in his direction. "The red tattoo. I never noticed it before, I suppose because of your armor." She chewed her lower lip and looked into his face.

Reflexively, he looked down, but he could just barely see it. Fortunately, it looked rather innocuous. Indistinct, actually. He relaxed a little. "That's not really a tattoo. More a birthmark."

"Oh, I'm sorry. It just seemed so . . . I don't know. It just seemed more purposeful than a birthmark. I thought perhaps it had some meaning. Please accept my apologies. I didn't mean to be rude."

Vheod just shrugged. Now, he realized, he was going to have to worry about what the Taint was doing during the entire time he spent with Melann and Whitlock.

"It's getting late," Whitlock interjected. He'd finished packing and prepared his bedroll.

Vheod appreciated the change in subject and was more than happy to lay back away from the fire and the light and stop feeling as if he was on trial. After his experience in the village so soon after his arrival, he never knew how the people of this world would react to him or his past, and he was already tired of thinking about it.

* * * * *

Morning came and with it a summer storm. Not like the dangerous storm of a few days before, but rather a cool rainstorm with little wind and only a smattering of thunder. The noise echoed through the mountains in ways Whitlock had never heard before, living in the relatively open Dales all his life. He liked it.

The rain really wasn't so bad. Whitlock appreciated the break from the heat, and he liked how the rain always made Melann so happy. He supposed it was the nurturing nature of the rain and the moisture that it brought to the growing things she loved so much. Anyway, he liked the shine on her cheeks when she smiled in the rain. It made him happy.

While he packed their already soggy things onto the horses, Whitlock noted that the rain would probably make for poor hunting. Most animals would find some sort of shelter. He would have to wait to get the group some food. That thought made Vheod's next comment so strange.

"What sort of bird is that?" the cambion asked.

Whitlock looked around, not for the bird, but for Melann, assuming she would answer his question.

Melann, however, was a few feet away, tending to her own horse. Whitlock sighed and looked to where the half-breed pointed. Sure enough, a large raven, black as night, sat in a tree not far away and watched them.

"That's a raven," he said dismissively.

Before Whitlock could turn away Vheod asked, "Is it an evil bird?"

"Evil?" Whitlock replied. "No. It's a bird. I suppose some people think they're a bad omen or something sinister like that, but it's just a bird."

"Sinister. An appropriate word. I don't like that bird."

Vheod was strange, to say the least. "Look, this isn't Hell, or wherever you're from. This is . . . the world. Here, animals can be just animals. You don't have to distrust everything."

"Did my brother just say those words?" Melann asked, approaching the two with a playful smile.

"I came from the Abyss, not Hell," Vheod said softly but succinctly. "There's an important difference, but I shouldn't expect you to understand that."

Whitlock turned. After all the liberties Whitlock had given this stranger, he wouldn't be spoken to like that. "Listen, you—"

"Wait. What's all this about?" Melann asked, stepping between them.

"Oh, he saw a bird and it spooked him," Whitlock said dismissively.

Both he and Vheod turned toward where the raven had perched, with Melann following their gaze, but it had gone.

"It's not even there anymore. Happy now?" Whitlock turned to finish his preparations. When he turned back again he saw the reassuring smile that Melann gave to Vheod. He did not like it.

Once they were back on the move, the rain diminished, and by mid-morning had stopped altogether. The trees dripped with a glistening shine, and the grass they passed over was slick, slowing them a little. The day remained cloudy and dark.

"According to Orrag's instructions," Vheod said, "we should probably arrive at the site tomorrow."

"Late tomorrow, perhaps," Whitlock added, looking at the mountains and comparing landmarks with the half-orc's directions. "Assuming he told us the truth in the first place."

They'd been moving at a dangerously slow pace compared to the earlier portions of their journey. That was to be expected, but the threat of the gnolls made the slow pace all the more nerve-racking.

"That's my brother for you," Melann said. She turned to Vheod. "Always the suspicious one."

Vheod didn't respond. Whitlock and Melann dismounted, and they prepared to rest for a while, using the opportunity of a nearby stream to water the horses.

Vheod turned with a start.

"What is it?" Melann hissed, turning in the direction Vheod was looking. Whitlock's hand was already on the hilt of his sword.

"In the trees, to the right," Vheod said, pointing.

At first Whitlock relaxed a little, thinking Vheod had seen another bird, but no, something passed between two trees—something humanoid. It was running away.

"A gnoll," Vheod said.

Whitlock leaped back into the saddle and pulled hard at the reins. His boots dug deeply into his steed's sides as he urged it to speed. Crossing the open space, he raced into the trees where the gnoll was quickly loping away. Whitlock drew his sword with a single smooth stroke. The gnoll was probably a scout, going to warn a larger group of their position.

He couldn't let it get away.

The gnoll ran, and ran quickly, but Whitlock saw an opening in the trees large enough to ride through, and he guided his mount into it.

Obviously sensing it was hopeless to attempt to outrun the horse, the gnoll wheeled and pulled at a spiked club that dangled from its belt. Grasping the club in both its clawed hands it planted itself, ready to attack as Whitlock approached.

So Whitlock did what the gnoll was not expecting.

Pulling his left foot up onto the saddle, he pushed off and leaped to the right, toward the surprised gnoll. He crashed into it with great force, knocking the gnoll off its feet. The flat of Whitlock's sword smashed into the creature's snout, and blood spattered over both of them as they rolled together. Whitlock used the gnoll's large, shaggy form to absorb the impact of his leap.

When they stopped rolling, the stunned gnoll lay on the ground under Whitlock and against a tree. The warrior placed his blade across the creature's neck, but it was still too dazed to even notice. Whitlock glanced up and saw that his horse had stopped about ten yards away and was circling back, out of the trees. He also heard footsteps coming up behind him—Vheod and Melann caught up.

"Melann," Whitlock said, "remember when those dwarves came to Archendale and they couldn't speak our language? That old priest—Thontoman, I think his name was—cast a spell that allowed him to speak with them. Can you do that?"

Melann was breathing heavily as she ran up. "No," she replied. "That's not a power at my command."

"I can speak to it," Vheod said. Whitlock noticed that the half-demon wasn't breathing heavily at all. Both Melann and Vheod approached and stood over Whitlock and his prisoner. "Assuming he can speak to anyone."

Whitlock slapped the gnoll's bloody snout a few times—not hard, but enough so it would notice. "Wake up," he spat.

The gnoll began to shake its head. Its eyes focused, and the warrior made sure it saw his blade before he put it back at its neck. "Don't try anything, monster."

Vheod concentrated for a moment, then bent over the creature to touch it.

"Do not attempt to flee, or you will die," Vheod said, in the common tongue.

The gnoll grunted and growled.

"What are you doing here?" Vheod asked.

The gnoll bared its teeth, and Whitlock could see its black gums. While it smelled of musk and feces, its breath was much worse, stinking of rancid meat.

"Tell us or you will die," Vheod's voice took on a cold quality that sent a chill down Whitlock's back.

The gnoll silently moved its head back and forth for a moment, then made noises like barking and grunting.

"He can understand what you're saying?" Melann asked from behind both Vheod and Whitlock. "You sound as though you're speaking normally."

Vheod didn't turn his gaze from the captive. "He can not understand the actual words I speak, exactly, but I can make him understand what I *mean*— and I can understand what he means."

She paused to consider this, and Vheod resumed the interrogation. "Why were you here? Were you looking for us?"

The gnoll responded with a few short grunts, then a string of unintelligible growls.

"It says," Vheod said, still focused on the gnoll, "that it wasn't here looking for us, but something else."

"They were expecting someone else along this path?" Whitlock asked.

"No, some*thing,* it said," Vheod reached into his pocket, and pulled forth the small green stone.

"Is this what you were looking for?" Vheod asked.

Though he couldn't understand the gnoll's crude speech, Whitlock could tell by the sudden look of recognition in its eyes that the answer was yes.

"What are they? What are they for?" Vheod asked sternly, still holding up the green stone that glistened like the wet leaves around them.

The creature spoke again, and Vheod translated, "It says they must gather these lost stones to bring to their master."

"Who in the Nine Hells is their master?" Whitlock demanded.

Vheod gave Whitlock a questioning look, but then asked the gnoll and got a reply. "It says its master is 'he who has called to its people.' 'He who will soon awaken from a long sleep.' It doesn't have a name for this master."

"That's why there're so many gnolls in the area," Melann interjected. "Someone has been calling them here."

"Chare'en," Vheod stated flatly.

"Is that what the creature said?" Melann asked.

"No, not by name." Vheod shook his head.

"Look," Whitlock said, "we can talk about that later. Are there more questions we need to ask this thing?"

Vheod proceeded to ask if there were more gnolls nearby, but the creature replied that most of the gnolls in this area were killed or chased off by something it didn't know or understand.

"That sounds bad," Whitlock said. He cleared his throat, not wanting Melann to hear the worry in his voice.

"Perhaps it means the crypt," Melann said suddenly. "Perhaps something about the crypt of Chare'en frightened the gnolls away. If we head toward it, we won't have to worry about them while we're there."

"Perhaps," Whitlock said slowly, "but that doesn't mean we don't have to be worried about whatever it is *they're* afraid of."

"True," she agreed.

Vheod sighed audibly. "I doubt there's anything more we can get from this creature."

"Now what?" Melann asked.

Vheod turned to her, his brows furrowed in confusion. "What do you mean?"

"I mean, what do we do with our . . . prisoner?" She looked to Whitlock, who still watched over the gnoll.

Whitlock raised his sword suddenly and brought the pommel down on its head. With a heavy thud, the creature's face fell to one side, and its eyes closed. Whitlock stood, brushed himself off, and walked to where the gnoll's weapon had dropped.

Picking up the club, he said "By the time the creature wakes up we'll be long gone and won't have to worry about any others it might talk to."

Melann sighed, turned and walked back to her horse. Whitlock heard her mutter a prayer to Chauntea under her breath, imploring her to guide them along the right path.

Whitlock lingered back to walk alongside Vheod for a moment. He recognized Vheod's surprise at their comparative leniency toward the gnoll, and knew what Vheod would have done.

He whispered tersely to Vheod, "We don't kill prisoners here, demon," then sped past him, going to gather his own horse.

Chapter Eleven

The travelers said little after their encounter and "conversation" with the gnoll. That night the ground was still wet from the morning rains, so they made their camp in the driest area they could find. The top of a large hill provided a small, flat area suitable for the three of them and the two horses. Their packs offered little to eat, but none of them really seemed to care. Clouds obscured the moon and stars more than the mountains ever could, conjuring an utterly black night. Their fire provided the only light, and they kept it very small so as not to draw too much attention.

As they prepared to sleep, Whitlock took Melann aside to speak with her. They stood in the edges of shadow and light, their faces masked in darkness but their eyes sparkling from the campfire.

"I've been thinking," he began in hushed tones, "about our new traveling companion."

Melann said nothing.

"What if this is all some sort of elaborate ruse? What if he's working with the gnolls for some purpose? His sudden appearance seemed awfully convenient, as did his supposed translation of what the gnoll was saying. How do we know if it really said those things?"

"I don't believe all that," Melann told him, "not for a moment. Why go to all that trouble?"

"To keep us away from the Crypt of Chare'en, for some reason," Whitlock whispered intently.

"Why not just kill us, if that was his intent? He's obviously powerful enough." She shook her head, then continued, "I just can't believe Vheod is somehow leading us into a trap or lying to us. Chauntea would never guide us into such a situation, and I still believe Chauntea is guiding us. She has to be—how else could everything that's happened be explained?"

Whitlock just stared at her, working his jaw, his gaze dropping to the ground.

"I hope Vheod is wrong about the nature of Chare'en," Melann said, "but that doesn't mean he's going to betray us. What it comes down to is that I believe in Vheod's sincerity. I envy the strength he must have to struggle against his nature and win. I can hardly imagine what it must be like to be in conflict with your own soul, or at least a part of it. Everyone's tempted by evil—that's a part of what evil is, after all—but his temptations must be unimaginable. You might think that makes it easy to expect the worst of Vheod, but I can only see it as a challenge worthy of the noblest of souls. Such a soul must belong to Vheod."

"I said, you've got a point."

"What?" Melann was shocked out of her speech by her brother. He must have spoken while she was rambling on. "Oh, sorry."

"I don't know why he wouldn't just try to kill us," Whitlock whispered, "so we'll assume you're right for now, but I assure you, I'm going to be watching him. If he's plotting against us, I'll know."

Melann sighed in exasperation, frustration, and fear.

* * * * *

In the morning, Vheod awoke from a night of fitful dreams. He'd dreamed of running about in a maze of underground tunnels. No matter where he went there seemed to be no way out. He felt as though the tunnels were leading him ever onward, toward some dark fate he could see coming but could not avoid.

The sun had already risen, but still cowered behind the mountains, giving the sky a light purple glow. The clouds still loomed above and gave no hint of parting that day. The air was moist but pleasantly fragrant in a way that might take him many years to truly become accustomed to. He was willing to try, he thought with a smile.

Melann was awake, not very far away, searching through some bushes for berries or other edible plants for breakfast. Vheod wasn't hungry, but thought to offer to provide some game for a meal. He stood, preparing himself for a short hunt. Melann turned at the sound of his rising.

"Good morning," she said, smiling. She held a small handful of red berries.

In the Abyss, plant life is twisted and evil—viper trees, clawgrass, and the blood-drinking thorns that Vheod remembered so well. Here it was pure. Vheod admired Melann's dedication to nurturing growing things. It seemed like a worthwhile purpose in life.

"Good morning," he returned, a little awkwardly.

Vheod gathered some of his things together. "Perhaps I can add to what you have gathered there. Surely there's some small animal or bird around here that—"

"No, I'll go." The voice came from behind Vheod. It was Whitlock. Vheod turned to see him already taking up a small crossbow he'd not seen the warrior use before. Whitlock scowled at Vheod and turned, walking out of the camp. Vheod watched him go but said nothing.

Melann walked over to Vheod, offering him some berries. "He . . ." Melann began to explain, but never finished. Vheod nodded sternly.

"I know he doesn't trust me. I cannot blame him for that."

Melann smiled, still holding up the berries. "We've had this conversation before," she said.

"Yes," Vheod said, taking a berry in his long fingers and popping it into his mouth.

Melann laid the berries on a cloth on the ground and searched through their packs, probably looking for any remaining bread or cheese. Vheod wished again that he'd thought to bring along his own supplies—not for himself, but to offer to Melann and Whitlock.

Vheod looked at Melann, and watched her prepare the food. He turned to look in the direction Whitlock had gone, and finally back to Melann.

"Not having grown up with siblings or a family of any kind," Vheod said, "I can only guess at the relationship you and Whitlock share. You must care about each other very much." He turned away, suddenly no longer able to look directly at Melann.

"I've never really worked with anyone or been cared for by anyone," he continued. "I've never encountered anyone worth caring about."

Vheod lowered his voice to almost a whisper. "Melann, I want you to know I am sorry about your parents. Even though I don't believe any good can come from visiting the place where Chare'en rests, I do hope you and your brother can find another means with which to lift the curse on your family."

"Thank you, Vheod," she replied, looking up at him only for a moment. She added, "We're not ready to give up."

"I know, and I even understand. That's why I'm going with you. I want to make sure that when you discover that—as I believe—you've made an error, I can be of some help in ensuring nothing goes wrong, and Chare'en is not freed."

Can a man trust his own feelings, Vheod thought, particularly a man whose soul is half demon? Vheod wondered how a cambion could ever truly know which half of him was guiding his actions. The fact that Chare'en was his great-grandfather, and the fact that the Taint seemed to be leading him along his current path, worried him. He couldn't share that worry with Melann, though—not yet.

Melann didn't say anything, nor had she apparently found any more food in her pack. She put the pack down with a sigh, and the sound was accompanied by a far-off cry of surprise and pain.

"Whitlock!" She turned toward the sound.

Vheod heard the yell and what seemed like the sound of a sword being drawn. He ran off toward the noise, followed quickly by Melann.

Wet grass under Vheod's feet made footing slippery as he loped down the hillside on which they had camped. He kept his sword sheathed in order to have both hands free to steady himself as he ran. He heard a resonant, high-pitched screech he couldn't identify.

At the bottom of the hill, a number of pine trees grew, their spread branches forming a thick, dark green wall. Vheod plunged into the trees. The needles scratched against him as he ran but didn't cut his leathery skin. The earth underneath his feet was covered with a thick carpet of brown needles and old pine cones, but the thick trees had never allowed grass or underbrush to grow. The ground under the needles was soft and moist and gave with each of Vheod's heavy, booted steps. He paused for just a moment to look behind him. Vheod couldn't see Melann through the trees, but he thought he heard her approach. Another high-pitched screech made him turn back the way he was headed.

Vheod heard another shrill cry, but this time it came from behind him. He stopped and turned yet again. He heard Melann cry out, "Vheod!"

He ran back. Melann lay on the ground at the edge of the trees. Her shoulder was bare, and crimson gashes gushed blood. Next to her stood a black bird at least five feet tall, with its outstretched wings measuring fifteen feet or more. The slashes must have come from this creature's talons, and it wasn't done with her yet. The gigantic raven raised itself over Melann, ready to strike her with its huge, black beak.

As he charged, Vheod yelled to draw its attention. The ploy worked, and the monster looked up. Vheod's blade sang as he slid it from its scabbard. The raven silently stared with shining eyes as black as oil. As Vheod burst from the trees, he saw that the sky was black with ravens. Most of them were smaller than the creature that stood over Melann.

He also saw that Melann was far from helpless. She cast a spell—more of a beseeching prayer—as he ran to her prone form. She waved her small holy symbol above her head, toward the sky.

A surge of energy washed over Vheod. Cool and warm at the same time, this pleasant power flowed through him, making his muscles relax and obey him with precision. His heart beat strong and steady in his chest, and all manner of fatigue fled. When the energy reached within him, he felt it wrap around his soul and gently caress it, as though he was being strengthened and supported in the battle he was about to fight. He realized this was a feeling he'd never felt before.

Vheod had been blessed.

A stinging sensation stabbed into his right leg. It felt like a dozen needles poking into his flesh at rapid intervals. He had no idea what it was, and when he looked down he saw nothing. He had to ignore it. He turned his attention back to the giant bird.

Melann was trying to scramble away from the distracted raven. It kept its wide eyes on Vheod and opened its beak, producing the high screech that Vheod had heard earlier. He leaped at the creature with his sword, and as he did, half a dozen of the more normal-sized ravens swooped down at him from above. The large bird pulled its head back, dodging Vheod's blow while its smaller brethren dived at him. Their beaks and claws struck like tiny, flying daggers, cutting into his flesh in many places at once.

The large raven, its wings still outstretched, thrust itself beak-first at Vheod. He realized just in time that the small birds only meant to distract him, and he swung his sword like a powerful club, batting away the sharp beak in a clumsy parry. Meanwhile, at least two of the small ravens landed on Vheod's shoulder and back and tore at his flesh with greater ferocity, their beating wings battering him into distraction. The movement all around disoriented him, but he planted his feet firmly on the ground and steadied his gaze on the real threat.

He lashed at the giant raven with his sword, but it quickly dodged the swings, using its wings to leap up into the air a few feet with a single beat. It stabbed at Vheod with its savage beak and even attempted to jump on him, tearing downward with its large talons.

Vheod lunged first to one side, then another to avoid its attacks.

A flash of light behind Vheod startled some of the attacking birds, driving them away. Melann had cast another spell. He was glad for the help, and grateful to see she was still all right. In fact, he was surprised at just how important her safety was becoming to him.

Still, one small raven ripped into the flesh on his shoulder, with repeated strike after vicious strike. Clenched in ferocity, Vheod's free hand lashed upward and grabbed the bird. With a look of hatred and anger in his eyes, in an instant he crushed the bird in his hand, squeezing the life from its soft flesh and brittle bones. The thought came from deep within him to thrust the raven up to his mouth and tear its head off with his teeth, but just at that moment he glanced to one side to see the shock and revulsion on Melann's face. He looked away immediately and threw the dead bird to the ground.

What was wrong? What did she see?

No!

He realized that she saw him for what he was—or what a part of him was. The look in her eyes made him realize it was something he no longer wanted to be.

Unfortunately, the whole event distracted him—just as the small ravens had intended. The large bird's beak tore into Vheod's arm and almost knocked him off his feet. He slashed at it with his sword to drive it back, and it fluttered into the air and down again a few yards away.

Vheod looked up and saw still more small ravens descending to attack. He knew he had to finish this battle quickly. Swinging his sword wildly to ward off any smaller birds around him, he lunged at the giant raven with renewed vigor. He focused on the blessing bestowed on him by Melann and mentally thrust that power into his arms. With a single mighty blow, he chopped the monster's head from its body. The dark, bloody mess fell to the wet ground in a heap, huge black feathers cascading down from the sky.

Before Vheod could even catch his breath, Melann shouted, "We've got to get to Whitlock!"

She ran into the trees, disappearing as if she had submerged herself in dark green water. Vheod dived into the trees behind her, the needles of the pines tearing into the small wounds that covered his body. This time he couldn't ignore the scratches, but he forced himself onward regardless.

Vheod ran, following Melann as she darted between trees. She moved fast, and he pushed himself to keep up. Despite her wound, her concern for her brother must have pushed her onward. Vheod, it seemed, was even more hurt than she; he kept her within sight, however. Too focused and wounded to say anything, he ran behind her. That alone kept him too busy to even think.

As quickly as they had passed into the thick expanse of trees at the bottom of the hill, they suddenly passed out of it as the land rose up to another crest. Coming out of the trees was like passing through a wall from one world to the next. As before, the sky was filled with ravens. On the ground, a giant raven's body lay sprawled, with feathers scattered everywhere. A crossbow bolt rose up out of its breast. That and a number of bloody sword cuts indicated that Whitlock most likely had slain it, yet the warrior was nowhere around.

A screech tore through the sky above them. Both Vheod and Melann looked upward as one, and to their horror they saw Whitlock's body held suspended in a giant raven's claws. Whitlock lay limp, his sword and crossbow fallen from his dangling arms.

"No!" Melann cried in terror.

Vheod kept a cool head. A keen mind is worth far more than a sword, he'd been taught. Sheathing his sword, he drew power from within him, calling on his inhuman essence. Using that power, Vheod rose off the ground, upward into the cloudy, raven-filled sky. He positioned himself so he would intercept the monstrous raven that carried Whitlock away. It seemed to be circling around to the west, which gave Vheod the opportunity to rise up ahead and underneath it.

Like black shadows, two more giant ravens swooped out of the sky toward him. Vheod called on a spell, reciting the incantation quickly and flawlessly. His outstretched hand launched red daggers of enchanted energy. The magical darts flew unerringly toward one of the monstrous ravens, striking its wings. The huge bird shrieked and plummeted to the ground. Still, the other soared closer. Vheod rose as fast as his tanar'ri levitation would allow, reaching upward to grab Whitlock out of the claws of his captor. The approaching raven spread his talons, ready to rake Vheod.

Before it could reach him, something streaked by the raven's wing, forcing it to veer to one side. Vheod looked down and saw Melann, surrounded by normal-sized ravens, holding Whitlock's crossbow. As he neared the steadily rising raven, Vheod flung his body toward it. His grasping hands found Whitlock's foot as the raven flew over. It wasn't the hold that he wanted, but he hung on with all his might.

The raven squawked in protest as Vheod's weight added to its load. The cambion knew he could use the magical lift to suspend him even as the raven dragged him along, but he wanted to force it down. The giant raven descended, shaking Whitlock and thus Vheod. Still Vheod clung to the warrior's foot. It worried Vheod that he saw no reaction from Whitlock as all this transpired. He looked to his face to see if he was breathing but couldn't tell.

Like a rain of knives, a torrent of ravens dived into Vheod, stabbing and tearing with beaks and claws. Using his free arm, he beat at the ravens to make them go away. As soon as he forced one away, however, another grabbed his flesh with tiny talons and began attacking with its beak. As one raked his face, his vision was filled with flapping black feathers. He wanted to reach up and grab Whitlock with his free hand, but he had to use it to protect his own face and eyes from the relentless attack.

Suddenly, he felt a raven land on his arm. He reach up to grab at it but missed. As he clung to Whitlock's foot, the small raven tore into the flesh of his hand then each individual finger. He clenched his fingers tighter and tighter, but they became slippery with his own blood. The giant raven carrying the two of them dropped lower and lower down into the trees. Still Vheod clung to Whitlock.

With a sudden jerk, the raven shook Whitlock and wrenched his boot free of his foot. Vheod suddenly found himself covered in ravens holding nothing but a boot. As the giant raven rose once again up into the sky, Vheod dropped. He frantically focused on his power to levitate, but it wasn't enough to completely compensate for the momentum that carried him into the tree tops. Branches and needles tore at his wounded, bloody flesh, and the ravens loosed him and flew away.

Vheod finally used his supernatural power to catch himself and slow his descent, sinking down from the tree tops. The ability granted him mostly vertical movement, and certainly not the speed needed to catch the huge raven now. He hit the ground and crumpled, closing his eyes. His wounds quickly dragged him toward unconsciousness.

Before the darkness could completely claim him, Vheod felt a soothing warmth flow through his body. He felt the pain from some of the larger wounds fade, while the sting of the smaller wounds disappeared completely. Despite a longing to enjoy this pleasure fully, letting him fall into a peaceful sleep, he forced his eyes open. Melann kneeled over him, Whitlock's sword and crossbow at her feet. Sweat and blood covered her body and stained her hair. It appeared the ravens had been as savage to her as they'd been to Vheod.

"Come, Vheod," she pleaded. "We can take the horses. We can follow the raven. It's got to land somewhere."

She was right. He rose, saying, "You should heal yourself first. You can't make it too far like that."

She nodded quickly and recited her plea to Chauntea. Her eyes contained an intensity Vheod hadn't seen in her before now. He watched as her own gashes and bleeding cuts disappeared, her healing magic sealing the wounds as if they'd never existed at all.

"You saw him," she said. Vheod wondered if she blamed him for his failure to bring Whitlock down. He'd been so close. . . .

"He was still alive, wasn't he?" she asked as she stood and grabbed her brother's weapons.

"Yes," Vheod lied. "I saw him breathing." He handed Whitlock's boot to her—he'd held on to it the whole time.

She forced a weak smile and took it. "We've got to get going, then. It flew to the west."

The two of them ran back through the pine copse once again. They crossed though the wooded vale. Neither spoke.

Crossing through the trees, they ascended the hill and reached their camp. Melann stored Vheod's sword and crossbow on her horse and quickly threw their packs over the steed's back. Vheod helped load Whitlock's horse.

Melann paused only long enough to ask Vheod one plaintive question: "What's going on?"

"Orrag spoke of someone called the Ravenwitch. He said I should beware her. This can't be a coincidence."

She only nodded and went back to her work. A tear—probably more from exasperation than anything—flowed down her cheek. Something inside Vheod grew tight at the sight of it.

When they were finished loading the horses, Vheod climbed into the saddle of Whitlock's mount. It snorted and stomped as if it sensed something wrong. It took Vheod a moment to realize that what it sensed was him. The creatures of this world would never let him forget how different he was. He jerked hard on the reins with a grimace crossing his face. His might brought the horse under control, but he kept the grimace. Melann looked away from this scene and mounted her mare. The two of them beckoned the animals to speed.

They headed west, looking upward for the raven.

The sky was still filled with birds, but the diabolical creatures no longer paid them any attention. As they flew to the west as one, they made it easy for Vheod and Melann to follow.

The saddle chafed at a wound on his leg that Melann's healing hadn't coped with—Vheod's body still sported a number of small scrapes and scratches, in fact. He looked down to his thigh and saw that his leggings were ripped open. He did remember a pain there early on in the fight. He saw that the Taint had been slashed by a raven's beak. The pain he remembered, however, came before ravens swooped down on him, Vheod thought, and it had been more of a prickling than the sharper pain he now felt from the wound.

Chapter Twelve

Melann hoped that keeping up with the ravens would be easier, but even with their swift, well rested horses she and Vheod fell behind. The birds didn't need to worry about the physical landscape, while Melann and Vheod were forced to guide their mounts around trees and rocks and ride up and down steep slopes. The ravens flew straight and swiftly together like a flight of arrows launched from powerful bows.

Melann thought about Vheod's words. She didn't like the sound of someone who called herself the Ravenwitch. What could this witch possibly want with Whitlock? Was it something special about him, or was he just a random victim of some horrible desire? Had they fallen into someone's trap, or was Whitlock simply in the wrong place at the wrong time?

She glanced at Vheod and saw the grim determination in his set jaw. Melann was glad not to be alone. If Vheod hadn't been with her, she was sure the ravens would've carried her off as well. His presence comforted her, though she was still just a little afraid of him as well.

The savage fury that Vheod displayed reminded her that he was, in part, a demon. When she saw him fighting with the ravens, for a short while it seemed he took on a completely different countenance. He'd seemed a different person—if a person at all. She didn't like thinking these thoughts, but they came to her unbidden. A part of Vheod was, and probably always would be, a monster.

The glimpse of the savage Vheod she'd seen seemed the exception, not the rule. If she could keep him from getting into similar situations, perhaps she could help him resist his evil nature. Of course, having him ride with her to encounter the ravens again—and perhaps their mysterious mistress—probably wasn't a good start. She vowed to herself to do whatever she could to help him fight to be the man he wanted himself to be. Perhaps that was part of the reason the Mother of All had brought them together.

Or perhaps Chauntea knew Melann would need Vheod's help to rescue Whitlock. She shuddered again at the thought of riding into unknown danger like this alone. Surely Chauntea was guiding her and taking care of her.

They followed the ravens, pushing their horses as much as they dared. The sky remained mostly overcast, and the air was cooler than it had been. Whitlock and his captor were out of sight, but Melann and Vheod moved fast enough to see the cloud of smaller ravens moving steadily westward. Once or twice they lost sight of the birds but saw them again once they crested the next hill.

They entered a wide valley filled with trees and lush greenery. Melann assumed that a river most likely flowed through the area, fostering and nurturing all the plant life. Once again, they lost sight of the ravens. The canopy of trees was thick, casting shadows over large areas, but letting in just enough light in others to produce a thick undergrowth of grasses, bushes, and climbing vines. The air was still.

Wordlessly exchanging glances of indecision, the two slowed a little and rode westward through the woods. As they rode, Melann wondered if they'd lost the ravens for good. Perhaps the birds led them into this wooded area for just that reason. They'd seemed rather intelligent, at least in their ability to coordinate their actions. Melann wondered if she and Vheod had been drawn into a trap—a fate as horrible as that which befell Whitlock. Melann steeled herself against her fear, but she remained wary.

* * * * *

Blood coated the blade of his sword. Vheod looked around and discovered he had no idea where he was, or how he'd gotten there. He stood on a smooth wooden floor, thin wisps of gray-blue mist coiled around his feet and partially obscured the floor, but he could see and feel enough to know it was made of wood. Rounded wooden walls rose to either side, each almost close enough to touch. Smatterings of black moss grew on the wood, clinging like perspiration. The air was cold, but damp. He held a torch in his left hand, which had been burning for some time, it appeared. He didn't remember lighting it. The light revealed that, forward and back, this passage of wood extended into darkness.

Where was he? What had happened?

He saw that the blood on the blade was mixed with some yellowish substance he couldn't identify. He was wounded, and while he remembered a number of scratches from the battle that morning—he assumed it was that morning—he seemed to have a few new cuts and something that looked like a bite on his leg. The Taint had moved to the back of his hand, and seemed no worse for the fact that it had been cut by a raven's beak earlier in the day.

Melann was nowhere to be seen. Vheod stood in a dark corridor that seemed to have been hollowed out of wood. He looked down the corridor and listened closely. He heard nothing ahead. He checked behind him, and this time he heard movement in the distance, impossible to identify.

Vheod decided to move back that way. Before he did, however, he whispered an intense, "Melann?" He repeated it a few more times. No response came. Nothing changed.

He walked down the wooden passage. The torchlight revealed no signs of boards or even tool marks on the wood. In fact, if anything, it seemed that he walked through a hollowed out log rather than a building made of boards. The curve to the walls and floor gave the impression that he moved through a natural passage or tube that extended through a tree, if such a thing was possible.

The passage took Vheod a few paces then reached a staircase leading down. The steps were of the same smooth wood as the walls and floor, but no tool had crafted these regular, perfect stairs. Some sort of sorcery must be involved here—wherever here was.

Vheod looked behind him, again hoping to see Melann. How could they have been separated? He looked down at the torch he didn't remember lighting, and the sword he didn't remember drawing.

Blood.

Lords of the Abyss, no! The very thought that he might have harmed Melann churned his stomach. How could he have done such a thing and not realized it? He looked at the Taint. Was it possible, he wondered in horror, that somehow something else had taken control of him? Worse yet, he considered that it might not be something else at all—perhaps the tanar'ri side of his nature had forced him to do things he now no longer remembered.

He couldn't remember ever losing time like this before, but maybe his dark, fiendish side did this to him from time to time. Perhaps he wasn't as in control of his life as he thought.

Vheod ran down the stairs, this time shouting, "Melann!" He so wanted reality to prove his fears wrong.

"Melann!" he cried out again as he reached the bottom of the winding stairs. Already he grew disoriented in this strange enclosed environment. Mist still swirled around every footstep he took. The bottommost step led him into a rounded chamber, the torchlight illuminating most of it. Vheod saw no furnishings, but there was still some sign that an intelligence had designed the chamber and lived within it. He now understood the movement he'd heard.

Ravens flitted about the room, roosting on a high shelf along the opposite side from the stairs he'd just descended. Their droppings stained the floor and gave the room an acrid smell. Black rose-covered vines ran up along some of the walls, entwining around the ravens' roost and down again. The ravens stopped when he entered, watching him with their black, soulless eyes. Emotionlessly they stared, as if waiting to see what he might do or say.

Vheod did and said nothing. He stared back in confusion. Ravens. He must have somehow arrived here while following the ravens that had taken Whitlock. The last thing he remembered was riding through a valley thick with trees, Melann at his side. She'd appeared so frightened. He'd wanted to comfort her, but things like that didn't come easily to him. He had no experience with such displays of emotion or caring.

"Melann!" he called again.

At the sound of his shout, some of the ravens nervously flapped their wings, and two or three even flitted to a higher perch on the shelf. A few cawed.

Vheod looked around him quickly. He stepped into the room. The chamber's only other exit was another curving staircase, leading down even further. Keeping a cautious eye on the ravens, Vheod went to the other staircase and went down. The ravens did nothing, though they watched his every move.

The stairs led Vheod down into yet another room that seemed identical to the first, including the climbing rose vines, though there was no roost filled with ravens. Instead, a wooden table and four simple stools filled most of the room. Vheod looked at the furniture and saw that it wasn't furniture at all. The stools and even the table grew up out of the floor, from the same smooth, uncut wood that made the rest of this place. Obviously, some sort of plant-affecting sorcery was at work here, though even that didn't explain where he was.

A few bird droppings scattered about the floor, just enough to indicate that the ravens—or some of the ravens—came down here occasionally, but this wasn't their main roost. The mist was even thinner here, and rose vines crawled all about the walls and on the table. Vheod didn't see any of the black moss here, or even in the room above, like he'd seen in the corridor where it had seemed he first arrived.

Another stairway descended farther, and Vheod left this room and the sounds of ravens behind. This stairway led down into silence but not darkness. Vheod saw that he no longer needed the torch he carried, for the room below was illuminated by a glowing sphere of soft, blue light. The sphere floated in the middle of the room, which seemed about the same size as the two above it, and round like those as well. These rooms seemed grown rather than built. As before, the room was all wood—almost. In this chamber, unlike those above, the wood on the floor parted, leaving patches of exposed, wet soil. Another staircase descended farther on the opposite side of the chamber, but Vheod could see that it sank down into the earth, not wood.

Near the bottom of the stairs, the climbing black rose vines formed a curtain so thick Vheod couldn't see what it concealed. Judging by its size, however, he thought it might be a door. He had little desire to descend underground at this point, so he hoped the answers he sought would lie beyond the curtain. He paused to yell for Melann again but received no response. In a change of tactics, he called out, "Whitlock?" but still no reply came.

Trying to avoid the long, sharp thorns the vines presented, Vheod gingerly pushed the curtain to one side. Even though he was careful, a thorn pricked him lightly, and he winced for a moment, then cursed himself for forgetting to use his sword to move the curtain again.

Again?

What did that mean? He definitely, for a moment at least, felt as though he'd moved this curtain aside before.

Using his sword to help this time, Vheod passed through the curtain and found himself back in the woods. These seemed to be the same trees into which he and Melann had ridden, though the exact surroundings were not familiar. In the distance, Vheod thought he heard running water, like a river or a stream. Ahead he saw their horses. Both lay slain on the ground, dozens of ravens picking at the flesh of their corpses.

He stepped out of the trunk of a giant tree, larger
than he really had the time or inclination to grasp. At
his feet, near the curtain-door, lay a giant raven like
those he'd fought earlier, dead. It had been hacked by
a blade, and its bloody corpse actually brought a sigh
of relief to Vheod. The blood on his blade was almost
certainly the same blood that stained the feathers of
the giant raven.

The blood was not Melann's. He hadn't lost control
to his darker side, or at least so it seemed. His memories had still left him somehow, for it seemed almost
certain he'd been here before and fought this monstrous raven. There were many unanswered questions, the most important of which was where was
Melann, and what was this yellowish syrupy substance on his blade?

As if in answer to his silent query, a creature trotted around the trunk of the tree to the doorway in
front of which Vheod still stood. This creature seemed
canine, walking on four legs. It stood almost chest
high to the cambion, and its flesh was a dark yellow.
Unlike a dog, which it resembled in the shape of its
face, its tall, pointed ears, and its body's shape, it had
no fur. Instead, covering its flesh were the same black
tendrils of rose vines that grew within the chambers
through which Vheod had just passed, and he now
noticed they grew so thickly over the surface of the
giant tree that he almost couldn't see its bark. The
only difference between the black rose vines on the
dog creature was that the thorns on it were pro-
nounced and appeared particularly dangerous.

The thorn-covered beast growled at Vheod and
leaned back into a battle-ready stance. Vheod had no
desire to fight this dog, but judging by the wounds on
its back and side and the yellowish substance that
oozed from them like sap from a tree, he'd fought it

before. Now the creature that he couldn't remember
wanted a rematch. Vengeance and anger filled its red
eyes.

"Fine," Vheod said to the beast resignedly. "If this is
what you want so badly, come and get it." He hefted
his blade, dropping the torch to the bare earth so he
could hold his sword in both hands.

The thorny dog leaped at him, snarling. Its yellow
teeth were the same color as its flesh, and its tongue
was simply a darker version of the same shade.
Vheod suddenly realized the dog was more plant than
animal.

He slashed with his sword but misjudged the
hound's speed. The dog ducked under the swing and
lunged at Vheod, teeth bared. Vheod's breastplate
protected him from the creature's bite, but the force
of the attack knocked Vheod to the ground. Worse, the
creature's thorn-covered hide slashed Vheod's arms
as he struggled to get the beast off him. He wriggled
free- and a half-hearted slash with his sword caught
the dog's underbelly, slicing into it. The wound oozed
more sap, and the beast howled and backed away,
angrier than ever.

The dog circled around Vheod, which gave him
time to regain his feet. Lunging at him yet again, the
beast went for Vheod's throat, but he was ready this
time. A quick thrust with his sword plunged the blade
into the dog's spine—if it had one—through the back
of its neck. Vheod pounded the hilt of his sword with
his off hand to shove it even deeper. Phlegmy sap
bubbled up from the wound, and the beast fell silently to its side with a gurgling noise. Vheod didn't know
if it could really be dead, for he wasn't sure what
actually defined its life.

He drew his sword out of the creature and wiped
the sap and the blood from it on the sparse grass; the

shade prevented much from growing around the looming tree. Vheod looked back to the horses and saw that the ravens had ceased their carrion feeding. Now they all stared at him. An urge to charge at them, scaring them off or killing them, rose to his throat and into his mind, but something made him look up.

Silent, staring ravens teemed over the impossibly high branches of the trees. Some appeared, at least at this distance, to be as large as the giant raven at his feet, or the one that carried Whitlock away. This wouldn't be a good battle to pick, he surmised. Not now. Besides, he wasn't sure what it could accomplish.

With the horses here, he reasoned, Melann could only be somewhere inside the tree. They must have entered together. Something stole away his memories, or his consciousness, or both. Perhaps the same thing had happened to her. Vheod thought of Melann wandering around inside the tree alone, and he picked up the torch again. It had gone out, but a few moment's work with flint and tinder nursed the flames back to life. Vheod thrust himself back through the curtain, this time remembering to use his sword to move the thorny curtain aside.

Something bid Vheod to check the stairway that descended into the earth. Though he thought it more likely that she was above, nearer where he found himself earlier, he crossed to the stairs.

The torchlight proved valuable as he descended. The passage at the bottom of the steps was low and narrow. Roots, some huge, some small, wrapped around the passage and sometimes bisected it. Small roots dangled from the ceiling, and Vheod had to be careful not to ignite them with his flaming brand. Moist earth was all around him, which produced a thick, rich odor. Soon after leaving the steps, the passage split into two. Vheod chose the left path, but it split again after fewer than a dozen steps. He could hear dripping water in the distance, but there was little sign of occupation.

Vheod had an idea. He kneeled down on the ground. Lowering the torch, he examined an area of soft earth on the floor between two roots. His search proved fruitful, for he found two booted footprints still fresh in the dirt. Neither was his, but they might have been Melann's. He pressed onward.

When he came to the next branching intersection in the root tunnels, he searched the ground for more tracks. Finding another boot print, he followed that branch of the passage. Occasionally, he had to duck underneath or climb over a root that stretched from wall to wall into the passageway. The going was slow, and the hanging roots and tubers continually made Vheod jump, for their startling appearance always resembled the movement of some creature. The weight of the earth above him and narrowness of the tunnel was oppressive. Perhaps it was only Vheod's imagination, but it seemed the passages continually became narrower and narrower. His hair and clothing was soon caked with fresh, black earth that clung to him when he brushed too close to a wall or the ceiling above him. The rich odor of the fresh soil became a thick, gagging, overbearing atmosphere of worm-laden dirt and mud.

He tracked the passage of the booted prints farther, but after two more intersections, he noticed something odd about them. It appeared that the person making these footprints was dragging something, or two things. Twin marks marred the earth. Farther on, Vheod found still more such tracks. Now, however, he could tell that the load the individual was dragging was a body—the marks he found were another pair of boots sliding along the ground. He hurried forward.

Finally, the narrow passage gave way to a larger chamber. The ceiling remained low, but the chamber stretched out to the left and the right farther than the light of Vheod's torch allowed him to see. His tanar'ri eyes allowed him greater vision in the dark than most men, but he still couldn't make out the extreme edges of the chamber. The torchlight passed over the dangling and protruding roots creating strange, snaky shadows. These serpentine shades danced and writhed in his flickering light, disturbed by his own movements.

The sound of dripping water was louder now. In fact, Vheod could hear what sounded like the gentle splashes of slowly running water somewhere ahead in the darkness. He advanced and saw that the chamber was cleft in two by a chasm at least fifteen feet wide. Gazing down into the trench, Vheod saw that water ran slowly over twenty feet below in an underground stream.

A single wide root stretched across the chasm like a bridge. Vheod approached and judged the root to be about three feet wide—enough to allow him to cross. He climbed on the rounded, twisted root, and made his way across. Numerous branching roots eased his passage, allowing him something to grasp as he walked across the treacherous, makeshift bridge. This tactic had forced him to sheathe his sword, but his weary arm was glad not to carry it for a while anyway.

His boot slipped on the soft, damp root, and his body slid to one side of the bridge. As his feet gave way underneath him, he flailed out with his free arm. He frantically grasped for anything he could get his hands on. He found himself dangling below the bridge, hanging from nothing but a single root strand. His shout of surprise and fear echoed throughout the underground chamber and across the submerged river.

He needed both hands to pull himself up and fast—before the root he clung to tore free. That would mean dropping the torch, however. Vheod considered trying to hold the torch in his mouth for a moment, but visions of his long hair catching fire forced him to drop it into the darkness and water.

Vheod heard a muted splash, then all went dark.

He cursed himself for a fool as he realized he could have thrown the torch to either side of the chasm, hoping it might rest, and if it went out, he would at least have a slowly diminishing light rather than the darkness that now enveloped him. Vheod's thoughts were interrupted by a sudden jerk and a cracking, tearing sound. He was breaking free from the root bridge.

Using his weight to his advantage, Vheod swung himself on the quickly tearing rootlet and grasped in the darkness like a blind man. His now-free hand found another hanging root strand, and he grasped it just in time as the first tore away. The sudden added weight, however, caused this new strand to begin to tear, so he thrust his hand upward to find another.

Somehow he managed to grab hold of yet another strand. Summoning all his strength, Vheod pulled himself upward so he could grasp another, higher strand. His hands clawed at the side of the massive main root as he found higher and higher minor roots that branched from it to pull himself up. Finally, he sat atop the bridge, straddling it like a wide horse. Vheod's tanar'ri vision began to adjust to the complete darkness enough to allow him to see a few feet ahead of him. Crawling and scooting along the bridge—not wanting to risk walking across again—he made his way across it to the other side.

Once on the opposite ledge of the chasm, Vheod stood. Without his torch, he could see only a short distance ahead of him, so he drew his sword to use to feel ahead in the dark. He didn't care for the bright light of day, but the utter finality of darkness was worse, and more limiting, though he could see a little. He preferred the light of an overcast day, or twilight—those were similar to the lighting conditions on the layer of the Abyss in which he'd grown up.

Where had he gotten a torch from anyway? Had Melann given it to him? Vheod seemed to remember vaguely there being a few torches mixed in with the siblings' other equipment on the horses. In any event, he moved forward into the darkness.

Since he couldn't see, after two dozen steps or so, he allowed himself the dangerous luxury of calling out again. The danger, of course, came from the fact than everything that might be down here would hear him—even something that meant him only harm.

"Melann?"

Vheod continued walking until his sword bumped into a wall. He followed it along, occasionally grasping the roots that reached out from the wall. He yanked them away from where they hung for no good reason other than to mark his path—a path he probably couldn't see to follow in any event. Vheod considered attempting to make another torch, since he carried flint and tinder with him in his pocket, but he didn't think he could make the moist roots burn well.

As he grasped a root projecting out of the earthen wall, it suddenly grabbed back. Vheod looked down at his arm and saw with faint vision a root about half an inch in diameter wrap around his arm. He tried to jerk it away, but the root held fast. He raised his sword, still tugging to free his arm. When he couldn't pull away, he tried to get as much of the root exposed between him and the wall as possible. Having done that as best he could, he hacked at it with his blade. It took two strikes to cut through the root, but when he'd succeeded, the severed part fell away, limp and lifeless.

"Hello?" A voice cried from within the sea of darkness. "Is anyone there?"

Vheod recognized Melann's voice and stumbled toward it in the darkness, moving away from the wall to keep out of the reach of any more strange, grasping tendrils. "Melann! It's me, Vheod."

"Vheod, I'm here!"

"Wait," he said in the direction of her voice. She sounded close. Vheod knelt down, setting his sword at his side. He took the flint from his pocket and tried to get a light, even a tiny spark that might set fire to one of the root tendrils he'd torn. After a few moments, he managed to get a spark to light the end of one of them. It wouldn't burn long, but it provided a tiny jewel of light for now.

Vheod saw Melann just a few feet away, up against the wall, held fast by a number of roots that had entangled themselves around her wrists and ankles, as though she was shackled. In fact, the roots that held her resembled conventional manacles too much to be coincidence. Someone was holding her here.

"Melann," he asked her, still a little worried to get too close to the obviously dangerous wall, "is there anyone near?"

"No," she replied, "I don't think so." Her voice was hoarse and dry. Sympathy welled inside him, and he longed to go to her, to free her.

"Who put you here?" Vheod nervously looked around, though he could see very little in the oppressive darkness. His tiny light was already dying.

"I don't know." Her voice seemed a little frantic. "I remember a woman with dark hair. I remember moving against my will, as if I was dragged, then I just remember being here. What happened? How did we get here? Where are we? The last thing I fully remember was riding through the woods with you."

"How long have you been here?" he asked her.

"Not long, I . . . I don't think . . ."

Perhaps their minds had been affected by the same thing, but she was abducted somehow, and he wasn't. Still there was much left that needed to be explained.

The light winked out. She gasped. Vheod stepped forward and grasped Melann's hand. He was close enough now to see her without a light. He could see her smile and visibly relax in the darkness when he touched her. He pulled her hand away from the wall as much as he could and chopped at the root that held her. He could see more roots uncoiling from the wall.

"Keep pulling as far from the wall as possible. I'm going to cut these bonds, and when I do, pull that part of you away." He didn't tell her why. He couldn't afford to have her worrying about advancing roots that she couldn't see anyway.

Melann did as Vheod told her, and he managed to cut away the roots and avoid being grasped himself. She thrust herself completely away from the wall just as more roots reached for her. He guided her away from the edge of the cavern. The roots on the floor where they knelt to catch their breath didn't react the way those along the wall had. Apparently the animate roots had been enchanted. Whoever lived in this tree fortress obviously used the lower level for a prison or dungeon.

Melann didn't speak for a few moments, and Vheod realized she was praying. When she finished, she raised her cupped hands above her, and they filled with magical light that illuminated the area around them much more brightly than Vheod's pitiful little flame.

When his eyes adjusted to the new light, he looked at Melann carefully. Moist dirt was caked all over her clothes, face, and hair.

"Are you all right? Are you hurt?"

"Other than some chaffed wrists," she said with raised brows, "I think I'm fine. You look as though you've been fighting."

"Do you remember anything, Melann?" He helped her to her feet, so that both of them were standing in the chill chamber. The air was still, but the water moving in the underground stream echoed in the distance. "Do you remember arriving at this . . . giant tree filled with ravens? Do you remember a thorny dog, or lighting a torch and exploring the inside?"

"The inside of a tree?" Melann asked, looking around.

"Yes," Vheod answered, nodding slightly. "We are below it now—in the roots."

"What you're saying seems to strike a familiar chord within me, like you're describing a distant dream. The events sound familiar, but I don't really remember them."

She brushed dirt away from her face and hair, then patted the soil from her clothes as well. She'd left her traveling cloak on her horse—as she'd done most of the time during the day. She wore only her light leather jerkin and gray cloth trousers, both torn and dirty.

"The same is true with me, I'm afraid. I've only been able to piece together what I've told you through interpolation. The last thing I clearly remember is riding through the woods with you."

"You said something about the tree being filled with ravens." It was a statement, not a question. She stopped brushing the dirt away and stared into Vheod's dark eyes. "Does that mean this is the lair of the Ravenwitch?"

"I think so," Vheod replied.

"Do you know where Whitlock is?"

"No, but I think I've got a good idea where to start looking."

Melann nodded, her eyes once again wide with optimism. "Well then, let's go."

Chapter Thirteen

Melann couldn't help but find the giant tree fascinating. As frightened and confused as she was, walking around inside a giant, living tree thrilled her. Despite the Ravenwitch's evil—at least, Melann assumed the witch was evil—she obviously knew wondrous secrets about the care and nurturing of growing things. Melann saw nothing to indicate that the tree had been mistreated or was unhealthy. On the contrary, it appeared to be thriving, as did the rose vines that grew throughout the interior, climbing and winding their way around everything. How they grew without sunlight was a mystery to Melann, but the interior of the tree was far more mysterious and wonderful. Obviously, somehow, the Ravenwitch had communicated with the tree on some level, coaxing it to take the shapes she desired. Corridors, rooms, staircases, doorways—the place was amazing.

Melann and Vheod briefly explored the subterranean root section of the tree, but Vheod seemed convinced that the Ravenwitch had Whitlock with her and that she would be in the upper reaches of the tree. Birds, he reasoned, stick mostly to the branches high above the ground, and Melann could find no reason to argue with him. The truth was, she really had no idea what to do next, but determination to find her

brother drove her onward. It was good that she had
Vheod to direct that driving need. She felt like some
sort of wild storm, full of energy but aimless and
without bearing.

Vheod, it appeared, didn't share her appreciation of
the tree, but she couldn't blame him. Anyone else
except perhaps a Brother or Sister of the Earth would
most likely find this place frightening and strange.
Remaining very quiet since he found her amid the
roots, Vheod seemed more pensive than she'd seen
him before. Of course, Melann was not completely
without fear herself.

Whitlock was somewhere inside the tree, and she
had to find him. She realized that if something happened to Whitlock, she would be utterly alone. Vheod
provided intriguing and pleasant companionship, but
she was entirely dependent on her family for support
and nurturing. As a garden grows dependent on its
caretaker, she found it difficult to imagine that she
could possibly succeed in her quest without her
brother—and that would mean losing her mother and
father as well.

Vheod had spoken about the loss of memories, but
Melann had assumed that she'd just been waylaid in
the woods and brought to the tree—perhaps by
magic. He was sure that the two of them fought their
way into the Ravenwitch's lair and something had
attacked their minds. He was convincing. The fact
that their horses lay slain outside of the tree certainly lent credence to his idea, but Melann simply
couldn't remember any of it.

They stood in the round chamber one story above
its almost identical counterpart on the ground level.
The wooden table and stools grew up from the floor in
a manner that occupied much of Melann's attention.
She marveled at the way they had been somehow

shaped, presumably as the tree grew. The whole room had obviously been shaped by careful planning and great skill with plants. Her mind drew back to the Ravenwitch. Melann considered their predicament, and the need to find Whitlock.

"At what point do you believe our minds were attacked?" she asked Vheod.

"Up high in the tree," he answered. "The first thing I can remember is standing in a woody corridor with rose vines and black moss and—"

Vheod paused suddenly, his dark eyes growing wide.

"What is it, Vheod?" Melann asked.

"Melann, you have some knowledge of plants, right?" Vheod asked with a rapid intensity.

"Well, yes, but I—"

"Have you ever heard of some sort of moss or fungus that can affect one's mind?"

"Well . . ." Melann ran through her training, and all she'd ever heard or read about mosses, lichens, and fungi. "Yes! There's something I believe is called, obviously enough, memory moss. It feeds on memories. Patches of it can be found in magical glens and enchanted areas, sometimes underground."

"Is it black?"

"I . . . I think so."

"Well, now we know what we're up against then, at least." Vheod leaned back against the wall. He seemed more relaxed. "Is there any way we can fight it?"

"I would imagine it could be burned," Melann told him. "But Vheod, I can't . . . I mean, I'm not supposed to . . ." She paused, with a pained expression.

"What is it?" Vheod furrowed his brow in obvious concern.

"I can't willingly destroy a growing thing—even something like memory moss. It's against everything I've ever been taught."

Vheod said nothing, just stared into her face, considering her words. He pulled away from the wall on which he leaned and folded his arms in front of him. Melann's spell of light illuminated his rough, angular face in such a way that his eyes seemed even darker and more distant than normal. Judging by the look on his face, Vheod was confused.

"Our Mother represents," Melann explained, "and is in turn represented by all growing things. Her teachings forbid the wanton destruction of her creations."

Still Vheod stood silent. He shifted his weight from one foot to the other.

"Melann, I don't understand. We're talking about something that attacked our minds. It may threaten us again in a similar—"

"I know," Melann interrupted, averting her eyes from him.

Sometimes clinging to her beliefs forced her into situations she truly hated. It seemed she should just be stalwart about what she knew to be right, but it wasn't that easy. Melann was not blind. She could see that sometimes the tenets of her faith presented obstacles.

Faith had never been easy for her. She'd been told as she rose in the ranks of the clergy that she showed strength and depth in that she agonized over, examined, and re-examined, every aspect of her religion. She saw it as a flaw herself and wished she could just be strong enough to never question.

"But you eat plants," Vheod reasoned.

"That's different," Melann said, shaking her head. She'd had such debates with many of those not within Chauntea's fold. "It's not the destruction of the plant for destruction's sake."

Vheod shook his head as well, folding his arms again. "You'll have to forgive me." His jaw was set squarely. "I am unused to such principles and such strict adherence to them. In the Abyss, the only principle was that which is most easily followed—'serve thyself above all others.' " His sneer was almost a smile.

He'd reached a point where he could almost joke about his past, Melann observed. Joke, that is, at least in a contemptuous way. He must have hated it there so much, she thought.

"But you obviously had principles," Melann stated softly. "You were different."

For just a moment, Vheod's eyes seemed to lighten as they stared into hers, though he remained silent. He looked away after a moment, glancing at the floor.

"More appropriate places will present themselves in which to hold this conversation, I'm sure." Vheod looked around, particularly at the stairs leading up and added, "In fact, I must say I'm surprised we haven't seen this Ravenwitch. She knows we're here."

"Perhaps," Melann said with a visible shudder, "she's otherwise preoccupied." Oh, Whitlock, she thought, where are you? What is she doing to you?

"Above this chamber, we will find a roost of ravens. Beyond that lies the passage with the moss. I'm afraid I'm going to have to try to burn it, Melann. Can you live with that?"

"We've got to get to Whitlock," was her reply, "but I cannot help in such a dire task."

Again Vheod breathed outward through clenched teeth. "I have made a lifetime out of completing distasteful tasks. I can do it alone."

Melann was sorry. She had no idea how to make Vheod understand. Surely his noble nature would recognize what she said to be true. "You won't harm this tree, though, right?"

Vheod replied with a question as he drew his sword. "How do you know the tree isn't a thing of evil? It's creator obviously is, isn't she?"

"I assume so, but a tree cannot be evil. It is but a tree. Besides, the Ravenwitch almost certainly didn't create the tree. She just shaped it, if it was her at all."

Melann considered that perhaps the Ravenwitch had killed the original caretaker of the tree or had forced another to shape it for her. She just couldn't reconcile in her mind that the same person responsible for the amazing nurturing and caring that went into the creation of this tree fortress could have sent foul, wicked ravens to attack them and abduct her brother.

"I think we'll learn soon enough," Vheod said, moving to the stairs.

* * * * *

Vheod's tall but graceful form emerged from the shadows of the staircase, illuminated by the magical light conjured by Melann's priestly faith. His long, cold steel blade bared before him, he advanced into the dark room he knew earlier had been filled with ravens. The chamber stank of bird droppings and feathers, and as Melann carefully followed Vheod up the stairs and into the room, they both could see that this indeed had been a roost for the black-feathered birds.

Now, however, the room stood empty and utterly silent. As Vheod moved to the center of the room, he looked all around and up onto the high shelf where he'd seen the ravens roosting earlier. The ravens were gone. He paused a moment to listen, motioning for Melann to remain at the top of the stairs.

Far above, he heard the distant sounds of shrill shrieks. The ravens had moved higher into the interior of the tree and now seemed to be agitated in some way. Vheod was too far away to determine more. He rushed across the room to the stairs leading higher up. Melann moved from the other staircase and followed him.

When he reached the top of that flight of stairs, Vheod paused. This was about where he first remembered being in the tree and thus perhaps where his memories were stolen from him. He looked ahead in the light as the illumination brightened with Melann's approach. She stopped quietly a few steps below where he stood, but Vheod could see in the magical light the black moss that streaked the wooden walls like blood from a wound or rust on metal. He was sure he hadn't seen this sort of moss anywhere else on the tree. It might not be the culprit that had stolen their memories, Vheod knew.

Even if it wasn't to blame, he had little to lose. Vheod sheathed his sword and began reciting the incantation for a spell he'd learned in a dark corner of Broken Reach. A tanar'ri wizard named Chirotobyn had taught him a number of minor spells in exchange for a full year of Vheod's service as a bodyguard. It had been a busy year, for Chirotobyn had many enemies. Vheod served his temporary master well, however, and even managed to get the tanar'ri to hold up his end of the bargain, though Chirotobyn had only done so at the end of Vheod's sword. In any event, Vheod now spread his fingers, thumbs touching, forming a fan with his hands. As he did, flames leaped from his fingertips, jetting outward against the walls of the corridor ahead of him. The fire splashed against the hardwood, which was too firm and solid to catch fire, though it blackened and scorched.

The moss, on the other hand, burned away just as Vheod had hoped. The passage through the tree filled with flickering light as the moss took the flame. As it did, the black, stringy substance changed its shape before his eyes. While Vheod watched, the moss formed a perfect image of his own face, howling in pain while it burned. The face contorted hideously, then reformed to gain the appearance of Melann's face.

Vheod looked away. He couldn't bear to see the wracked expression of the moss Melann face burning in the flames he'd conjured. Thankfully, the fire burned the moss quickly and thoroughly, almost disintegrating the stringy strands completely. What little remained fell to the floor as a dark powder. The hall went mostly dark again, lit only by the magical light Melann still held cupped in her hands on the staircase below Vheod.

The horrible display on Melann's face seemed to confirm in Vheod's mind that the moss had somehow stolen a portion of their memories. A useful defense, he mused, assuming the Ravenwitch herself had some immunity to the affect. Obviously, when the memory moss struck, the witch or her servants had grabbed Melann. Perhaps they had come back for him, but he'd already wandered off to another portion of the tree fortress. His tanar'ri nature probably allowed him to shrug off the effects more quickly than they—whoever *they* were—had predicted.

Vheod turned to Melann and again motioned for her to wait. Her face showed concern. She wasn't the type who liked to wait while others went into danger—Vheod had realized that early on. He wanted to make sure the corridor ahead was safe, and he'd also observed that neither Melann nor Whitlock possessed his skill at moving quietly. Obviously, they'd not grown up in an environment filled with fiends that would slay them at the slightest provocation.

Vheod hunched down so he was almost crawling on hands and knees and crept forward down the corridor. The illumination behind him enabled him to see enough—more than if he weren't half tanar'ri. As he slipped silently down the passage he felt a strange tingling sensation on his wrist. He didn't need to see at all to know it was the Taint, but he had no idea what the feeling meant. He pressed forward.

The passage twisted and turned but sprouted no side passages. It almost seemed to Vheod that he and Melann had climbed up through the trunk of the tree, and now he crept inside one of the gigantic branches. The corridor split into two, and Vheod had no idea which way to go. He also had passed far enough away from Melann's light that he could really see just a little more than nothing. He would have to go back and get her. Before he did he allowed himself another moment to just listen. Again he heard the high shrieks of upset ravens, and though they seemed closer, Vheod's ears detected the sounds of fewer of them now.

Worst of all—or perhaps best of all—amid the squawking birds he heard what sounded like a man moaning in pain.

Whitlock.

Vheod ran back down the corridor as quietly as he could, but as quickly as he dared. The light grew brighter with each step, until he reached Melann once again at the top of the stairs near the scorched corridor walls. She looked at him with silent expectation.

"I think Whitlock is ahead somewhere. We must be careful, and as quiet as possible."

"Is he all right?" She asked emphatically, the excitement and anxiety a living thing in her eyes.

"I don't know," Vheod said in a forced whisper. "I think he's alive, but I think he might be hurt or in danger."

"Then let's go," Melann stressed, attempting to press ahead of Vheod.

The cambion turned to the dark passage and stepped forward so he remained in the lead. He drew his blade and began to creep silently ahead, if for no other reason than to encourage Melann to be as quiet as she could, and slow down her too-anxious pace. Vheod didn't want them to foolishly stumble into some unknown danger.

Melann's devotion to her brother was the most sincere thing Vheod had ever encountered. She was everything he'd always wanted to be himself—honest, true to herself and others, noble, generous, kind. . . . At many times in his life he'd thought such things were only fabled concepts, not real. Her purity of heart had quickly become the most important treasure he knew of. Melann herself had just as quickly become the center of his thoughts. He knew now that he would do anything for her.

Vheod and Melann reached the point where the passage branched off into two passages, separated by only a narrow angle, as if they stood at the juncture of two tree limbs. They followed the sounds of ravens that seemed to come from the right, with Vheod still in the lead and Melann anxiously dogging his heels. Vheod saw light ahead and tried to pause, but he knew Melann's understandable efforts to urge him ahead would quickly spoil any chance they had of approaching undetected. Both could hear the pained screeches of ravens entwined about a human moan. Behind him, Vheod could hear Melann discarding the light and preparing a blessing for the two of them. She obviously thought they were going into danger and battle. Vheod couldn't help but think she was right. His instincts screamed of danger ahead. As he began moving swiftly down the passage toward the light, he once again felt the rush of power flow over him as Melann bestowed Chauntea's blessing on them. He also felt a prickling pain at his wrist—where he knew the Taint to be. He knew there was no time to think of that now, as he rushed into the well lit area at the end of the passage.

A starry sky above Vheod and a cool summer breeze brought him to the realization that he was outside. The passage he'd come through led through a limb of the gigantic tree and out onto a platform formed by the spiral entwining of a number of the huge tree's branches. The platform reached a diameter of at least thirty yards, but for the most part its surface stretched emptily into the night, except for numerous thorn-covered black rose vines. The ever-present climbing vines snaked in every direction. Some of those hanging on higher branches within the tree's gargantuan canopy dangled down above the platform, while others stretched down and grappled the wood of the platform in a taut web of black flowers and thorns.

At the center of the platform, the network of vines grew thick, and to Vheod's surprise the vines held a number of ravens. Coils wrapped around the birds like constricting snakes. Many of the birds screeched in protest, while others hung limply in the black tendrils. Looking closer, Vheod saw thin trickles of red blood inch in grisly streaks down the vines to the center of this hideous black web. Whitlock hung suspended above the platform wrapped tightly in biting strands of black roses. The thorns dug into his bared flesh so that the ravens' blood flowed down the vines and into his wounds. The man moaned and weakly thrashed in his taut bonds, but his eyes were closed and he showed no signs of conscious awareness.

Vheod and Melann sprinted forward out of the tunnel and across the platform. The footing was uneven and tricky, but the urgency of the situation pressed them onward, guiding their feet.

Before they could cross even half the distance, a shimmering wall of translucent blackness erupted before them. Vheod could just make out a female form, clothed in long black dress, on the other side of the wall, standing below where Whitlock hung. He hadn't seen her when they began running, but she'd obviously seen them. The magical barrier rested on the platform and stretched around in what appeared to be a semicircle. Vheod knew he could get around it, but surely its creator was aware of that simple fact as well.

She wasn't trying to stop them, just delay them.

Obviously, time was of the essence here, and Vheod surmised that Whitlock was the key. Melann drew her mace and slammed into the barrier forcefully but to no avail. She began to run around to the right. Vheod, however, took a few steps back and hefted his sword in a way that offset its center of gravity, pointing the blade almost parallel with the floor. Taking a few steps forward again, he threw his arm back and flung the sword so it spun through the air, over the conjured wall of energy. The whirling blade cut a swath through the air, and the woman behind the translucent screen watched it fly over her head.

"No!" the woman shouted in protest.

Vheod hoped Chauntea's blessing would help guide his reckless heave. He almost prayed.

The spinning blade flew toward Whitlock, and Vheod saw the look of horror cross Melann's face as she ran to the right edge of the wall. Wordlessly, she watched as it chopped at the air, angling over the wall and down at her brother.

The blade struck true. It cut through the vine that supported the bulk of Whitlock's weight. With that vine severed, a number of the others tore with the sudden weight of his body, and Whitlock came crashing down amid rose petals, thorns, and blood.

The black-clad woman screamed in frustration.

The energy wall faded away.

The woman looked at Vheod, dark eyes smoldering. Her skin shone in the moonlight like smooth, milky alabaster, her long dark tresses merged with her flowing dress so that in the dim light they made it difficult to distinguish where they ended and the garment began. A cape made entirely of raven feathers draped from her neck and dragged well behind her in a long train. She raised her long-nailed fingers like claws, as though she prepared to loose some dark spell, but then she stopped.

Melann ran to her brother, passing the woman to one side. She was too preoccupied to pay the black-clad woman any heed. Likewise, the woman ignored Melann. Once at her brother's side, Melann began pulling the thorny vines away from him. Whitlock stirred enough to indicated that he was at least alive and partially conscious. Melann's sobs of fear and relief were the only sound other than the cries of pain and protest from the trapped birds.

Until the mysterious woman spoke. She focused on Vheod for a moment, as though studying him.

"Child of demons," she said. "Chare'en's blood flows through your veins."

Vheod stared back at her. He felt helpless and naked before her gaze, particularly without his sword. This woman—the Ravenwitch—was beautiful and terrible at once. She reminded him of Nethess, the tanar'ri marilith that had hunted him his last days in the Abyss. Something inside him roused at the sound of her dark, throaty voice. It was like nothing that caused him to care for Melann. In fact, it seemed his desire came from all the parts of him that lay dormant while he thought of the pure-hearted priestess. This Ravenwitch appealed to that small part of him he didn't want to admit existed. She reminded him of everything in him that missed the Abyss and his former life. She was the catalyst that brought to the surface the lure of the darkness in his soul. The revel of dark power, the taste of innocent blood, and the beckoning need of betrayal and corruption churned within him.

Vheod felt the power of Melann's blessing drain away, almost as if it pooled at his feet and evaporated. He glanced at his left wrist, and saw the Taint. It formed a leering, fiendish face with a look of triumph and exultation.

"You have come to free Chare'en," the Ravenwitch stated. It wasn't a question.

Chapter Fourteen

Whitlock's wounds appeared much worse than they really were. He had lost a great deal of blood, but the injuries weren't deep. His naked, cut, and torn flesh was covered with ravens' blood, and a fair amount of it had poured into his wounds. The Ravenwitch had made him a part of some evil ceremony or ritual, but Melann didn't know enough about her to even guess at what its goal had been.

The Ravenwitch seemed to have turned her attention toward Vheod. She didn't even seem to care that Whitlock had been freed from his bonds or that Melann was in the process of preparing a healing blessing.

Vheod stared at the Ravenwitch, speechless. His arms hung limply at his side, and his face showed that her words had struck him with a wound more grievous than any weapon could possibly inflict.

"Do you deny that you are the descendant of the balor, Chare'en?" the Ravenwitch asked him, stepping toward him.

Melann watched as Vheod's face changed. The look of pain and horror shifted with disquieting swiftness to one of deep need or hunger. She continued to tend to her brother's wounds, but her eyes couldn't leave Vheod.

"Vheod?" Melann's tone spoke a thousand questions, the answer to any of which might easily break her heart.

"I deny nothing, witch," Vheod said. The beginnings of a smile came to his lips. Rather than gladden Melann, the sight of that smile terrified her.

"You have come here in error then, cambion," the Ravenwitch told him softly. "Your master isn't here. His prison lies in a cavern miles to the south."

Vheod began to speak again, but stopped. Melann, from behind the Ravenwitch, still kneeling at her brother's side, interrupted him. She could think of nothing more to say than simply, "Vheod?"

The sound of her voice seemed to bring about another change in him. He looked past the Ravenwitch to Melann. He stared at her a moment as she helped her brother. Vheod's face changed, and his eyes seemed to grow softer. He looked to the Ravenwitch again, but the smile had vanished.

"I have no master, *witch*!" He shouted in defiance.

The Ravenwitch was silent for a moment, her body perfectly still, then slowly turned and looked back and down at Melann and Whitlock. Perhaps she'd simply followed Vheod's gaze, or maybe she had some dire plan for the siblings. Melann would believe anything at this point.

Still looking at Melann and Whitlock, the Ravenwitch said simply, "I see."

"You mistake me for someone or something else, I think, witch," Vheod said, seemingly steeling himself as he straightened his back. The muscles in his neck and arms tightened. "I've come to ensure that Chare'en is *not* freed. I don't wish his evil loosed on this world."

The Ravenwitch turned back to Vheod. She moved even closer to him, close enough for her to lay a long-fingered hand on his shoulder. Vheod remained rigid.

"If that is truly your goal, cambion, then you will fail." She said.

"Do not threaten me," Vheod spoke through clenched teeth.

"I do not threaten. I speak of the future, and the certainties I have seen in divination. You will free Chare'en."

Vheod remained silent.

"I suspect, then, after you free him and he gathers the army of creatures that already amassed waiting for him, you will fight at his side. The two of you can carve a fiendish kingdom of evil for yourselves. You'll fight even against the arrayed armies of Cormyr and the kingdoms to the south, spreading destruction as only tanar'ri truly can. I don't wish to oppose such a powerful menace. I want to survive." The Ravenwitch gestured with open palms toward Vheod, but Melann was sure her narrowed eyes concealed something.

Melann looked down at Whitlock and called on the power of Chauntea to heal her brother. As she prayed, a bluish-white glow flowed from her fingertips to Whitlock's flesh. The light caressed his bloody wounds, erasing them from his body as though they had never been. Whitlock's eyes fluttered open, and he opened his mouth to speak, but all he managed was to cough up dark blood—raven's blood.

"What have you done to my brother?" Melann demanded, interrupting the strange, disturbing conversation Vheod and the Ravenwitch were having. She held on to Whitlock as he spat out the blood and moaned.

"I did nothing," the Ravenwitch said, circling around Vheod then turning to face Melann from behind him. "I was about to grant him the greatest gift within my power. A blessing, really,"—she shook her head slightly—"but you stopped it. Without the infusion of ravens' blood, now that the magical process is ruined, he'll be nothing but a human." She looked at Vheod from behind him. "Your tendency to thrust yourself into situations you don't fully understand will be your downfall, cambion."

Vheod turned to face her. "I am certain whatever you were doing to him was something that was rightfully ended. Do not attempt to trick me with sly wordplay, Ravenwitch. I lived for years among the sharp and slippery tongues of the tanar'ri, skilled in eons of temptation and betrayal. You will not fool me with your lies."

"But," the Ravenwitch retorted, "I was going to make him my servant. He would have been granted great gifts—flight, physical power, virtual immortality. . . ."

Realization of the importance of the ravens' blood washed over Melann. "You were going to make him into some sort of lycanthropic slave—a wereraven! You were going to turn my brother into a horrible monster." Melann stood, clenching her hands into fists. Her body was tense with anger.

"Something like that," the Ravenwitch replied casually, "though I wouldn't choose to use quite those words. One thing is certain: Your brother would have stood a much better chance of surviving as my servant than he will otherwise, once Chare'en is loosed on the Thunder Peaks and into the Dalelands. Mere humans will fall before his might quickly and easily."

"I won't let that happen," Vheod said quietly, but firmly.

"Did you not hear me, cambion? You will cause it. That is why you are here." The Ravenwitch offered a single open hand held flatly toward him as if to suggest that she offered a simple truth.

"No!" Vheod spat. "In fact, the truth is that you are the one, are you not? I was warned about your evil.

You plan to free the balor Chare'en, don't you? You probably worship him, don't you? Foolish mortal woman—you'll bring about your own demise."

"No," the Ravenwitch replied. Her voice was still calm and flat.

Melann noted that other than her initial shock at their sudden arrival, the Ravenwitch had remained decidedly unemotional. Somehow that caused Melann to hate and fear her more.

"I don't worship demons," the Ravenwitch continued. "I don't look forward to a future where gnoll armies with fiendish commanders lay waste to the countryside." Only on speaking of gnoll armies did her voice falter, or betray any emotion at all. "I know the future though, and I don't fight against the inevitable. I am many things, perhaps, but I am not a fool.

"There is one, however, who does worship Chare'en, serving him and putting events in motion to help free the balor, and of course there are the gnolls." Her disdain for the gnolls became even more clear with the look of fire that flashed in her eyes when she said the word.

"What about the gnolls?" Vheod asked her.

The Ravenwitch moved back to where she'd stood before, between Melann and Vheod. Melann helped Whitlock to his feet and over toward Vheod. She hoped they could just flee, once she got the three of them together. She didn't care about exacting revenge on the Ravenwitch—she'd never been interested in such pettiness. She was, however, tired of hearing the witch's half-truths and strange words. She just wanted to get away from the Ravenwitch and away from the giant tree. She needed time to think. Again Vheod had terrified her. The darkness in his soul was strong—stronger than she'd originally assumed.

"The gnolls," the Ravenwitch said finally, "or rather their ancestors, once worshiped and served Chare'en when he was free in Faerûn. They were his army. Now, I suspect, they somehow hear his call once again. Don't be so foolish as to think Chare'en doesn't know you're coming to free him. I suspect he's quite eager to meet you."

Melann didn't know if it was right that she and her brother spend any further time with Vheod. She believed Vheod fought against his evil nature, but for the first time she seriously worried about what would happen if he lost that fight.

To the surprise of the other three, Whitlock managed to speak as he regained his feet. "So then, everything Vheod said was true. Chare'en wasn't an ancient sorcerer, he was—is—a demon, and if we go looking for the remedy for our family's curse, we'll free him."

"Yes, Whitlock," Vheod answered. He frowned, and Melann knew he wasn't happy to be right.

The Ravenwitch shook her head. "You won't free him," she said to Whitlock, and pointed at Vheod. "He will."

"I told you, woman, I will not." His muscles tightened further, and his eyes smoldered with anger. "Particularly now—we won't even go there."

"And we'll never find the staff we were told might lift the curse," Melann said, her voice cracking with sadness. She looked down at the ground, still helping Whitlock along.

"Oh, I imagine that if you go to Chare'en's prison, you'll find the staff you seek," the Ravenwitch said.

"What?" Melann looked up. "You mean it *is* there?"

"Almost certainly. Many things of great and wondrous power lie in the balor's prison, but you'll never get there without your friend."

Vheod remained silent. Melann noticed him glance down at his wrist, where his crimson tattoo lay. That struck her as strange. She was certain she'd seen it near his neck before. Had it moved? How could she have not noticed? What else didn't she know?

"If we try to leave this place," Melann asked her slowly, with a narrowed gaze, "are you going to try to stop us?"

"Of course not," the Ravenwitch said. "You both misjudge and misunderstand me." Melann thought of how the witch had sent her ravens to carry away her brother against his will and determined that she did *not* misjudge her. The Ravenwitch continued, "I know Chare'en will be freed. I know his reign of terror will spread and his armies will swoop over the land— here. I don't want him to think of me as his enemy so I do not obstruct the actions of his heir and savior." She bowed slightly toward Vheod.

Still obviously fuming with anger, Vheod remained silent. With Melann and Whitlock now at his side, he began walking toward the entrance to the passage through the branch that would take them back to the ground. The ravens around them let loose shrill cries in the moonlight, but he seemed unmoved.

Vheod stopped. Looking back to the Ravenwitch, he said, "You don't know me. The future is always uncertain. My destiny isn't preordained. I make my own way. Don't judge me by what you assume I am. I am more than that. I always have been, and I always will be."

As they walked away, the Ravenwitch said something that puzzled Melann, though her words were directed at Vheod. "It is a terrible thing for a creature to deny its own nature," she said. "Unlike most, you have a choice—you have two natures. Choose one, and don't deny it."

* * * * *

Vheod and Melann searched through the packs on the dead horses outside the Ravenwitch's tree. Each horse was already cold in death. Melann took out some clothes for Whitlock and helped him put them on. Vheod removed the useful supplies, including some rope, a few empty bags, two bedrolls, some cooking gear, six torches, a knife, Whitlock's sword and crossbow, a quiver of a dozen or so crossbow bolts, and three mostly full waterskins.

They didn't have Whitlock's armor, Vheod's sword, or any food. Melann made a comment about how they'd not eaten all day as she helped Whitlock, who remained weak after his ordeal. Melann's priestly magic had aided him a great deal, and perhaps even saved him from death, but a number of his initial wounds from the battle with the giant ravens remained and weakened him.

"We need to get away from this place," Vheod told her, "then we can rest. I'll try to find us some food then."

He loaded the supplies into two backpacks and handed one to Melann. She said a quiet blessing over the dead horses and thanked them for the help they had given the three of them. They both shouldered the packs and helped Whitlock to his feet. With his arms draped over their shoulders they walked away, into the deep woods.

Following the nearby river, the three travelers made their way south. They walked for a little over an hour, then stopped to rest for the remainder of the night. Vheod hoped the distance they put between themselves and the Ravenwitch would be enough to protect them from any treachery on her part. He didn't trust anything the witch did or said.

"We never asked about the green stones," Melann said as she unrolled a bedroll and made Whitlock comfortable.

"What?" Vheod said, turning to her.

"The Ravenwitch said a lot of things back there, but we never asked about the strange green stones the gnolls seem to be collecting."

"I wouldn't have believed her anyway," Vheod said.

"Do you think everything she said was a lie?" Melann asked as she collapsed to the ground herself, wearily laying back on her own bedroll.

"I know her kind. The Abyss is full of creatures like her. They lace their lies with hints of the truth, just to make the lies more believable." Vheod looked at Melann. She seemed to be carefully studying him.

"She confirmed your belief that Chare'en was a fiend, not a wizard," she said after a moment.

"Yes. As I said, traces of the truth." Vheod picked up a twig from the ground and whirled it around in his fingers.

"What about what she said about you? About you freeing him? Serving him?"

"Lies," Vheod said harshly and quickly in response to Melann's words. He didn't look up at her, still staring at the small stick he spun in his hand.

"Vheod," Melann said gently, "I've spent some time with you, and I'm a good judge of character. I know you're struggling against the evil nature of your heritage." She paused, swallowing hard. The words appeared to come to her only with difficulty. "But haven't you considered the possibility that perhaps you've been set up? That somehow Chare'en—your ancestor—might have planned all of this?"

"I am in control of my own destiny," Vheod protested, shaking his head. He snapped the twig in his hands and tossed it aside.

"But what if you aren't? What if there's a part of you—the evil, fiendish part—that actually conspires against you? I've seen that evil nature well up inside you. It could be capable of anything."

Melann's words cut into him like a sword. Vheod stared at the ground where he sat next to the reclining siblings. Whitlock had fallen into a much-needed sleep. Melann was quiet.

Vheod started to get up after a moment. "I'll see if I can get something for us to eat."

"No, Vheod," Melann said, still lying down. "Wait until morning. Whitlock's asleep, and I'm exhausted. We couldn't eat anything now anyway."

Vheod sat back down.

"Are you sure you don't want a bedroll?" Melann asked. "I can sleep without one for once."

"I'm sure," Vheod told her, as he had on previous nights.

They both lay on the ground in silence, listening to the wind gently tug at the tree branches above their heads.

"Vheod?" Melann asked quietly. "Thank you for my brother. I could never have rescued him, and could never have gotten out of there on my own. Thank you." Her tired eyes closed even as she finished speaking. She soon fell asleep, but sleep did not come that night to Vheod.

* * * * *

By the time Melann and Whitlock were awake, Vheod had already built a fire and was roasting a pair of rabbits that he'd killed with Whitlock's crossbow. The sun had risen a fair height in the sky, and the day once again promised plenty of sun and heat.

Whitlock appeared considerably better, and another dose of Melann's priestly healing seemed to restore him almost completely. He smiled when Vheod offered him some of the rabbit, and he ate hungrily. Melann also smiled silently as she accepted some of Vheod's breakfast.

Vheod had thought all through the night. Try as he might, he couldn't rule out that perhaps a part of him had conspired with other evil forces. That foul portion of him, which claimed obvious links to Chare'en, might have planned to come here so he could free his great-grandfather. Perhaps the Taint was the representation of that dark side. It certainly hadn't reacted well to Melann's holy blessings and had most certainly played a part in leading him here. It brought him to Destiny's Last Hope and the abandoned temple of the enigmatic Arach and Gyrison. Perhaps those priests had been disguised fiends, working to get him to come here to free Chare'en. If these things were true, then he'd done everything they'd wanted him to do. He was a prisoner of his own destiny.

"Vheod," Whitlock said, swallowing his food, "once again I owe you my thanks. I didn't trust you, and you still went to great lengths to save me."

"Perhaps you were right," Vheod whispered.

"What?" Whitlock asked.

"Perhaps you were right not to trust me. Perhaps I am a fool for trusting myself."

"Look," Whitlock continued, "the Ravenwitch—she's insane—mad and evil. I don't credit her with one word of truth. As far as I'm concerned, the things she said change nothing."

"Nothing?" Melann interjected. "You mean you still think we might be able to lift the curse on our family?" Vheod couldn't tell if she was hopeful or incredulous.

"I think that we would be fools to end our quest on the word of someone who was in the process of changing me into some raven creature." Whitlock almost laughed. Vheod had to admit, in the light of day, miles away from the tree, it did almost seem absurd.

"And even if every word she said was truth—" he glanced at Vheod, then back to Melann— "and I'll admit I probably didn't hear everything, she did say the magical staff we seek might actually be with Chare'en, whatever his nature."

"So you want to press onward," Vheod said.

"Of course," Whitlock answered.

"You never have told me," Vheod said, "how you came to find out about Chare'en and the staff in the first place."

Whitlock and Melann exchanged glances, as if to decide who would relate the tale. Melann began to speak. "In Archendale, we conducted research. We knew that ages ago an ancestor of ours had offended some powerful wizard, and that the wizard cursed him and his entire line. The curse strikes down family members erratically, sometimes in childhood, sometimes as adults, sometimes skipping entire generations altogether. Each time it's the same thing—a wasting malady weakens and finally overcomes them. That was really all our family knew.

"We were lucky in that we encountered a pair of traveling sages passing through our town. When we spoke to them, they told us that the wizard—who's name, they said, was Chare'en—had kept a magical staff that could lift any curse he had bestowed. The staff, they said, was buried with him in his crypt."

"These sages," Vheod asked, following a hunch, "what do you remember of them?"

"Not much," Whitlock replied, shaking his head. "I think their names were Gyrison and ah . . . Arach."

Vheod's mouth dropped open in surprise. Did that make the whole tale more believable, or less? He really couldn't be sure. Thinking back, he knew he'd never told Melann and Whitlock the names of the priests he'd encountered in those spider-infested woods.

"I'm afraid that after hearing what the Ravenwitch had to say," Melann spoke up, "I believe we've either been lied to or we've made some horrible mistake."

"If we don't go and find out for ourselves, we'll never rest," her brother said. "We'll never forgive ourselves if Mother and Father succumb to the curse. As much as ever, we've got to go. We've got to find the crypt of Chare'en—or his prison, or whatever it is."

Melann sighed heavily. "You're right, Whitlock. You're absolutely right." She turned to Vheod. "We have to go. The Ravenwitch said we wouldn't find anything without you, but I would understand if you didn't want to go."

Vheod couldn't help but admire their convictions, and their bravery. This was the point at which circumstances put his convictions, and more, his faith in himself, to the test. The Ravenwitch had said he'd come to Toril to free Chare'en. The Taint seemed to be leading him onward, and he had little remaining doubt that the Taint was evil and untrustworthy. Still, he had to believe he was ultimately in control of his own actions.

If I can't trust that much, he thought, I should just give up on myself right now. If I can't believe that I control my own actions, I don't want to live.

Besides, if the Ravenwitch had been lying and Gyrison and Arach spoke the truth, then he could be on hand to make sure that Whitlock and Melann didn't free Chare'en accidentally.

But there was more to it, as well. He only now considered that if they parted company, he would leave

Melann. He didn't want to do that—the sudden pain at the thought of not seeing her again scared him. He cared for her deeply. He also liked the part of himself that found the wonderful qualities within her attractive. He thought about how a part of him had initially reacted to the Ravenwitch, and it frightened him. Was there really a part of him that missed his life in the Abyss?

In short, he liked himself more when he was with Melann, and he feared being apart from her.

"We'll have to be wary of gnolls, of course," Vheod stated.

Both Melann and Whitlock smiled.

Chapter Fifteen

Everything was working perfectly. Wind tossed Orrag's thin hair about his head, but he didn't notice. His hideous face was gripped in an evil, toothy grin. He and his small band of followers crouched in the trees watching as the gnolls finished their work.

The gnolls had arrived before Orrag and his men and cleared away all of the debris. The cave-like entrance, free of the fallen rock that had buried it for years, lay exposed for the first time in centuries. Convenient. Already his men had hidden the digging tools they'd brought in the underbrush.

Of course, now there were two hundred gnolls between the crypt entrance and Orrag. He turned and looked at his men. They numbered six—no match for that many gnolls. Two of them had some particular talents that might help.

"Gyrison, Arach, come here," he whispered.

Two figures, still crouching, sneaked to his side. They joined him as he watched the gnolls. The shorter, rounder of the two spoke up. "What is wrong?"

"Yes, what is wrong?" the taller one also asked.

Gyrison and Arach had taken some getting used to on Orrag's part, but they were useful. "Can you do something to help get these gnolls out of the way?"

"They're here to help free their master," Gyrison said.

"Their shamen must have foreseen Vheod's coming," Arach added.

"See how they assemble the stones of the ancient idol they once worshiped?" Gyrison pointed at some of the gnolls carrying green stones.

"The idol of their—" Arach began

"Fine," Orrag interrupted. "Whatever. That doesn't change the fact that if we try to go in there they'll tear us apart."

Arach and Gyrison stared at the gnolls quietly for a moment, never once looking at each other. Then, almost at the same time, they both began softly chanting and making rhythmic hand gestures.

Orrag could hear a rustle in the leaves. He looked around, startled, but saw nothing. The gnolls obviously heard it too. The creatures stopped what they were doing and looked into the forest around them.

A horn sounded nearby, then another, and another—each from a different direction. The sounds of soldiers rushing into battle filled the wood. The gnolls grabbed their weapons and shields. They quickly formed defensive lines as a few barked orders.

The sounds of hundreds of men became the sounds of thousands.

The gnolls howled in fear, and one by one they retreated into the woods. They scattered, wide-eyed, clearly fearing for their lives. As soon as the morale of a few had broken, the gnolls fled in droves, until all had left the clearing around the entrance.

"Excellent," Orrag said with a grin. "The ruse won't last long, but it should be enough." He licked his yellow, pointed teeth with an almost-black tongue, but kept smiling as though this were the happiest day of his foul life.

Gyrison and Arach ended their spell. The sounds of charging soldiers and blaring horns faded away.

"We must hurry," Arach said to Orrag.

"We must get inside," Gyrison added.

"I'm here for the same reason you are, friends," Orrag said, not dropping his toothy smile for a moment. "You don't have to tell me."

The small group rose from their hiding places, still staring at the entrance. They'd traveled without stopping for the last few days to get here as quickly as possible, but now Orrag wanted to move slowly. He motioned for the rest to follow him, and they crossed the clearing to the cliff. Orrag gazed into the dark opening.

"The brother and sister I told you about either didn't make it or have been slowed down," Orrag told them. "Unfortunately, since the gnolls will return soon, we can't wait for them." He turned toward the others. Looking each of them up and down, he finally said, "Unther, Panish, grab Wenmer and bring him here."

The man named Wenmer cried out in surprise. Two of the others grabbed him by the arms and dragged him forward. Orrag commanded the remaining man to light a torch, and he led them into the opening in the cliff.

The smooth-cut passage went straight back from the entrance, stopped, and turned to the left. When it stopped again, Orrag motioned for his men to bring Wenmer forward.

"Hold still, man," Orrag told the captive as he fought to get free. "The guardian must be appeased. I've been preparing for far too long to let anything distract me from my goal."

Orrag ran his hand over an amulet suspended around his neck then drew his knife. He looked for Arach and Gyrison, but they remained outside. No matter. He didn't need them anymore.

"Great and powerful Chare'en," Orrag began to invoke, "Lord of the Seven Vengeances and Master of the Hosts of J'Duna . . ." His voice became a mumbling chant in a language men were never meant to speak.

Wenmer cried out, but his screams were not heeded. The other men looked neither at Orrag nor at Wenmer, as if they had neither the strength nor the stomach to confront either. The two holding Wenmer kept him as still as they could.

"Orrag!" Wenmer shouted, "you promised if I would help you, you'd give me gold. You promised me power from this demon we would free! Don't hurt me! I'll help you!"

Orrag didn't stop.

"You betrayed me. You lied to me!"

Orrag didn't stop.

Wenmer continued to cry out and struggle, but neither helped him.

Orrag's dark ceremony and Wenmer's pleas for mercy ended abruptly and simultaneously as Orrag's knife slashed the young man's throat. Blood spattered on the ground.

The men let Wenmer fall, and Orrag's grin returned. When he looked at his remaining lackeys, who all now stared at Wenmer's body, Orrag knew he'd better say something. "He was never a true follower." He shook his head, attempting to shape a look of regret.

"I knew that from the start," he continued in his lie, "but his death serves us, Chare'en's chosen. His loss is our gain."

The three men said nothing, alternately looking at their dead comrade or at their leader.

"Now come on!" Orrag couldn't spend all day coddling them. If they had to be sacrificed as well, he could still probably succeed without them.

The four of them followed the passage and eventually came to a small chamber. As they did, Orrag heard sounds from behind. He turned and saw Gyrison and Arach catching up with them. The strange pair had evidently collected the stones the gnolls had left behind and now carried them awkwardly, using the fronts of their brown robes as pouches. Without a word, they came into the room and dumped their burdens on the floor.

"What's all this?" Orrag asked.

"You knew that the stones were not without meaning," Gyrison said.

"Didn't you?" Arach asked.

As they spoke, the two got on their hands and knees and began arranging the stones on the floor in some sort of pattern.

Orrag stood watching for a few moments. The other men did the same. "Is this really important?" Orrag asked.

"Yes," they both answered in unison.

When they were finished, they stood and turned back to the half-orc priest and his followers.

"You can handle the rest," Arach told him.

"We have things to prepare for the master's arrival—in his real home," Gyrison said.

The two of them suddenly changed. The illusion of their appearance faded away, and they stretched their black, batlike wings behind them. Hideous, monstrous faces replaced their simple human features, and long, obsidian claws stretched out where soft hands once folded gently in front of them.

"Don't fail the master, human," one of them—Orrag could no longer tell them apart—said.

In a flash of fire and light the two demons departed, back, Orrag was sure, to the netherworld of the Abyss. He wasn't sorry to see them go. His men stood rigid, covered in sweat. The sight of those two should keep them in line, Orrag thought.

Everything was working perfectly.

Now all he needed was a little help from his ally, Vheod.

Chapter Sixteen

"I'm not as stupid as you must think," Whitlock told Melann in a low whisper.

The three of them had walked the entire day and the summer heat had them all soaked in sweat. Hiking through the rough terrain, climbing over rocks and up and down steep slopes, proved to be a great deal more work than riding had been, and so the heat took its toll. They still hadn't reached the crypt of Chare'en, which they now knew to be the *prison* of Chare'en. They made camp, and Vheod moved out to find more game for their meal. Whitlock lent him his crossbow on a somewhat permanent basis, since Vheod hadn't been able to retrieve his sword, leaving him without a weapon.

With Vheod gone, the siblings spoke of the matters at hand.

"What do you mean?" Melann asked forcefully but quietly. She'd gathered some roots and leaves from edible plants.

Whitlock arranged the wood for a fire to boil what she'd gathered. "I've got eyes, sister," he said. "I know you're attracted to Vheod."

Melann didn't reply, but stared at him silently.

"I just don't think it's a very good idea." He pulled flint and steel from his belt pouch, striking it to set fire to the kindling he'd piled.

"You don't think *what's* a good idea?" Now Melann's nostrils began to flare. Her face reddened. Whitlock knew she was angry or embarrassed. Perhaps she was angry because she was embarrassed, or embarrassed that she was angry.

"You and Vheod," he replied, spreading his hands wide and dropping the flint. "It's not that I don't trust him, though I don't mind telling you I certainly didn't before. The growing attraction between the two of you made it worse, not better." He picked up the flint and began working it against the steel again.

"As I was saying, I do trust him now—he's earned that from us—but let's face the truth here, Melann. He's a *demon*."

"He seems to prefer tanar'ri," Melann replied.

"Whatever," Whitlock shot back, irritated. "It doesn't change the fact that he's not human."

"And he's only half tanar'ri," she said in his further defense.

Whitlock looked up from his work and grimaced.

He began working at the fire again and said, "So you're in love with him, aren't you?"

"To be truthful, Whitlock, I don't know," Melann said, then looked off, down the hillside where Vheod had gone to hunt. "I thought I might be, but then I caught more than one glimpse of his dark side—and it really frightened me."

Finally, a blaze started in the twigs and grass Whitlock had gathered. He prepared the wood to add once the fire really got going in earnest. He made a grunting noise and seemed to pause in thought for a moment. He didn't speak until the fire really started. "That's for the best, Melann," he said, looking up at her.

She'd filled their small pot with water and set it over the fire to boil. Melann placed the roots into the water right away, for they would need more time to boil than anything else. Once softened, they would complement just about anything Vheod might bring back. Of course, they were better heavily seasoned, but Melann was quickly growing used to doing without such pleasantries.

She wondered if she was indeed carrying out Chauntea's will. Everything she'd been taught had been about the Mother of All's love for growing things, and about nurturing and caring for others. Now Melann found herself wandering through the wilderness, fighting for her life at every turn against enemies she didn't even know she had. Where was the divine direction she'd come to count on? Melann suddenly felt very alone and distant from all she knew.

Vheod returned with three quail. Soon the three travelers feasted on the roasted birds, garnished with the boiled roots and leaves that Melann found. By the time they finished, the moon had risen high into the night sky, and a cool wind blew away the day's heat. After dinner, Melann prepared for sleep, knowing the next day they would probably come to the end of their long journey. Orrag's directions indicated that they were only three or four hours' walk from where Chare'en lay—either entombed or imprisoned, depending on which story one believed.

Melann watched as the others also prepared to go to sleep, even Vheod. She knew he'd not slept the night before. She could almost imagine what had been going through his mind, or at least she thought that she could. She knew what it was like to fear what the future might hold. Each day that passed for her brought new doubts. Melann continually wondered if she was good enough, if she did the right thing. For Vheod, it must be even worse. As frightening as it was to see the darker side of her new friend, it was more troubling still to realize that even he was just coming to fully realize what he was—and what he was not. Vheod, she surmised, felt as confused, and perhaps as alone, as she did.

As Vheod laid back into the cool night grass, she moved to him and knelt wordlessly at his side. He looked at her and opened his mouth to speak. Melann put a single finger to his lips to quiet him. Whitlock's soft snores already accompanied the crackling of the dying fire. Melann took Vheod's hand in hers, feeling the coarse, hardened skin that covered his fingers. Kneeling there, under the stars, Melann silently gazed into his deep, dark eyes, until he fell asleep. She slept at his side.

* * * * *

By morning the night's cool breezes had transformed into chilling winds. Dark clouds sped over the tops of the mountains like swarming warriors preparing for battle. Vheod saw that he was the last to wake. He thought for a moment about Melann, and remembered her holding his hand until sleep claimed him. She'd said nothing. It seemed almost like a dream now.

But no, that had been no dream, for Vheod's dreams had been filled with images of death and destruction. Haunting crimson images of battle and horrible monstrosities gathered in his mind, and he felt it better to just forget about the entire night. This new day held enough on which to focus itself. Today they would reach the prison of Chare'en.

At least, Vheod thought, there they would all find answers to the questions they'd asked for the last few days, or even for their entire lives. A cure for

Melann and Whitlock's family curse, the truth behind Vheod's real reason for coming here, perhaps even the real purpose of the Taint—the day was fraught with possibilities. Most of them were quite terrifying.

They ate some of the previous night's leftover food, washing it down with cold water from the stream at the bottom of the hill on which they had camped. Vheod took some time after the meal to make minor preparations to cast some magical spells that day. Some wizards needed to study in books or scrolls to prepare spells, but the Abyssal magic Vheod had learned required only that he ready some of the particular mental concepts in his mind—focusing on the central idea of each spell and placing it within his mind's eye.

When Vheod was finished, he helped Melann and Whitlock get ready to break camp. The three of them spoke little as they packed their two backpacks, Vheod and Whitlock hefting them when they were ready to move. The fire had long since died, but Melann made sure to scoop dirt onto the warm ashes to make sure that there was no chance of the surrounding vegetation catching fire.

The terrain presented a number of difficulties, as the rough, forested hills of the past few days became rocky cliffs and pathless treks up steep slopes. Vheod wondered if they would even have been able to bring the horses through this area, had they lived. By midmorning, they had rounded a steep mountain and walked through a nearly level pass between it and another towering peak. The wind still tousled their hair and clothes, and the gray clouds concealed the sun. They knew from the landmarks around them that the end of the journey lay at the end of this very pass.

Vheod led the way through the tall pine trees. As he always did when he got nervous, Vheod looked for the Taint. He couldn't find it again, so he assumed it hid under his breastplate or clothes. A noise behind him made him stop. He turned.

Whitlock motioned for him to come back. Vheod stepped quietly and slowly toward the warrior, watching him for some clue as to what was wrong. Melann stood next to Whitlock but seemed as confused as Vheod felt. Whitlock pointed down.

"Gnolls," Whitlock whispered. "Lots of them."

Vheod looked down and saw numerous prints of large feet. His gaze followed them along and noticed that branches of trees had been broken and other growth disturbed by their passing. Whitlock was right. As Vheod looked around, he now saw that dozens on dozens of the creatures had probably passed through this very area, though he admitted to himself that if he didn't already know there were gnolls in the area, he couldn't have identified the exact type of creature that had made this disturbance. He wondered if Whitlock also made that assumption, or if he could see something Vheod couldn't.

It didn't matter. What did matter was that the three of them would need to be particularly cautious. Vheod knew that through a minor spell he could render himself invisible from sight, but that wouldn't help his companions. They would all have to just take their chances together.

This area seemed drier than most of the mountainous region through which they'd traveled. The needles of the coniferous trees showed brown patches and snapped off at the merest touch. Brittle, fallen branches crunched under their feet as they resumed their march, each step kicking up a small amount of dust that lay under the carpet of rust-colored needles. The thinner trees didn't provide as much cover as Vheod wished, but he did his best to use the concealment that remained in case there was someone or something watching for them.

Finally, after about another hour's careful walk through the thick trees, the three of them rounded a ridge and found themselves staring at a cliff face partially obscured by boulders and loose stones. While some of the rocks hadn't moved in lifetimes, it was apparent that others had recently been moved aside, which judging by their size was no small feat. These recently displaced boulders surrounded a dark, rectangular opening that led into the cliff. An open area at least two hundred yards across stretched in front of the opening.

Vheod had no doubt in his mind that Chare'en lay within the cliff, through that doorway, but who had cleared away the boulders? The trees surrounding the area had been chopped down too, probably to facilitate the work uncovering the doorway.

Taking a deep breath, he started for the opening, but Whitlock's hand on his shoulder stopped him. Vheod turned and saw that the man wanted to talk. He followed Whitlock and Melann back a few paces but toward the cliff's face. The three of them crouched amid the trees, behind a far-tossed boulder.

"This is it, isn't it?" Melann asked, staring at the opening rather than the two men.

Whitlock didn't respond, instead telling Vheod, "We've got to look around the outside here and make sure that if we go in, nothing comes in after us. We don't want to get trapped in there."

"I suppose that's prudent," Vheod stared with dark, passionate eyes, "but don't you think that the sooner we can get inside and look around, the sooner we'll be able to leave? I mean, if the staff you seek lies within, the sooner we find it the better."

Melann's expression indicated that she agreed, but Whitlock was adamant. "We've got to be smart about this. Now's not the time to be headstrong."

"If we hadn't plunged 'headstrong' into the Ravenwitch's tree, you wouldn't be here," Vheod said immediately.

Whitlock dropped his gaze to the ground. His shoulders slumped slightly.

"No," Vheod said, shaking his head, "forget I said that."

Melann forced a smile. "We're all nervous," she said, placing her hand on Whitlock's shoulder. "Everyone wants this to end well—whatever that means."

"What do you think might be around here?" Vheod asked.

"Look around!" Whitlock's whisper was harsh. "This area looks just like the one we passed a few miles back, but it's even more clearly been occupied by gnolls for some time."

"Then where are they now? Inside?" Vheod motioned toward the opening in the cliff.

"No, I don't think so," Whitlock said, looking around. "Something tells me they left this area—but not long ago." Whitlock kneeled down and examined the ground carefully, looked around him, then straightened up. "In fact, the tracks even suggest that they left in a hurry. See how there's lots of scuffling and smeared prints? They'll probably be back."

Whitlock's skill as a tracker certainly impressed Vheod. Nevertheless, he felt an eagerness to get inside that doorway. Maybe it was just that he wanted to get the whole thing over with—maybe because a part of him was anxious to find out which portion of his nature was truly in command of his life. He would see if someone, perhaps even himself, schemed and manipulated him into coming here to free his ancestor. If he was truly meant to free Chare'en, and the balor waited inside, he would see if he could keep himself from committing such an atrocity. Somehow the answers would all be found beyond that doorway.

Vheod handed Whitlock the crossbow. "Here, you scout around the perimeter of the open area and cover me with this." He turned to Melann. "You stay here and watch this side of the entrance. I'm going to sneak in and take a brief look around on the inside. If it's clear out here and within, you can follow me through the doorway."

Whitlock scowled. "Fine."

He accepted the crossbow and took the time to cock and load it. Vheod drew the knife he'd found in their packs earlier, then cast the brief spell that allowed him to fade from sight. Melann gasped softly, obviously unprepared for Vheod's tactic. Her wide eyes searched in vain for him, but she said nothing. By the time he disappeared, Whitlock was already creeping through the trees.

Invisible, Vheod moved very close to Melann, so that his mouth was very near her ear. Her mouth opened slightly, and her eyes flashed, indicating that she could feel his presence near her.

"I'll let you know where I am," he whispered.

He wanted to touch her soft cheek with his own, but he didn't. Instead, he turned and moved very quietly into the cleared area, toward the open doorway.

Inside, Vheod's tanar'ri vision allowed him to see a fair distance using just the daylight filtering in through the cloud of dust at the door. Ancient, stagnant air hung in the doorway and grew thicker as he entered. A passage, cut through the stone with regular angles and keen workmanship, extended into the cliff at least twenty-five feet, but then ended. Only after he crossed most of that distance did Vheod see that corridors probed deeper into the stone to the left and right of there. He approached this juncture and looked down both options.

To the left, he saw a fair amount of rubble and loose dirt scattered about the floor. The passage extended deeper into the darkness than his supernatural vision could penetrate. At the edge of the darkness, however, amid the broken stone, Vheod thought he could see a dead body, perhaps that of a human or something human-sized.

Looking to his right, Vheod saw only a strange cloud of sparkling greenish flecks hovering in the air, churning like dust. Vheod tentatively reached out to touch one of the shining motes. When he did the cloud stirred violently. He heard stone agonizingly slide against stone, and a terrible, heavy footfall, then another.

Backing away, Vheod saw a large shape lumbering out from the cloud of swirling specks. Something lurched out of the darkness. He backed a few steps, eyes wide. His muscles tensed and his mind raced. What was this thing? What magic was this?

It stood at least a foot taller than Vheod. The top of the creature's head came within a foot of the ceiling. It was humanoid in shape, but the entire, gigantic figure was made of stone. In one fist it clenched a long, broad-headed spear, though Vheod didn't think the stone of the spear was actually separate from the stone of the hand that appeared to grip it. The living statue had been carved with an intricate, ornate pattern on its body, granting it raiment and facial features. The hands of time had clawed away at the fine detail, so now the lumbering giant seemed mostly crude in construction, except for a few spots that retained the designs, betraying its former beauty.

Vheod found nothing beautiful about this animate mass of stone, though, and backed away toward the entrance as fast as he could. He had no intention of attempting to fight this thing with just a knife—if he could fight it at all. What worried him most was that the construct advanced toward him even though he was invisible.

Afraid to turn his back on the advancing monstrosity, Vheod continued to back quickly away. The animated statue stopped. Vheod stopped. Obviously, this thing was a guardian—perhaps it wouldn't follow him out. Still, it halted in the juncture of the two passageways, and Vheod imagined that it would react with hostility if he attempted to get past or even approach it.

Perhaps a spell could destroy it, Vheod mused, staring at it from just a few steps from the entrance. Obviously, it was a creature animated by magic, and perhaps that would be its undoing. Unfortunately, Vheod's spells were minor. He doubted he could do anything that might affect a giant stone statue given life by sorcery. Then, he considered—

His thoughts were suddenly torn away from him by the sound of Melann's scream from outside. He whirled around and ran, still magically hidden from normal sight, into a danger even greater than that of the magical statue.

The gnolls had returned.

Chapter Seventeen

A raven is not a creature that enjoys disappointment. Take something away from one, and it only gets angry. Denied completely, and the raven sulks.

The Ravenwitch sat before her divinatory pool, watching black rose petals float about the surface. She leaned heavily on the water basin, sighing. One by one, she poked the petals down into the water. Some sank to the bottom; some bobbed back up.

With a dramatic gesture she brushed at the surface of the water, sending a petal-laden wave splashing to the wooden floor. She stood as she did this, glaring down into the pool then up at the ceiling.

"Damn them!" she screamed, clutching her hands into fists.

She was without a manservant and without even so much as a good candidate. What was worse, she'd slain dozens of her own ravens to execute the process that would have granted that young man—Whitlock?—the power and abilities required of her servant. The ritual had been ruined, and the cursed one who ruined it was beyond reproach. She didn't dare retaliate against the descendant of Chare'en, when the balor would rule over all the Thunder Peaks in so short a time.

She slumped back into her chair. What good could come of revenge anyway? She'd lived long enough to know that in the end, it earned nothing. What was lost, was lost. She had more important things to worry about right now, like how to cope with the coming events. The Ravenwitch enjoyed things as they were. She was more than pleased with her tree, and the flock flourished nicely—even despite the losses it had suffered lately at the hands of . . . what was his name? Vheod? As well as those who'd died by her own hand.

The Ravenwitch hadn't liked that at all. She would never have had to attempt the blood ritual in the first place had the gnolls not slain Yrrin—the gnolls that sought to serve Chare'en. Everything seemed to point to the same conclusion. His release would bring only change and hardship for her.

She sighed again.

Her attempts at divining potential futures based on different approaches she might take—defiance, subservience, friendliness, outright attack—had all been horribly skewed. Something was upsetting the tides of time here. Some presence had thrown off all her divinations.

Perhaps the young demon Vheod was to blame for that too.

How could she know?

No, the Ravenwitch thought, at this juncture the only way to predict the future with any great accuracy was to control it. She had to take some sort of action, not sit here gazing into mist-shrouded "ifs" and "what-might-have-beens."

Gathering her feathered cape behind her, the Ravenwitch stood and glided out of the room, down a passage through the heart of the grandfather tree, and into a chamber ill used of late. This oval-shaped room was filled with shelves sunk into the wood of the walls. Each shelf was lined with books. She owned thousands of tomes, some acquired long ago, some more recent, some bought, some stolen. A few she'd even written herself.

With a fevered intensity, the Ravenwitch pulled books from shelves, placing them on a table located in the middle of the room. Her long, black-nailed fingers glided along familiar paths across the well-worn shelves, deftly finding each tome she required. She ignored the dust accumulated from neglect, carefully brushing away the spiders without harming their delicate webs.

Utilizing magically conjured light, the Ravenwitch read through the night, pouring over histories and accounts of days long lost, as well as texts regarding the fiendish denizens of the Lower Planes. The stacks of books pulled down from the shelves towered above the table at which she sat. Much to her delight, her research proved fruitful, as she found more than one reference to the balor Chare'en. Apparently, he'd come to Toril in the last, fading days of Myth Drannor, in the Year of the Toppled Throne, as a part of the Army of Darkness that warred with the elves of Cormanthyr.

Chare'en remained long after those battles, attempting to raise up an army of chaos and evil in the Thunder Peaks. Most of his servitors were—not surprisingly—gnolls. The gnolls worshiped Chare'en and erected a huge idol dedicated to the tanar'ri made of a strange, semitransparent magical stone not native to this world. The green, glassy idol stood as a testament to the balor's dark power.

Chare'en's defeat came, hundreds of years ago, at the hands of a human wizard named Piotyr Braendysh who had crafted an amulet that rendered him immune to the balor's power. Using his own sorcery, Piotyr destroyed the green idol and imprisoned

Chare'en in a cell made of some of the statue's shattered remains. The rest of the stone was scattered throughout the mountains. Braendysh then sealed the prison with his magical, rune-covered staff and buried it deep underground.

A raven burst into the room, coming to rest on the chair next to the Ravenwitch. It cawed softly.

She turned to the bird and stared into its opaque black eyes. "Yes, my darling, I know morning has come. Go and find yourself something to eat in the woods with the others. I shall be fine here."

The raven squawked shrilly and flew from the library.

An amulet that rendered him immune to the balor's power. Interesting. With such an item, the Ravenwitch would have nothing to fear from the future. Chare'en would mean nothing to her. But where would such an amulet be now? It could be anywhere in all Faerûn. She sighed. There was no time to search for it. If it was lost—buried in some vault or fallen amid some ancient ruin—she would never find it soon enough for it to be of any help.

No, the only way she could hope to find the amulet would be to presume that someone else found it first and had it with him now. Perhaps a person who knew about the coming of Chare'en and the power of the amulet—or at least something of its history—had already discovered it. More than likely, that person would be nearby, concerned somehow with the current events.

This required some thought.

Chapter Eighteen

Gnolls swarmed from every possible angle, as though they'd been scattered and were regrouping. Unfortunately, their chosen rallying point lay within the clearing right outside the entrance to the prison, at the edge of which stood Whitlock and Melann.

Prison, Whitlock thought. The prison of Chare'en.

Had he already completely given up on the idea that this might be the crypt of Chare'en—the goal of the entire journey? If this was a prison, and Chare'en was a demon and not a wizard, what in Helm's name were they doing here?

The situation at hand hardly presented Whitlock with the opportunity to think about that at length. Fortunately, it appeared that the gnolls were expecting to find him and his sister here even less than Whitlock expected the gnolls to return right at that moment. Bestial eyes stretched wide, and howls of surprise and confusion seemed to occupy the gaping mouths of the creatures rather than commands or warnings. Whitlock's combat training and experience took over as he looked all around him, sizing up the enemy and possible strategies to defeat them. He fired the loaded crossbow at the first gnoll he saw through the trees and watched it drop into the foliage at its feet.

His instincts quickly determined that their only option was flight. Turning to look for Melann, Whitlock saw that she was already casting a spell on the gnolls nearest her, wrapping them in divine energy that held them in place. Effective, but not enough considering that the monsters numbered at least a hundred, if not more.

Careful not to interrupt her spell, Whitlock shouted when she was finished, "Melann, run inside the . . . cave." He wasn't sure whether to call it a crypt or a prison, at least not out loud. There was no time to consider it now. He hung the crossbow on a hook on his belt.

Melann turned to him, her eyes betraying utter terror. Whitlock ran, not into the mountain, but along the edge of the clearing that surrounded it, racing to reach his sister. His sword sang in his hand, and he threw himself at the nearest gnoll. Steel met flesh, but the warrior was interested only in reaching Melann. As he ran toward her, she moved to meet him.

"Into the cave!" he shouted again.

The gnolls began to recover from their surprise and confusion, surging toward the humans. Whitlock pushed away an onrushing beast-man, using his charging momentum to add to the force of his blow.

Melann used her mace to fend off the only gnoll near her left mobile after her spell. Rather than fight it, she ducked under its muscular, hairy arms as it slashed at her with a crude axe. She ran to her brother. Whitlock held his ground, waiting for Melann to reach him. Another gnoll rushed toward him and he slashed at it with his blade.

The creature lunged to his left to avoid the sword stroke, then raised its spear high above its head. Plunging the weapon down at Whitlock, the gnoll was caught off guard as the warrior threw himself at its feet. Whitlock crashed into its lower legs, so as the gnoll lunged forward with its spear, it not only missed him, but toppled over the top of his now crouching form. The impact to its legs only sent it over the top of him that much harder. Whitlock gained his feet much faster than his foe did, and two well-aimed chops from his sword ensured that the gnoll would indeed never rise again.

Pain arched through Whitlock's arm and he whirled and saw that another gnoll had approached while he'd fought with the other. The bestial humanoid's spear point dripped with Whitlock's blood, and the gnoll pulled back for another stab. Whitlock's empty arm went limp, and he could do little but swing his sword to block the second spear thrust. He was weak with pain.

Suddenly darts of reddish energy struck the gnoll, overcoming it and sending it crashing to the bare earth. Whitlock turned again, this time to see Vheod standing at the entrance to the cave. His spells had cleared a path for the siblings to reach the opening in the cliff face. Melann reached Whitlock's side and reached toward his wounded arm.

"There's no time," he told her, pulling his arm away.

He ran to Vheod and Melann followed. Turning to look behind him, Whitlock saw the gnolls rushing after them, appearing more numerous than the trees from which they poured forth. Whitlock and Melann had to cross almost two hundred yards between the edge of the clearing and the rectangular entrance. Their feet slid in misplaced steps on the open, gravel-covered earth. The gnolls followed them into the clearing, emerging from the trees in greater and greater numbers like grain pouring into an empty bowl.

Whitlock and Melann scrambled over the jumbled rocks that lay at the bottom of the cliff wall. The hot summer sun beat down, and the cacophonous growls and roars of the gnolls behind them deafened them to all else. Sweat and blood covered Whitlock's upper body as he ran toward the opening in the stone wall. Vheod stood at the entrance, calling out to them—no, to Melann—as they approached.

The opening showed signs of great activity—the gnolls had apparently uncovered this entrance, probably within the last day or so. Large, bestial footprints and claw marks covered the surrounding rock. There was something else, too, but the situation provided no time for a detailed analysis. Only when they were inside did Whitlock realize in surprise that he could see Vheod. When the cambion had entered he'd rendered himself hidden from sight.

"Don't go back very far," Vheod told them in a harsh tone. "There's a stone guardian blocking the way."

Whitlock looked down the passage that led into the earth but saw only darkness. Small bits of stone lay scattered amid the smooth rock floor, and dust churned in the sunlight around them, stirred by their activity.

"If we can't go inside, we're doomed!" Whitlock said.

"We can at least make a stand here," Melann said hopefully. Whitlock knew that defensive position or not, the three of them could never defeat so many enemies.

"Perhaps we can defeat two foes at once," Vheod told them as he grabbed Whitlock's crossbow from his belt in a swift motion. Whitlock handed him a quarrel and watched silently as he loaded and cocked the weapon. He had no idea what the cambion had in mind.

Melann invoked the power of Chauntea in the form of a blessing. Vheod turned to her and said, "I believe we're going to need that."

"Here they come," Whitlock shouted, looking up at the approaching gnolls. "What's the plan? We don't have any time." The gnolls slowed. They appeared to approach the entrance with trepidation—or was it reverence?

"This is going to be extremely dangerous," Vheod said with a calmness Whitlock found disturbing. "When I begin to run, follow me. Even if you can't see me, just keep to one side of the passage or the other and run as fast as you can. When you reach the end of the corridor, turn to the left and stop."

"What are you going to do?"

"There's no time to explain," Vheod said. "Just trust me."

As much as it surprised Whitlock to realize it, he did trust Vheod. How could he not? Despite all of Whitlock's initial reservations and suspicions, Vheod had twice saved his life.

Whitlock looked Vheod in the eye and gave him a short nod. "Whatever you say."

Vheod turned to look at the oncoming gnolls. They would reach the entrance in a second, but Vheod seemed to be waiting for something. Melann visibly held her breath. Whitlock gripped his sword's hilt more tightly—both in anticipation and to help distract him from the pain in his other arm. They stood just inside the cave, and Whitlock noticed for the first time that cool air drifted slowly out of the corridor behind him.

Vheod turned away from the gnolls and fired the crossbow down the corridor and into the darkness. The sound of the grunting, growling brutes was louder than the sound of their heavy footfalls on the bare earth, and even louder than the first few gnolls clambering over the rocks in their way. Whitlock couldn't hear if the quarrel struck anything in particular.

The sounds of the gnolls wasn't loud enough, however, to overcome the heavy thud that Whitlock heard deep in the darkness a moment after the quarrel was released. Another scraping thud followed, and Whitlock saw Vheod's body tense.

"Get ready to run," Vheod whispered, staring down the dark passage.

Another thud was accompanied by the sound of stone scraping against stone. This time the sound was louder—or perhaps closer. Whitlock turned to look back outside, and saw that the first ranks of the approaching gnolls were less than a dozen paces away. He looked back to Vheod for some sort of sign, but the cambion just stared into the darkness, ignoring the oncoming gnolls. More heavy thuds followed, and Whitlock realized that they were footsteps. The creature making those sounds, he guessed, must be huge, heavy, or quite probably both.

"Vheod?" Melann whispered. The name asked many questions, but Vheod answered none of them.

The gnolls were close enough that Whitlock could smell their musky scent. He was ready to run on Vheod's signal, and he kept an eye on the humanoids that were rapidly descended on them. He was ready to turn to face these enemies, ignoring Vheod, when he glanced into the darkness one last time.

Looming out of the tenebrous shadow, a tall, indistinct man made of stone approached them. It carried a long spear carved from the same stone from which its body had been made, obviously long years before. The animate statue bore no expression, but its malignancy was obvious.

"Now!" Vheod's deep voice resonated throughout the hall. "Run!" Though he was prepared, surprise still gripped Whitlock as Vheod raced toward this new menace.

The statue lashed out with the long, wide-headed stone spear, but Vheod flattened himself against the wall at the last moment, and the spear struck behind him, producing a flash of sparks along the stone floor.

The gnolls reached the entrance. They were coming in.

Vheod slipped past the statue, which continued moving forward.

"Run!" Whitlock shouted to Melann as he leaped toward the oncoming stone guardian. He paused for a moment, stepping to his left. The statue countered, coming at him with its spear point aimed at his head. Whitlock feinted with his blade, drawing the construct's attention for a moment. A blow from the statue was too powerful and heavy to parry, so he had to remain light on his feet if he was to survive. He lunged to his left to avoid a thrust from the guardian's spear. The sound of charging gnolls rose behind him, and he expected a blow from one of the brutes against the back of his head at any moment. Nevertheless, he stood his ground until he saw his sister dive past the statue to the right.

Her movement drew the statue's attention momentarily, but it was enough to give Whitlock his chance to escape as well. As he ducked and tumbled forward, he felt the movement of air next to his ear where an axe blade or spear point slashed by him. Melann's blessing must be helping somehow, he reasoned. Whitlock actually scrambled under the statue's legs, dodging its weapon and its heavy, crushing footstep.

Now, Vheod's plan became obvious. His crossbow bolt alerted the guardian and brought it toward them. However, with so many intruders, the statue didn't turn toward the three of them after they managed to slip by it. Instead, it threw itself into combat with the oncoming gnolls. A forceful spear thrust pierced the midsection of an oncoming gnoll and proved that the brutes were too large and clumsy to dodge past the guardian as their human targets had.

Whitlock watched for a moment as the gnolls attempted to turn and flee from the animated statue only to run into their frenzied comrades behind them. The statue mercilessly, indiscriminately, slashed and stabbed at their backs. Already Vheod and Melann had disappeared into the dark corridor. Whitlock followed.

* * * * *

Vheod's only regret was that his spellcasting had caused his invisibility to falter. Other than that, everything had gone better than he could have dreamed. Now they'd just have to get deep enough into the caves so that when the gnolls retreated from the guardian, the stone statue would be too far away to turn on them. Of course, they would almost certainly need to return this way when they left, but Vheod hoped the guardian statue had been prepared only to keep out intruders and might not notice someone trying to leave.

Vheod's vision allowed him to see well enough to round the corner to the left. He stopped and waited for the others, noting that the turn to the right led only to a dead end—it was really more an alcove—in which the statue had waited. The magical cloud of greenish particles was gone.

At Vheod's feet lay a blood-soaked human body. He couldn't make out many details, even with his tanar'ri darkvision, but the man had apparently died within the last hour or so. Melann hurriedly, quietly walked down the passage, feeling along the right side wall. Her face showed terror mixed with relief.

"This way," Vheod whispered.

Her head turned suddenly toward the sound of his voice. She paused wordlessly, then came toward him with small, careful steps. Obviously, she couldn't see at all. He reached toward her and grasped her arm, pulling her close to him.

"What now?" she whispered in his ear.

Her presence gladdened him. At least his plan had worked well enough to get her past the statue. Glancing around the corner, he was equally glad to see Whitlock making his way along the left-hand wall. The statue engaged the gnolls behind him.

It worked.

Vheod called out softly to Whitlock and brought the three of them together in the darkness.

"What's that smell?" Melann asked.

"There's a body on the floor. Someone was killed here very recently."

"Someone?" Whitlock asked in a forced whisper. "Not a gnoll?"

"No, not a gnoll. I don't know who it is," Vheod replied.

Both Melann and Whitlock paused in silence, as if considering this. Melann stared straight ahead, knowing that she could see nothing. Whitlock still glanced from side to side, as if some action on his part might suddenly allow him to see. The underground passage was cool. A slight breeze originated somewhere deeper in.

"We need light," Whitlock stated.

"Whitlock's right, Vheod," Melann said. "We can't fumble through the darkness like this. It's too difficult. It's too dangerous."

Vheod produced one of the torches he had managed to recover from the dead horses' packs. Even in the darkness, he was able to produce enough of a spark with his flint and steel to light some tinder, then the torch. Soon, flickering light illuminated the well-crafted passageway. All three of them could see where the statue had once stood, the corridor ahead of them, and the corpse at their feet.

Whitlock knelt next to the body, but Melann interrupted him, using her divine power to heal his injured arm. The process took a few minutes, during which Vheod anxiously watched the passage around the corner where the gnolls fought against the guardian. The bestial warriors struggled against the stone statue to no avail. He was surprised to see that they didn't turn from the overwhelming might of their foe. Instead the humanoids threw themselves at it. They must really want to get inside—was it really only to get at them? Somehow Vheod doubted it. This underground structure held more secrets, that seemed evident.

The body at their feet held no recognizable features for any of them. All three of them, in fact, were certain they'd never seen the individual before. He wore a leather jerkin and carried equipment and supplies befitting someone who knew he was going underground—torches, rope, pitons, and more. Vheod also noted that the dead body was well armed with a short sword and a number of daggers.

Vheod took the sword and daggers, shrugging his shoulders as he stood back up and looked at his companions. "We may need these." Whitlock replied with a grim nod. Melann said nothing.

"We should get moving," Whitlock said. He took the torch from Vheod.

Whitlock led the three of them down the corridor as Vheod tucked the weapons in his belt. The hauntingly cool air currents chilled their summer-accustomed flesh. The smooth angular walls and floor were coated with a thick layer of dust, though in places the flickering torchlight indicated disturbances suggesting that others had passed through there before.

"That man was not killed by the stone guardian . . ." Melann said to no one in particular.

"I don't think the guardian was activated until we got here," Vheod replied.

". . . I think he was a sacrifice," Melann continued. She turned to Vheod with an intense glare in her eye. "His throat had been cut. I don't think he was killed in a fight."

"The gnolls?" Vheod asked.

Melann raised her eyebrows and shoulders in unison, shaking her head slightly. She turned away.

"I think it must have been the gnolls," Whitlock said from ahead of them. "Take a look at this."

Whitlock moved to one side to allow the other two to see beyond him. The passage gave way to a small chamber with smooth stone walls and powerful arches supporting the ceiling. In the center of the room, hundreds of small green stones glittered in the torchlight. They lay in a carefully constructed pile.

"Those are the same stones the gnolls were gathering," Melann said.

"Yes," Whitlock replied. "They must have been bringing them here as an offering or something."

Vheod entered the room and approached the stones. He could see that they'd not just been piled on the floor, but had been placed in a deliberate pattern. When he stood next to the pile, directly over the pattern, he could see what was intended. It formed a crude depiction of a leering, fiendish face.

Instinctively, he brought his left arm up to look at the back of his hand. There the Taint emblazoned on his flesh, mockingly took the same shape as the pattern on the floor. The leering face was a shape that the Taint had taken numerous times before. He never thought about it before, but it was the shape the tattoo took most of the time. The stones had been positioned here in the same manner.

The same leering, mocking face.

"Damn," Vheod said quietly.

Melann came to his side, looking down at the pattern of stones. She looked at the Taint, then into his eyes.

"I don't think you should be here," she told him. Her voice was soft.

"You're probably right," he said slowly. Sighing deeply, he continued, "I've been led here, Melann. Everything that's happened to me since I arrived in this world, or perhaps earlier than that—perhaps even my entire life—has led me here. It's as though I have no will of my own. Like what I want to do with my life doesn't matter. Everything I've done, every person I've ever met, has been part of a manipulation to bring me here. Even you and Whitlock, unknowingly, have been a part of it."

"But," Melann interrupted, "who has been doing this to you?"

"For all I know, I have."

"I don't understand."

"Neither do I," Vheod said, shaking his head and stepping away from the stones, "but I do know that all my life I've borne this Taint and that sometimes it acts as though it's an intelligent force of its own. It leads me places. It set into motion the events that brought me here in the first place. The Taint led me to Arach and Gyrison. It led me to Orrag. It . . . it led me to you."

"Why?" Melann asked. "Why did it do all of this? What is it?"

"I don't know," Vheod said, looking at the tattoo.

"Can you get rid of it somehow? Can you use magic? Can you cut it off?"

"In the first battle with the giant ravens, the flesh where it rested was slashed, but it didn't affect the Taint."

Melann grew quiet, obviously overwhelmed by the situation. Vheod couldn't blame her.

Finally, she said, "Is Chare'en—the demon—imprisoned here like you said?" She paused, and knelt down to look at an individual green stone. "If so, why are we here? Does that mean everything we've been told, and all we've relied on to save our parents and possibly ourselves, has been a lie?" She stood again.

"Perhaps." Vheod lowered his head.

"If you even so much as suspected this, why did you come at all?"

"If it wasn't true, then you might come here and free Chare'en accidentally. I thought you might need my help." He looked back up at her.

"By the Mother of All," Melann said, "it's my fault."

"No, it's not. Don't you see? Even if everything I feared was true—I still had to come here. I need to know who's controlling my life. If Chare'en—my own fiendish ancestor—is here, then it's not only my responsibility to make sure he doesn't cause any harm, but it's also imperative I come here to prove that even if forces have manipulated to bring me here to free him, I won't do it.

"I am my own man. I have to prove that—at least to myself."

"I understand," Melann said after a moment, "but there's such a risk."

Vheod's shoulders fell. He shut his eyes.

"No," Melann said. "I didn't mean that. I have faith in you, Vheod. You can do it."

Whitlock suddenly returned, though Vheod hadn't noticed he'd left. "I looked ahead—the passage continues beyond this chamber. It leads fairly far into the mountain, and I'm pretty sure I heard something moving around up there. I think we should probably check it out. Besides,"—he looked back the way they'd come—"there's no way to tell if and when the gnolls or that guardian statue might show up at our backs."

Melann looked to Vheod and nodded solemnly, with a smile of support. "Let's go check it out," she said.

Vheod arched his back, thrusting his chest ahead of him. He took a deep breath. "Yes," he said quietly, "let's go."

The passage was indeed long, and the temperature dropped slightly with each step down its length. Ahead of them they saw light and heard movement. They continued without discussion.

At the corridor's end, a huge set of brass doors barred the way. Runes, glyphs, and other symbols covered the entire surface of both doors. Four figures stood before the portals, obviously attempting to open them. As Vheod, Whitlock, and Melann approached, three turned to face them while the largest among them continued to work at the doors, thrusting his weight into pushing one open.

The figures were human men, each brandishing a short sword, a dagger, or a long, curved knife. Two held well-burnt torches high above their heads. They glowered silently as Vheod and the others approached. Their eyes showed only malice.

"Hello," Melann said tentatively.

Whitlock and Vheod both tightly gripped their already drawn swords. No response came. The three of them stopped about twenty feet away from the doors, the menacing figures in front of them.

Finally, the large figure turned toward them. Vheod recognized him, as did Whitlock and Melann, judging by the looks on their faces. But then, of course they did, Vheod realized.

The man was Orrag.

Chapter Nineteen

"I was wondering when you would get here," Orrag said with an evil grin. "I was starting to worry."

"What are you doing here?" Vheod demanded, pointing at Orrag with the short sword.

"I'm here for the same reason you are, friend," the half-orc said to Vheod, never dropping his toothy smile for a moment. "To free your ancestor, the great and powerful Chare'en, Lord of the Seven Vengeances."

Vheod had never heard that title before. How had Orrag? He felt Melann and Whitlock's gazes fall on him, but he didn't turn from the villainous half-orc.

"I'm here for just the opposite reason, as you well know," Vheod said. "Was everything you told me in Tilverton a lie?"

"Of course not," Orrag replied with his phlegmy, rough voice. "If it had all been a lie you never would've found your way here."

"Listen, you," Whitlock interrupted, "I don't know what sort of game you're playing, but we won't be your pawns. Why did you give us directions to this place if you knew it wasn't really what we were looking for. We sought the crypt of an old wizard—not a demon's prison."

"Simpleton," Orrag said. "You'll die not knowing."

The four men who stood around Orrag tensed. Two of them took menacing steps forward but stopped when they saw their leader made no hostile moves. Orrag continued to smile.

"Why all the elaborate deceptions?" Vheod asked and lowered his sword.

"Only you can free him, Vheod. I may be a devout servant, but the spells that imprison him can only be broken by a blood relation. Braendysh, the wizard who created this prison, saw to it." Orrag drew forth a long, curved scimitar from his belt, still grinning.

"I was so sure that Chauntea led us here," Melann whispered. "I was so sure."

Orrag spoke. "Now, Vheod, join me in opening these doors, and let's finish what has been started."

"If you think," Vheod retorted without hesitation, "that for one moment I might consider joining you in your sick plans, you're as dim-witted as you look."

"Vheod," Orrag said, still smiling, "this is your destiny. Don't fool yourself." The smile faded. "This is who you are."

"Never!" Vheod suddenly launched himself at Orrag, with sword in hand and denial as a battle cry.

* * * * *

Melann's world crumbled around her as surely as if the stone of the walls tumbled down around them all. How could she have been so wrong? The whole thing—the whole quest that she and her brother had undertaken—was a lie. It had all been a trick from the beginning. She'd told herself that Chauntea wanted ed her to undertake this journey, and as proof to herself she observed how everything seemed to work so well to lead her down this path. Now she saw that she'd been fooled as much as Vheod. She wondered if Vheod, like she, had been the primary instrument in his own deception.

Poor Vheod. She'd only helped his enemies in maneuvering him into this situation. Now he fought not only for his life but for his very soul. With every movement he must be questioning himself, she realized. She'd told him that she had faith in him, and it was true. Despite all reason, she truly believed that in the struggle against his own evil nature he was strong enough to win. That didn't mean it was going to be easy for him—nor did it mean he might not be killed if he wouldn't submit.

Melann had faith in Vheod but not in herself. While she never doubted Chauntea's power, she certainly doubted her own ability to devote all of her time and attention to the Mother of All's causes. She had become caught up in this personal mission to come here and find something to assuage the curse that plagued her family. Now that obsession with her personal goals had brought everything to ruin. There was no magical staff to remove the curse; there was only some demonic creature about to be loosed on the world.

Vheod had, at first, seemingly caught Orrag off guard with his attack. Though he seemed as surprised as the half-orc by Vheod's actions, Whitlock appeared more than happy to leap into the fray and help. Orrag and his followers outnumbered the two warriors— they needed her help. Melann reached through the cloud of despair that surrounded her and grabbed the wooden amulet bearing Chauntea's symbol.

No. She couldn't bring herself to call on her goddess's power. Her hand dropped to her belt where she kept her mace. She drew it out and stepped forward to where Vheod and Whitlock already fought Orrag and his men. Vheod engaged Orrag directly, but the four thugs threatened to overwhelm her brother almost immediately.

Melann hefted her weapon with both hands and attacked one of the men. She smashed the mace into his shoulder and spun him around to face her.

"Chare'en will show you vengeance, woman!" the cutthroat shouted as he slashed at her with a curved knife.

The wicked blade cut through the air, but she stepped backward to avoid it. All these men must worship Chare'en, she realized. Melann found it difficult to imagine such a horrible thing. How could they revere a demon? How could they worship the evil and death it represented? Her revulsion drove her mace in powerful strokes, first onto the villain's arm, which replied with a snap of bone. The knife flew from his hand, and she lifted the weapon over her head to finish him off.

Her foe was driven by powerful emotions of his own, though, and weaponless, he lunged at her using his weight to knock her back. Savagely he tore at her with his remaining arm and even with his teeth.

"Animal!" she grunted as she pushed him away.

Melann bore no regret as she smashed her mace into the man's face. He slumped to the floor. She'd never fought a human before, let alone killed one—though these fiend-worshiping cultists hardly carried themselves as men—but there was little doubt that he was dead.

Melann suddenly couldn't see the battle around her. She could only see what her willful actions had brought her to as she looked at the blood that coated her weapon.

She began to sob.

* * * * *

Whitlock had thrust himself, sword first, into the fray. As Vheod attacked Orrag, he positioned himself to fend off the other men who accompanied the half-orc. It was all he could do, however, to parry their attacks with his blade. He missed his shield, not to mention his armor. He dropped his torch to the ground, hoping it would burn long enough so that he could see in the coming fight. Orrag's henchmen who brandished torches did likewise as they moved to attack.

Melann moved forward and attacked one of his foes, drawing the cultist's attention to her. That helped considerably, as Whitlock thrust his blade offensively toward one of the three remaining men. Two had short swords, the other—the fastest and most dangerous, Whitlock judged—fought with a dagger in each hand. With three foes instead of four, Whitlock could press them back with his own jabs and feints while still maintaining his guard. Fighting multiple gnolls a number of times over the last few days had forced him to become accustomed to this sort of fighting, and while these fiend-worshiping cultists weren't without skill and determination, they didn't possess the size and strength of the gnolls.

Whitlock at least had a chance. Defeating all three of these men would almost certainly still be the most difficult battle of his life. One of the swordsmen moved in close to eliminate the advantage that Whitlock's long sword granted him. He countered that move with a punch to the man's stomach that caused him to double over. Whitlock raised his sword to capitalize on his advantage, but the double-dagger man lunged forward, forcing him to duck aside. He still brought his blade down on the first attacker, but it was mistimed and only barely sliced the cultist's leg.

Whitlock then backed away a few steps. Behind him Melann still fought with her foe, though it sounded as if she was getting the best of him. She'd done nothing but impress Whitlock in battle and stressful situations. His little sister had certainly grown up. He should have told her how proud he was to fight along side her and how willing he'd become to rely on her skill and intelligence, but he'd not. He rarely thought to say such things.

The man with two daggers—a bearded tough with dark hair—leaped at him again. Whitlock countered with a wide stroke, forcing his foe back, but it was just a ruse. One of the other men—a long-haired, stout man with a sword—stabbed at him when his guard was down. The blade cut into his side, and Whitlock knew his only hope was to go on the offensive.

Slashing wildly, he forced all three of his opponents back a step then lunged at the heavy-set swordsman with long hair. Whitlock's blade sank deeply into the man's guts, but the fellow made no sound other than to whisper, "Chare'en." His eyes closed as he fell to the ground, but Whitlock couldn't take the time to watch. Freeing his blade he stepped around the fallen foe, putting him between Whitlock and the other two cultists.

Now that he was turned around, he could see that Melann was in the process of dispatching her foe. As the cultist she fought fell, his comrades' attention was drawn to him. Whitlock used the opportunity to grab the dead man's short sword. With two blades, he was more likely to match two foes. The thug whose leg he'd cut came at him with an animalistic growl. Whitlock parried his blade with the newly acquired short sword, then swiped at him with his other weapon. His opponent retreated a pace.

The bearded dagger-wielder jumped, and Whitlock turned to see the man already high in the air. With a shrill scream, the dark-haired man crashed into Whitlock, and they both tumbled to the stone surface of the corridor. The short sword fell from Whitlock's hand and skittered away along the floor.

"Your soul will go to feed our master," the cultist said through clenched teeth as he and Whitlock lay in a tangled heap. If he didn't get this man off him quickly, one of those daggers would almost certainly find its way into his heart, Whitlock knew.

Focusing all his might, ignoring his assailant's words and the foulness of his breath, Whitlock flung him off and rolled to his feet. The swordsman hadn't yet advanced. Perhaps the wound Whitlock had dealt him was worse than he'd had thought. Spinning around to face the dagger man, he saw that his opponent had already regained his feet. He also saw that one of the man's dagger blades ran red with blood. Only then did Whitlock realize he'd been stabbed while the two lay on the ground.

Don't look down, he told himself. I don't want to know how bad it is.

"Whitlock!" Melann yelled from somewhere off to his right.

Probably losing blood fast, Whitlock pressed the attack. His sword caught the dagger-wielder with a slash across his chest. The man winced in pain but still stabbed forward with both his blades. Whitlock stepped back but used his sword's length to his advantage and brought it up then down on the cultist's neck.

He turned to face the last remaining foe, already weakening, but he saw that Melann stood over the man's fallen body. Her blood-covered iron mace was clenched tightly in both hands. She didn't look at the swordsman but at Whitlock. Her mouth open, she followed him with her gaze as he turned toward her and the last downed thug, then as his knees gave out from under him and he collapsed to the stone floor.

* * * * *

Vheod didn't care how many men Orrag had with him. It only mattered that he kill the half-orc before he could complete his baleful task and free Chare'en—or worse, somehow force or trick Vheod into freeing the balor. Orrag's counter to Vheod's strike was powerful. The half-orc was as strong as he was massive.

Gritting his teeth, Vheod launched a flurry of attacks against Orrag, but each time the larger man parried them or somehow managed to step back out of the way. Vheod was more accustomed to a longer, heavier blade than the one he now used, but he would adapt.

"Don't be foolish, Vheod," Orrag told him with the last parry. "You're not fighting me, you're fighting yourself here. Don't struggle against your own nature. Accept what and who you are."

"Shut up!" Vheod stabbed at his tormentor and ducked past his scimitar, but Orrag's leather armor turned the blade enough that he barely drew blood. "You're the fool, Orrag. You think you serve Chare'en? He's a tanar'ri! As soon as he's free he'll slay you as eagerly as he'd slay anyone. In fact, he might take particular pleasure in your destruction and make it specifically horrible. That's what tanar'ri do, Orrag—they kill, they torture, and they betray. Only a simpleton trusts a tanar'ri."

Just ask Whitlock or Melann, Vheod thought to himself. They trusted me, and look where it got them. Vheod sighed heavily.

"Oh, I'm not worried about any such thing," Orrag shook his head weightily back and forth, his fleshy cheeks swinging like pendulums. "I'm in control of this situation."

"You're more of an idiot than I ever imagined if you really believe that," Vheod said, "but even if you think you're safe from Chare'en, I assure you, you're not safe from me!" He stabbed again with his sword. Vheod's powerful thrust almost knocked Orrag from his feet as the half-orc attempted to counter the blow.

"You came here to free Chare'en!" Orrag spat as he steadied himself. "Why do you fight it?"

Vheod was suddenly filled with dread. He stepped back a pace. "You, or perhaps Chare'en . . . you're in contact with the Taint, aren't you? That's how all of this is happening, isn't it."

Orrag's dark, bulging eyes opened wide for a moment as he reacted with a start. "What are you talking about now?" Orrag seemed genuinely confused.

He didn't know about the Taint? Could that be possible? Vheod took the time to glance at the mark, which remained on his left hand. The mocking face leered outward, but not at him—at Orrag. It almost seemed to be laughing at the half-orc.

Why?

Vheod pressed his attack again and saw the beads of sweat gathering on Orrag's brow. The half-orc roared in frustration and pushed Vheod's attacks away yet again. When Vheod stepped forward with a flurry of blows, Orrag surprised him with a powerful swing that would have cut the cambion open if he'd not still been wearing his breastplate.

Only vaguely aware of the battle going on at his back, Vheod silently hoped Melann and Whitlock were all right. Once concern for Melann's safety entered into his mind, he knew he had to end this fight with Orrag as quickly as possible to insure that she was unharmed. While he knew she could take care of herself, he also knew he cared too deeply about her not to know for sure that she was safe.

Calling on the fiendish nature of his being, he brought forth a wave of oily blackness that occluded all light. It swarmed around him like water pouring into a basin, and he sent it forward to surround Orrag. The darkness had no effect other than to prevent his opponent from seeing, but that was all the advantage Vheod needed. Orrag stepped out of the swirling shadow, only to be knocked back into it by a forceful blow from Vheod's blade. The cambion felt his sword cut deep into flesh.

From within the swirling cloud of conjured blackness, Vheod heard a loud thud, then a softer one, but he could no more see in this magical darkness than Orrag could.

"It isn't fair," came the half-orc's gruff and gravelly voice. "I had it all planned, but you weren't supposed to attack me. That's not how it was supposed to happen." These words were followed by a grating sound that startled Vheod.

With but a thought and a focus of his tanar'ri nature, Vheod dispelled the darkness he'd brought forth. Orrag lay on the floor in front of the bronze, rune-covered doors, covered in blood.

The Taint visibly laughed on the back of his hand, but Vheod had no idea if it was laughing at Orrag, at him, or at both of them.

The doors, also now covered in blood, stood open.

Chapter Twenty

Melann cradled her brother's unconscious, blood-soaked body in her arms as she knelt on the stone floor. Her lack of conviction had brought her here—deep inside the prison of a demon, having just killed two men, and with Whitlock dying in her arms. If she'd only remained focused on Chauntea's will and not her own, none of this would have happened. How could she call on Chauntea's mercy to heal her brother's wounds? How could she expect the Mother of All to answer her call when she'd so obviously and blatantly gone astray? She didn't deserve the aid of her god, and now her brother would pay the price for her shortcomings.

Perhaps it was for the best. Whitlock had fallen in battle, and he certainly would have wanted it that way. She knew that death and failure were inevitable now for all of them. Melann looked down into her brother's face and thought of how he'd always considered her the cheerful one. She'd always seen the best of things—always believed in what was good. He'd told her once that that was what made her so well suited for the priesthood. Compliments came rarely from Whitlock, so she always remembered the comment and took it to heart. Finally now, her optimism had been proven wrong—she had to accept that. The gnolls had them trapped here amid the dead and dying, along with an imprisoned demon.

She had failed and failed utterly.

Tears rolled down her face, but she ignored them, instead wiping the brow of her brother.

Worst of all, with each step she'd taken toward failure, Melann had told herself she was following Chauntea's will. She'd deceived herself, and she'd done so happily. She'd wanted her own will more than she'd wanted to serve her patron. No deserving priest would ever do that, she knew. Melann had dragged herself toward this end, convinced that she'd been led by Chauntea and by good fortune.

In her delusion, she'd also brought her brother and Vheod to their sad end as well. Though Vheod had proven to be the master of his own life, just as he'd wanted, Melann was certain that none of them could escape this place and this end. Her own selfishness and hubris had brought them too deep to escape now. She looked down at Whitlock and knew that she was right.

The flames of the dropped torches around her died, but she made no move to correct the situation, for she'd neither the power nor the strength.

Vheod, she saw in the flickering light, stood over the body of Orrag. Melann could at least see that the offer Orrag had made Vheod—one the half-orc seemed to honestly believe Vheod would accept—was the test of inner strength he knew was coming. At the very least, she was right to have faith in Vheod.

Not that it mattered now.

Vheod moved through the growing shadows toward the doorway that now stood open after the battle. The bronze doors had somehow given way during the fighting. Melann couldn't remember when that had happened, but they were indeed open now and revealed a gigantic room beyond, awash in a faint glow that at first seemed green, then changed to red.

Through the wide doorway, the huge room appeared full of a multitude of objects making vast and dramatic movements. Vheod approached slowly, drawn by curiosity—she hoped. Had he completely overcome his evil nature? What lay in that room that compelled him so? She shuddered. Had she been wrong about everything?

As he moved closer to the entrance, her own vision was drawn with him. She could see now that what she'd believed to be many moving objects was really a single object of many parts, all of them spinning and moving about the room, yet connected to one another. Spheres and other three-dimensional shapes, crafted from tarnished bronze, rotated rapidly, like a gigantic orrery animated with life—frantic life. The parts of this immense device, which must have been at least a hundred feet high, moved rapidly but with such precision that they produced almost no sound other than the whip of displaced air.

A metallic smell rolled through the open doorway, mixed with dust and ancient, stale air. Vheod continued inside, until Melann could no longer see him. Remaining where she was she could just make out that at the center of the spinning, rotating, orbiting arms, and rings and other portions of the device, was an oval made of green stone. Through the translucent shell of this colossal egg, a humanoid figure writhed. The thing in the glassy container must have stood twelve feet tall, and huge wings jutted from its back.

Chare'en.

This was the prison of the fiend—a prison made of the green glassy rock that had once comprised an ancient idol dedicated to him. A painful chill ran slowly through Melann like a wave of nausea, and as it passed over her she grew numb. She became completely unfeeling as though she was wrapped tightly in a prisonlike shell of her own. Now every lie she'd been told was indeed confirmed.

Now, every hope she'd possessed was truly dead.

She heard Vheod's voice come from inside the strange chamber. "Melann," he cried. What could it be? Was there really any more that could happen? If it was over, couldn't it just be truly over?

"The staff!"

What?

"Melann! The staff—I believe I've found the staff you seek. I've found the key to removing your family's curse."

Eyes wide and staring straight ahead, she still knelt on the cold stone, too shocked to move. Too afraid that if she even breathed what Vheod just said might somehow not be true, or that she would realize she heard him incorrectly.

Warmth cracked and penetrated the despair that encircled Melann. All the hope she'd lost, all the faith that had fled from her—both faith in herself and in her goddess's willingness to provide for her—came flooding back. It overwhelmed her. She'd given up believing in the lies she'd been told. Now, now was there yet some grain of truth in the stories of the dead wizard named Chare'en and the magical staff that lay in his crypt? Could it be true?

Her spirit was almost torn asunder. Never before had she found such a pit of despair within her, and now to be pulled out so quickly and completely to learn that her greatest wish had come true was almost more than she could take. She steadied herself with a hand on the stone floor.

Melann told herself that she dare not believe it before she saw it with her own eyes, but it was too late. All her hopes and faith now rested on the words of Vheod—noble Vheod who had overcome the temptation of his own evil soul. He'd rejected Orrag, and now his strength brought him to the staff that would lift the curse on her family. She owed it all to—

Whitlock!

Melann realized that before she could do anything, she had to save her brother. She lowered his body slowly to the ground and stood up. She took a deep breath, then another.

Her hands raised above her head, and she whispered, "Great Mother, please . . . I don't know if I've followed your will to come here or not, but I need your help. I probably don't deserve your attention now, but my brother is dying." Summoning what inner strength remained, she performed the healing rite and lowered her hands to Whitlock's bleeding abdomen.

Before her eyes, the gaping wound exposed by the tear in his shirt blurred and disappeared, leaving only healthy flesh.

"Oh, thank you! Praise Chauntea—provider and nurturer of life."

Whitlock remained unconscious, but Melann knew he would live. His condition was still fragile, he needed rest, and any undue stress might still pose a danger to him. She should remain at his side.

But the staff! How could she not go see the object of their quest? It was the culmination of all their dreams and plans. They could cure their parents and ensure that their family was free of the affliction forever. She and Whitlock could live out their lives without fear of the curse. That staff meant freedom and peace. Melann looked down at her brother and smiled. She stood and walked into the strange room from which Vheod had called to her.

Once inside, Melann saw the contents of the room in greater detail. At the center was the glass prison, eighteen feet in height and more than half as wide. Orbiting around it, however, were strangely shaped objects of all sizes—some as large as a horse—that rotated, rose, fell, and circled around each other. All these objects were connected together in a complex web of metal supported at the center of the room around the area of the floor on which the oval vessel of green, glassy stone rested. The spinning spectacle of metal whirled at great speed all around the prison, filling the room that stretched at least three hundred feet in all directions, but it never touched the green glass egg itself.

Vheod stood before the glass prison, reaching toward it. What was he doing? Was he compelled by his evil side, even now, to liberate dread Chare'en? Was there no end to his internal struggle?

"No, Vheod, don't! Not after all you've already overcome," she shouted at him from just inside the doorway leading into the vast chamber.

"But," he said, turning his head toward her, "the staff . . ."

Melann looked more closely at the prison. There, barring the seal that held the two halves of the egglike vessel together was a wooden, rune-covered staff. Both the staff's ends were capped in silver, and the runes that ran up and down its four sides were inlaid also in silver. It sparkled with a radiant beauty that seemed out of place here. The silver glow that came from the staff extended from it like tethers lashing it to the prison, holding it against the seam over a silver seal.

It was clear that to remove the staff, the seal had to be broken.

The figure inside the glass prison shifted its position and flexed its wings. It seemed as though it was listening to the conversation. It seemed that it was preparing to escape its imprisonment.

"Without it, your parents will die," Vheod told her. "You may die."

"That doesn't matter now," she told him.

"I can't believe that." He shook his head slowly, his gaze never dropping from hers.

"You have to believe it, Vheod. I'm not worth it. No one person is."

"That's not the way I see it," he told her firmly. "If I thought that I wouldn't be here. I wouldn't have survived in the Abyss."

"That's not what I mean."

"I can't let you die, Melann. I can't let the misery and pain of your family's curse continue."

Melann looked away from him. As she was drawn to look even closer at the massive figure within the translucent prison, she saw that its face was shaped like the stone pattern the gnolls had made with their green rocks. It looked just like the Taint on the back of Vheod's hand.

Melann then knew the truth. Orrag was not the voice of temptation, he was yet another pawn in the whole vast plan. Apparently, only Vheod could remove the staff and free Chare'en, but Orrag could never have convinced him to do it—the balor in the prison knew that.

No, Orrag did not provide the temptation here. She did. Every portion of the Taint's—of Chare'en's—plan had come together.

"Vheod, you can't let them win!" It's not your fault, she thought. It was the Taint—it was Chare'en all along. Even the curse on her family was but a stepping stone to this moment when Vheod's human side would act out of what Chare'en certainly saw as the human weaknesses of love and loyalty.

"No," Vheod said, "I love you too much to let you fail." He reached toward the silvery staff.

Melann ran to him, hands outstretched, attempting to cross the distance that remained, all the while dodging the veritable maelstrom of metal parts to the grand device surrounding the prison. Her mouth formed a silent scream of protest, and her eyes were wide with fear and despair.

She was too late.

Chapter Twenty-one

FREEDOM.

"No, Vheod, No!"

FREEDOM.

"Vheod, don't you see? They've won! By the Mother, *it's free!*"

FREEDOM.

"They've not won," Vheod proclaimed. "I have."

FREEDOM.

With the staff removed, the silver seal burst asunder.

FREEDOM!

With no more seal holding the seam shut, the egg-like prison split apart.

"No!" Melann fell to her knees before she ever reached Vheod.

Humid air belched forth from the opened capsule. The figure that emerged dripped with foul fluids. Burnt red skin pulled taut over sinewy muscles and sharp, wicked bones as it moved, stretching wide, bat-like—dragonlike—wings with a wet, fleshy crunch. Clawed hands clutched a long, black, many-tailed whip covered in spikes and a jagged sword of black iron, both dragging along the ground behind it, creating sparks of protest. The prisoner's wide head sported a flat face framed by broad, slightly curled horns.

A mouth of jagged teeth like rusty nails curled in what might have passed for a smile in some unthinkable nether plane. Powerful lungs inhaled deeply, expanding its chest to a surprising degree, and it exhaled a single word that echoed throughout the room.

"FREEDOM!"

"I've won," Vheod said, holding the silver-runed staff above his head, "because I can give you what you need and still stand against the evil of Chare'en!"

Vheod tossed the staff to Melann and spun on the creature emerging from eons of imprisonment, drawing forth the blade with which he'd defeated Orrag. A wild look filled his dark eyes as he stared at his ancestor. He tossed the small sword back and forth from hand to hand as he poised tensely for battle.

Chare'en looked down and studied the cambion who stood before him. Black eyes like lances bore holes into Vheod, but he stood his ground. The balor threw his head back in a barking, echoing laugh.

"You are mine to control little man," the demon said. "You dance like a puppet on my strings, and you always have. You stand against what I tell you to stand against."

Vheod's long red hair had been smeared with dirt, sweat, and blood, a little of each marring his dusky face as well. Mouth grim, he worked his jaw but stared up at the balor in front of him with only victory blazing in his eyes. A smile creeped across his lips, and he finally spoke. "I reject you, great-grandfather. You don't control me."

Chare'en's laughter exploded forth like a burst bubble. "If I did not control you, I would not be free." The words slid from his mouth like snakes.

"Vheod," Melann said, raising her head. Through

the fear and despair, she choked out, "The Taint—it's the Taint. It's not you, you're not evil. It's not your fault."

She was wrong, of course. Vheod knew that he was indeed evil. He was half tanar'ri, and tanar'ri were inherently malicious, cruel, and all that was wrong. That is what they were on some important, fundamental level. He couldn't blame the Taint, or Orrag, or even Chare'en for his own nature, not any more than a child can blame his parents for his eye or hair color.

At the same time, however, he was half human. Rather than worry about his nature, he could overcome it. Facing it head on, he could challenge evil and defeat it. Right now, that meant facing and defeating Chare'en once and for all. He would show himself and all the world that he was master of his own life, and his own destiny, by taking the offensive.

Nevertheless, Vheod had to admit to himself that it had seemed a better plan before actually seeing the towering figure of the balor standing before him, quite literally dripping with power, rage, and evil. Even if he died Vheod would still have won. He still would have fought against evil rather than having been mastered by it.

"Your freedom means nothing," Vheod said through teeth gritted with determination. "I will destroy you."

Again Chare'en threw back his head in a spasm of laughter. This time Vheod used the opportunity to his advantage. Summoning his strength, he grasped the hilt of the short sword in both hands and launched himself into the air. He came down with a stabbing strike over his head, plunging the sword into the huge tanar'ri's belly.

* * * * *

In the walled city of Tilverton, a less than reputable weaponsmith named Hirtho makes his living by selling low-cost, simple weapons to criminals and thugs. Hirtho once worked for a group in the city called the Fire Knives, an evil, roguish group that plagued the city. Eventually, the Fire Knives were completely driven out of the city, and Hirtho looked into a new line of work. His father had been a blacksmith, and Hirtho had learned a little of the trade when he was young. Possessed of none of his father's skill or artistry, he nevertheless discovered that the right clientele would be willing to buy his crude weapons for low prices. Because of his connections, he knew where to get cheap steel "liberated" from merchant caravans.

Hirtho thus led a simple but comfortable life off his ill-gotten gains. One of his many sales went to a young man named Wenmer who was hired as an enforcer for a local criminal and—according to some—priest of some mysterious evil god. Little did Hirtho know, the young enforcer would be killed before he ever drew the blade—by his own criminal boss as a blood sacrifice no less. Hirtho would never have believed that a cambion from the Abyss would then take the sword and use it against that same criminal. The idea that one of Hirtho's crude creations would have been used in an attack against a balor—perhaps the most powerful of fiends in all the Lower Planes—would have been inconceivable to the shady smith.

Vheod shouldn't have needed to know the blade's short and lackluster history to realize that his actions were foolhardy. He shouldn't have been surprised when, on coming into contact with the flesh of dread Chare'en, the ungainly sword shattered into thousands of metal shards. The force of the blow and its results sent Vheod sprawling backward through the air, where he struck the stone floor with great force.

* * * * *

Chare'en appeared more stunned and surprised than hurt. In fact, he didn't appear hurt at all.

Vheod's vision swirled around him. He closed his eyes tightly, hoping to steady his vision. When he opened them again, Melann was kneeling over him.

"Vheod, get up," she begged, her voice thin and panicked. "He'll kill us all!"

She was attempting to lift him from the ground by his shoulders, and he allowed her to help him stumble to his feet. The demon's black gaze fell on them both.

"Now, young mortalheart, I swear by the Abyss that gave birth to us both," Chare'en said in a voice like polished obsidian, "you will *die!*"

Vheod and Melann ran, scrambling across the stone floor as fast as they could. The spine-covered whip slapped and scraped the ground behind them as Chare'en swung it over his head and crashed its tails where they had stood. The two of them ran, dodging the moving and whirling parts of the still rapidly moving metallic device.

Chare'en bellowed in rage, shaking both of them, body and soul. They reached the doorway and passed through the open bronze portals. Vheod looked around, blankly surveyed the bodies of the fallen thugs, Orrag, and Whitlock. He ran to where Whitlock lay.

"Is he . . . does he live?" Vheod asked, not looking back at Melann.

"Yes," she replied, "but he shouldn't be moved."

"There's nowhere to move him to anyway, I'm

afraid." Vheod took Whitlock's sword and turned back to Melann. She'd begun some sort of prayer.

Next to her, Vheod saw Orrag's fallen body by the doors. The floor shook as Chare'en followed them, loping slowly with legs cramped from centuries of captivity. With each step, the balor grew stronger. Vheod stepped up to the doorway but still looked down at Orrag. Surely the half-orc would have brought something of power with him here to this place. He seemed like a crafty planner—wouldn't he have brought along some sort of fail-safe plan?

Vheod reached down and picked up the falchion the half-orc still clutched in his quickly stiffening fingers. Orrag, obviously not wanting to inflict serious injury on Vheod, hadn't really attacked him with the weapon. Perhaps it was a magical blade—Orrag's backup?

Chare'en reached the doorway as Melann finished chanting the mysterious invocation. Lines of blue fire traced a complicated pattern across the floor inside the doorway. "By the power of Chauntea, Mother of All," Melann shouted at the fiend, "you cannot cross this line, demon!"

To Vheod's surprise, Chare'en stopped. He studied the line of power and seemed to consider it, as if evaluating its power and limitations. Or perhaps he considered his own. Vheod couldn't be sure. Nevertheless, anything that stopped the balor's advance was mighty indeed and was an advantage that shouldn't be wasted.

Unfortunately, even as thoughts of escape began to form in Vheod's mind, he saw a glint of metal behind the balor. On the floor, near the middle of the chamber, lay the silver-runed staff. In her haste to help him, Melann had left the staff behind. He knew he couldn't leave without it.

Besides, he thought, the intention behind his actions had been to slay Chare'en. He had to attempt to do so, or die trying. As he watched, Chare'en's flat black eyes rolled slightly. Vheod knew the balor was calling on his own inner, Abyssal power.

Melann didn't pause to observe. Instead, she used the time to begin calling on the power of her goddess yet again. While she chanted quietly, Vheod loosed a spell of his own. Daggers of light flew from his hand and screamed toward Chare'en's broad chest. They disappeared inches before they would have struck him, as though they'd never existed. Vheod realized that the balor's presence and power rendered many minor magical spells useless against him. Vheod cursed his luck and his trivial magical skills, then tumbled through the doorway and off to his right.

At almost the same time, a shining blue warhammer of heavenly might appeared in Melann's hands. She flung it into the air at Chare'en but turned to watch Vheod leap past her protective barrier.

"By all the Gods of Faerûn, Vheod," she shrieked, "are you mad?"

Vheod realized that the barrier obviously was meant to keep Abyssal creatures at bay. He was able to cross it one way, but due to his nature, would it repel him as well? He would never get the chance to discover the answer, for as all this occurred, Chare'en summoned forth the power within him and with a wave of his clawed hand dispelled the blue fire barrier with a snap of coarse, black lightning.

"I shall be denied nothing, regardless of which of your weak goddesses you call on!" His words curdled the air with his anger and hate.

The hammer Melann had conjured forth, also of bluish, goddess-granted fire, struck the tanar'ri noble. This spell passed through the balor's resist-

ance to magical energies and staggered him slightly.
Vheod used both that distraction and the fact that
Chare'en had needed to drop one of his weapons to
dispel the barrier, to aid in his attack on the balor's
flank. Daleland broadsword in one hand and curved
orc steel in the other, he slashed and stabbed at the
fiend. His blades found their mark, and Chare'en bled
an odiferous corruption for which no earthly name
applies.

"Melann," Vheod shouted, "get the staff! I'll hold
him . . ."

Black blood raged to Vheod's head, and as he'd
done before, he lost himself to the hatred and darkness of the tanar'ri portion of his soul. He struck blow
after blow with his blades, hammering Chare'en with
fury and might. The ferocity forced the balor back a
few lumbering steps. He unfurled his wings in anger,
but as he did a spinning sphere carried through the
air by a curved metal span smashed into one of them,
almost knocking Chare'en down. Even more surprising, as it struck the tanar'ri, the sphere stopped spinning—though it continued its revolution about the
room—and a face within the metal surface groaned
with wide eyes and a large, open mouth. Vheod
watched in surprise and fascination, but the device
continued to turn, and soon the sphere was rounding
its way to the far side of the room.

The device was alive.

Vheod had had no idea.

* * * * *

Melann did as Vheod had suggested. She ran past
Vheod and Chare'en as they fought, circling around
to the left as she entered the chamber full of whirling
metal spheres and supports. Vheod appeared so small

next to the terrifying fiend. She could never have imagined such a horror. Chare'en was the embodiment of anathema. He was living despair, destruction, and desecration. Melann now suddenly understood evil much more intimately than she'd ever wanted to.

Fortunately, the spiritual weapon that Chauntea had granted her still beat on Chare'en's body, aiding Vheod in his fight. The fact that her god's magic worked even in the face of such terrible power served to strengthen Melann's faith in her patron. She had no idea what she would do or think if it had failed.

Melann reached the staff and grasped it. Though it was wooden, it felt cool and smooth, like silver. The staff had been carved with four flat sides, each with etched runes filled with silver inlay. The ends were each capped in silver, all of it shining as if the object were brand new. In its texture and balance it was light and somehow pleasant to hold.

A cry of pain made her spin on her heel, looking back toward Vheod. Chare'en had managed to grasp the cambion in the tendrils of his many-tailed whip. Blood flowed from numerous wounds inflicted by the barbs and spines on the whips. As Vheod struggled to free himself, Chare'en laughed and burst into infernal flames.

Or at least, that was what Melann thought at first. Instead, she saw after her eyes adjusted to the unpleasant light of the piercing flames, that the tanar'ri had somehow immolated himself, sheathing his body in flames that seemed to inflict no pain on him whatsoever. The fire lapped at Chare'en's flesh like waves of water, and as he continued to laugh the balor pulled Vheod closer and closer to him and to the conjured fires of chaos and evil.

Melann bounded toward this scene as Vheod still strained at the coils of the whip that trapped him. She raised the staff, gripping it in both hands, and charged Chare'en with it as if it were a spear. The heat of the fire forced her back. She couldn't get close enough even to strike. With a mighty yank, Chare'en drew Vheod into the flames and held him close in a fiery, life-quenching embrace.

"No, please, don't," she protested in vain. "Vheod! I love you!"

She wasn't sure until now, but it was true. Vheod's nobility, strength, and passion were greater than anyone she'd ever met. Now, it would seem, he would be taken away from her before she could ever tell him, for the roar of the flames drowned out her words.

To her surprise Vheod still struggled in the grasp of the fiend. While the flames obviously burned him, he withstood the heat with a greater fortitude than she would have believed possible. His Abyssal heritage must give him such strength, she reasoned, but could it be enough? She was near exhaustion and thought if she could only reach Vheod, she might possibly be able to call on the power of Chauntea once more to heal him, but then she would be of no further use.

She charged forward again and was again repelled by the flames. The twisted laughter of Chare'en still filled the room. It drew her attention, however, to the orrery-like rotating device spinning almost silently in the room. She had seen it earlier strike the demon and almost knock him down. She'd also seen the face within the metal that appeared when it struck him. Perhaps she could get it to strike again—but if she did, it would strike Vheod as well.

Melann ran back to the center of the room. The base of the device was an immobile tripod of metal that surrounded the now-open glass prison. The top of the tripod, where the three supports joined, held a spinning disk from which curved metal supports extended at various lengths into the chamber. At the end of each was one of the metallic, three-dimensional shapes that whirled in circles. Some moved up and down as well as around. Most were joined to other shapes by further metal supports, so that the entire superstructure moved as one—around, up and down, with many of the individual parts spinning on their own.

Melann tucked the staff into her belt at her back and began to climb up one of the legs of the giant tripod. The support was about as thick as she was, and so by wrapping her arms and legs around it she was able to quickly inch her way up the outer surface of the leg. Near the top, she reached up and grabbed onto the disk that turned horizontally. She was surprised by the force that tore her from the leg. As she held on with all her might, she whirled around on the spinning disk.

Pulling herself up on top of the disk, she found she could stand on it and maintain her balance between the various supports that sprouted forth and connected to the rest of the structure. The whole thing obviously functioned by magic, for she found nothing resembling a mundane mechanism at the center of the device to turn the disk. She reasoned that perhaps the device was some sort of magical generator that powered the prison to hold Chare'en. No other explanation for its existence seemed to make sense. Experimentally, she leaned against one of the supports and began to shake it using her weight. To her surprise, she was able to cause the entire device to waver slightly.

As she turned, Melann saw Chare'en and Vheod. Again to her surprise, she saw that Chare'en had dropped Vheod to the floor, where the cambion writhed in burned agony—but he was alive! Chare'en reeled backward, but Melann had no idea why. She turned past them and no longer could get a good view of what happened.

By the time the device circled her around, Melann could see that Chare'en clutched at something sticking in his left eye. As the fiend staggered backward he roared in pain. With his movement, however, Melann saw past him to the doorway.

Whitlock stood between the open bronze doors, a crossbow weakly dangling in his hand. As she passed around past the scene again, Melann determined that her brother would almost certainly drop at any moment. She had to do something—now was her chance.

Once again, despite the growing dizziness she felt from the rapid rotation, Melann grasped one of the supports and began attempting to shake it. Throwing her weight into it, she caused the device to shudder and shake. With each moment, it grew more violent. The shapes, one by one, stopped spinning on their own. Each formed a humanlike face in the metal surface, each turned toward her. As they rotated around the central axis, shifting up and down, near and far and throughout the room, the faces all moaned with voices of metal fatigue: "*No!*"

She ignored them. Melann didn't stop.

"We maintain the prison of the balor, Chare'en. We were placed here by Braendysh. It is our duty for all time to ensure he does not escape . . ." the voices continued.

"You failed, whatever you are," Melann whispered as she shook the support. "It's my turn now."

As the support wobbled more and more dramatically, the voices moaned and protested more.

Meanwhile, she saw Chare'en remove the crossbow bolt from his eye and toss it to the ground. Black and green fluid poured from the wound, but already the flow began to ebb. Suddenly, two of the metal shapes clashed together as the device swayed and shook, and the different moving parts began to turn out of sync. The whole structure careened out of control. Supports began to bend and tear apart.

Melann's eyes grew wide. "What have I done?" she shouted, though only she could hear herself.

The floor was fifteen feet below her at least, but she had to get off the device, and quickly. She stood on the disk, retaining her balance, when a powerful shudder echoed through the chamber. As she'd hoped, a part of the magical generator slammed into Chare'en. The tanar'ri was carried across and around the room a fair distance. Unfortunately, the same shock sent Melann tumbling off the disk to the ground below.

She landed with a crack, and the arm that she reflexively put out to cushion the long fall snapped like a tree branch. Pain shot through her body as she rolled along the floor.

Long, agonizing moments passed while Melann couldn't bring herself even to open her eyes. In her self-imposed darkness, she could hear the once nearly silent device screaming like a thing in pain. Another moment passed before she realized that she screamed in pain right along with it.

Somehow she dragged herself to her feet, clutching her broken arm. She thought it likely that she might have broken a rib or two, judging from the pain in her chest. Luckily, her legs seemed relatively unharmed, and she was able to stumble to what she believed was where Vheod lay, which fortunately was near Whitlock and the exit.

Melann got lucky, or perhaps Chauntea continued to watch over her, for after only a few dozen short, stumbling steps she came to Vheod. She looked down, and what she saw made her no longer feel quite so much pain herself. Vheod's clothing—apparently as well as the straps of his breastplate—had burned away, leaving him with little covering his bloody, black flesh. He was horribly burned, and he curled up like a dying animal.

Collapsing near him, Melann called one last time on the Mother of All, asking her to heal Vheod with the goddess's life-giving touch. Melann's good hand radiated golden energy, and where she passed her fingers, Vheod's burned flesh healed. Using this divine power, Melann was able to heal a great portion of his wounds. He sighed with the pleasure of reduced pain and began to writhe. His body had thrown him into a state of shock, but he recovered with a start.

Looking up, Vheod's eyes widened in surprise. "Abyssal hosts!" he cursed. "We've got to get out of here!"

Melann managed to follow his gaze and saw that the device spun entirely out of control now, the parts bending, snapping, and crashing into each other. His wounds at least partially healed, Vheod had strength enough to help Melann to her feet. Grasping his arm tightly around her, he brought both of them toward the only exit from the chamber.

A hemispherical portion of the device crashed next to them, a horrified metal face screaming in frustration. The still rotating generator dragged the hemisphere along the ground toward them, sparks flying about it. Vheod managed to pull them both out of the way, and they reached the door.

Whitlock lay at their feet, once again bleeding dangerously. Before Melann could even think about tending to him, a tremendous cacophony of metal and screams came from behind them. The entire device—tons on tons of metal—crashed to the floor in a single, unbelievable blow. Even through the crash they could hear the voice of Chare'en from across the chamber.

"*No!*" the tanar'ri cried.

The voices of the magical device suddenly cried in unison "It is our duty for all time to ensure he does not escape!"

The silence that followed seemed as abrupt as the crash. Dust roiled in the air as Melann and Vheod stared into the room where their foe had stood. Now they could only see bent and broken metal.

It was over.

Melann fell to her knees and with her unbroken arm tore away the remainder of Whitlock's shirt. Tearing the cloth into strips, she began to bind the re-opened wound in his abdomen. She rolled his heavy body over to get around to his back, then brought the strip around again and again. A few bits of metal still bent under their own weight creating a small creaking sound.

Vheod stood over her, still staring into the chamber. In the brief instant that she looked at his face, it held only one emotion: disbelief. She turned back to Whitlock. A few more bits of metal clanked against each other or the stone floor as the debris settled.

"No," Vheod whispered.

Melann looked up from her work. She'd almost finished tending to her brother's wound. In the far side of the room, in the little light they had she saw some of the pieces of metal still settling. They moved and shuddered. The movement grew more intense—not less. It was not settling.

It was not over.

Chare'en rose up from the shards of metal and the debris that had brought him down. Blood and bile-oozing gashes cut long streaks through his red, glistening skin. One of his horns was broken, and his fleshy wings were tattered and probably near useless. His sword and whip were nowhere to be seen.

He laughed. His low, evil chuckle echoed through the room. "Braendysh created that cursed contraption. It was filled with the spirits of those he claimed I had wrongly slain. They spent these last eons willingly exacting their vengeance on me by keeping me prisoner. They have been set free, but so have I. You cannot kill me. It is not within your power."

Shadows appeared to gather around them. Melann could swear that the darkness grew and moved in the air surrounding her, her brother, and Vheod. Only now did she notice that Vheod still clutched Whitlock's sword in his bloody hand.

"While I yet live," he whispered, "I have the power to do anything I desire. I control my limits, not you." Blood ran down his face, but Vheod ignored it. His hair was burned and caked with blood, and his nearly naked body glistened with sweat in the dying light. "Now it is time to end this."

"I can help insure it's the ending that you want," a lush voice from behind them said.

The Ravenwitch stood in the corridor, surrounded by her black-feathered servants.

Chapter Twenty-two

The growing darkness had in fact been the ravens filling the small room that gave way to the prison chamber. Vheod looked at the Ravenwitch over his shoulder. "I don't have time for you now, witch."

The Ravenwitch flowed toward him like black water given life. A long cloak of black feathers rippled behind her, as did her long, ebony tresses. She smiled a thin, tight smile but didn't reply. As Vheod and Melann watched, she stopped at Orrag's body and knelt beside it. Pulling his shirt away from his neck, she pulled out an amulet on a chain. It glittered with gold and some small sorcerous symbols.

Taking it from the half-orc's corpse, she handed it to Vheod. "If anyone concerned was in possession of this amulet, it would be this one. He'd been planning for this day for some time, and while not exactly a tower of intellect, he had a sort of craftiness that suggested he would plan ahead."

Vheod took the amulet and turned back to the chamber. Chare'en slowly advanced through the debris and dust, breathing heavily.

"But what is it?" Vheod asked with an intensity burning in his eyes.

"Braendysh needed something to defeat Chare'en," she told him. "This protected him and enabled his victory against the demon so long ago."

"Why are you helping us now?" Melann asked, her voice betraying all her suspicions.

"I am helping myself, not you." She looked over Vheod's shoulder into the room and a look of mixed fascination and horror crossed her countenance. "Surely we can discuss this some other time."

Vheod placed the amulet around his neck and turned back to Chare'en. He hefted the broadsword, wiped his brow of sweat and blood, and moved into the chamber, almost immediately having to climb up and over some of the scattered metal debris. He noticed he was suddenly accompanied by dozens of ravens that flew into the room and hopped about the wreckage around him. Biting his tongue, Vheod did his best to ignore them.

The tanar'ri and the half-tanar'ri met near the center of the room, but closer to the entrance than the opposite side. Chare'en flexed his long claws at the end of his powerful arms. His sneer betrayed hundreds of jagged teeth. Visible, dark green breath snorted out of his wide nostrils. Already his eye was healing, for blows from unenchanted weapons or attacks could never permanently harm him.

Still, the balor breathed heavily. Chare'en couldn't conceal the fact that he was quite hurt.

"I suppose," Chare'en said heavily, "you might expect me to ask you one last time to concede to my will and serve me." He paused and took a labored breath. "I do not need you any longer, boy. I am free. Letting you live now would be akin to mercy, I would suppose, and you should well know that I could not abide that."

"I know all too well what you're like," Vheod told him. "I harbor a bit of you within me."

"If that were true, you would not face me now—for you would know that I would destroy you."

Vheod shook his head. He almost smiled. "I know something that you do not."

A sharp laugh escaped Chare'en's toothy grin. "We shall see."

The balor raised his muscular arm and brought it down on Vheod. He raised it again with a horrid smile, thinking to find the cambion smashed beyond recognition. Instead, Vheod stood his ground, unscathed.

Vheod breathed a sigh of relief. Even up to the last moment, he questioned the words of the Ravenwitch. However, at least so far, she'd apparently spoken the truth. Chare'en could not harm him.

This changed everything.

Chare'en struck at Vheod again and again. With a wrinkled brow, he looked down at the cambion. All at once, his eyes filled with recognition, then something else crossed his face. Could it have been fear? Vheod hoped so.

Vheod struck at the balor, sinking his sword deep into tanar'ri flesh once again. "You are nothing but an abomination here, Chare'en," he said. Another stroke, another hit. "You will be destroyed this time." Another strike.

Vheod's blows forced the tanar'ri back. Chare'en clawed at his foe, but to no avail. The magic of the amulet seemed to provide complete protection. As Vheod attacked, the ravens in the room did as well. They came at the huge demon from all sides, buffeting his face with their wings and tearing at his already open flesh with beaks and claws.

Vheod jumped up, thrusting his weight against Chare'en's chest and striking with his sword. The force of the blow knocked the balor back, tearing his side as he pushed against a sharp metal shard. Vheod dropped to the ground but stumbled over some debris. As he did, Chare'en lashed out, attempting to grab the amulet away. Vheod was just barely able to pull back and dodge the blow.

"I must destroy you, Chare'en, for this world and for myself. Neither deserves to have to worry about your manipulation or threats." Vheod chopped at the balor with his blade yet again.

Chare'en's face was full of pain and worry now—but both emotions fled, pushed away by anger. Chare'en began drawing on his internal, sorcerous nature. He began summoning power—a lot of power. The ravens began to scatter, though some remained to peck and claw at their enemy.

Chare'en's arms raised above his head, and he gazed upward as black and violent fire wrapped around his hands then the air between them. The demon lowered his gaze back down to Vheod, and a smile crossed his thin, black lips.

Vheod didn't wait to see what would happen next. He leaped upward at his huge foe, this time throwing his shoulder into Chare'en's chest. Hands still blazing with black fire, the balor flailed his arms to keep his balance. His nearly useless wings fluttered, and it wasn't enough. Chare'en fell backward—backward onto the broken remains of his glass prison. The bottom portion of one of the vertically split halves rose up slightly from the debris, its jagged edge protruding like a spike that thrust up through the tanar'ri as he fell. Blood and black bile spurted in all directions, and his hands exploded in unreleased dark sorcery.

Chare'en let loose a high-pitched wail. His eyes shot forth dark bolts of raw, evil power. His body shook violently, then crumbled abruptly into a fine reddish powder that rose in a cloud around his former prison, settling down on and around the broken green shards.

Vheod breathed a slow, easy breath. Chare'en was gone, his physical form destroyed. This world wouldn't need to know his abrasive touch. It was safe. He was safe. Melann and Whitlock were safe. Vheod breathed again. He looked back to the entrance, where he could see Melann laughing—though he knew it was through great pain that she did so.

Vheod looked on the shattered glassy stone that lay all around him. In each piece, he saw his own reflection, and he knew that like his great-grandfather, he too had been in a glass prison. All his life he'd looked around himself and believed himself to be free, never realizing that transparent walls of destiny surrounded him. He now knew that his own nature was in fact his greatest enemy.

Vheod looked down at the Taint. It rested as it often did, on the back of his hand. He knew he could never completely rid himself of that nature, no more than he could rid himself of his heart or his brain. It was a part of him, as true as any other, but that didn't mean he was its slave.

He could take control. Now that he saw the walls, he could break through them, just as Chare'en's own glass prison had shattered.

* * * * *

With Chare'en destroyed, the Ravenwitch and her cadre of ravens simply left. Vheod had walked back to where she and Melann stood and said, "I'm not sure how to say this, but . . . thank you."

The Ravenwitch showed no sign that she even recognized the words he spoke. She made a small sound that apparently the ravens all understood. They began to fly out as a flock then the Ravenwitch just turned and left. Vheod and Melann let her go.

Eventually, after they rested a while, they carried Whitlock through the underground passages and found the exit. All around lay slain gnolls. Though many looked as though the guardian had killed them, a significant number of others sported smaller wounds, indicating tiny talons or beaks. A great many black feathers lay scattered about the fallen, as well as a few dead ravens. The guardian was nowhere to be seen. Vheod did, however, notice that there was a little more stone rubble near the entrance than he remembered.

The three of them rested not far away for two full days, until Whitlock was feeling better. Melann administered both conventional aid and magical healing, which brought relief to all of them. During that time, they discussed what they would do next.

"Obviously," Whitlock said, still somewhat weak from his wounds, "Melann and I need to return to Archendale with the staff. We can lift the family curse and present the staff to my father." Whitlock smiled broadly, and Melann joined him in his smile.

"Actually, Whitlock," she said, "I'm not going to return with you right away."

"What?" he asked with a wrinkled brow and a sharp frown.

"You see, Vheod's going to look for his family. With all that's happened, he can do that. He could use some help; he's still very new to this world.

"It won't take both of us to carry the staff," she told him. "You'll be fine to travel by tomorrow." She paused, looking her brother in the eye. "You understand, don't you?"

Whitlock stared back at her for a long while. He finally replied, "Yes, I suppose I do," and managed a smile.

Melann saw now that Chauntea had never abandoned her, and that she had never abandoned Chauntea. The goddess represented goodness, order, purity, the sanctity of life, and the nature of all growing things. As long as Melann, as a representative of the Mother of All here in the world of mortals, dwelt on those ideals, upheld them and lived her life in a way that fostered and encouraged those beliefs, her will and the goddess's will would not be in conflict. She'd finally found peace with herself in that fact. She'd found the frame of mind required of her to truly serve Chauntea in the best possible way.

For now—and maybe forever—that way meant helping Vheod. Not only did she love him for what he was, but she felt compelled to stand at his side to help him become what he could be. She smiled at the thought of it. She was suddenly bound on another quest, confident this time that it was the right thing to do.

* * * * *

Vheod left the siblings alone while Melann told Whitlock that she had decided to travel with him. He was still anxious to find the human part of his heritage. It would be good to develop actual ties with this world. Such ties would allow him to feel like he belonged here, which at the moment, was the second most important thing to him.

The most important thing, he'd realized over the last few days, was Melann. He loved her. She was everything he wanted to be, and he wanted more than anything to be with her and to help her in whatever she set out to do. He wondered still if he actually deserved to be with her. The Taint, glaring up at him from his arm, certainly made him question that. Did the dark side of his soul represent a danger? He certainly hoped not, but how could he ever be certain?

Can a man overcome his own inborn nature?

The answer depends on the man.

An Excerpt

Silverfall

Stories of the Seven Sisters

Ed Greenwood

**Available in August, 1999
From TSR**

The Chionthar runs slow, cold, and foul past the mud-choked pilings and wharves of the Caravan City. If she'd still needed to breathe, its muddy bottom would have been Qilué's grave. As it was, she gave herself over to waiting in the numbing cold until all her slayers turned away. She knew well the impatience that ruled most dark elves, as it had once governed her, before she'd truly come to know and embrace Mystra.

She gave the goddess wry thanks now for this highlight of her career and concentrated on ensuring one of the spells she'd awakened in her last struggle was working properly.

1

Yes, *there*: the faintest, most blurred of touches told her she was linked to Brelma, through the bites she'd landed a time or two, not all that long ago. Right now the lady drow was striding rather grimly through the disarray of the grandest room in the Eldeglut mansion, looking urgently for the glass of wine she'd been in the middle of when all the trouble with the spy had started. Good. That was a link Qilué would follow in the days to come.

It was probably time to call on one of her other active spells and end her drifting in mud that was rather too rich in long-dead, rotting fish—and hungry, very-much-alive lampreys with a taste for recently delivered bodies—for her liking. Being dead, Qilué judged, was decidedly undignified, chilly, and boring.

* * * * *

It was the practice of the barge merchant Welver Thauburn to shift his most valuable cargoes a little way downstream and across the Chionthar, early in the dark hours of a night—a little thing, but it baffled a surprising number of thieves into spending fruitless, cursing hours groping blindly up and down the wrong riverbank. Welver kept an eye and ear out for such nuisances as crossbow bolts and strong swimmers at such times, but he was entirely unprepared for the sudden eruption, from the waters not an arm's reach away from where he sat against the rail of his best barge, of a bound and blindfolded woman's body.

It burst up into the air, hung almost above him for one terrifying moment, dripping as it blotted out the stars, then flew rapidly and silently away to the northwest. Welver stared after it, hastily drained his hip flask of Old Raw Comfort, then hurled the flask into the river, vowing to give up strong drink forever. Well, perhaps after this coming dawn, when he'd drunk dry the keg waiting for him in his cellar. . . .

* * * * *

"Simylra," Cathlona Tabbartan asked archly, shifting her peacock-feather fan to better display the dusting of diamonds in her upswept hair, "tell me, pray: *who* is that vision of manliness below? In the silver and green scales."

Her companion leaned forward over the balcony rail, in a gesture designed to display her diamond-dusted, fur-supported breastworks to all of reveling Waterdeep. "That, I declare, must be Lord Emveolstone," she said, then gave a little shriek of excitement—not the only one to rise just then from an otherwise breathless female throat—and gasped, "Oh, but cousin Cat, look you now upon a dragon incarnate! Could it be that Danilo Thann?"

Cathlona bent forward over the rail in a near plunge that sent the spindle-shaped, rose-hued crystals of her pectoral dancing against her heavily rouged chin, and said, "I-I can't tell who it is; that dragon head entirely covers him. . . . He must be looking out of its jaws!"

The lord in question was wearing a splendid silver specimen of what by now were over two dozen ridiculous dragon suits that the two cousins from Amn had seen grandly entering the festivities at their first Waterdhavian nobles' revel. They couldn't even recall the name of the noble family hosting this costume ball, but it was certainly grand. Servants were plying all of the guests with decanters of drink and silver pyramids of sugar-dusted pastries, and Cathlona, for one, was already feeling rather sick.

She righted herself hastily, looking a little green, gave her cousin a weak smile, and sat back to fan herself with rather more enthusiasm than grace. "My word, Simmy—how're they going to dance in such arrays, do you think?"

"The costumes *do* come off," her cousin said testily, "and I'll thank you not to call me by that—that disgustingly silly nickname!"

"There are no silly names," a glorious voice drawled near at hand, "in the presence of such beauty."

The cousins turned as one to stare at the speaker—and emitted identical gasps of hungry awe.

The object of their attention was a man whose fine features were adorned rather than ruined by a finely upswept mustache, its chestnut magnificence overwhelmed by the curly sweep of hair that must have reached to the man's waist but was bound up in a scarlet ribbon to keep it clear of the spotless green shoulders of his elegantly cut festive jacket. He was lean and lithe beneath the devastatingly simple lines of his garb, but from the lace at his wrists to that at his throat, every curve of his form betrayed sleek strength and flaring, ready muscle. As for his gray silken breeches, with their discreet codpiece—why, the tight bottom they displayed to the world as he bowed and turned to leave them made both cousins gasp again, then swallow . . . then turn to each other to share an incredulously delighted squeal.

As he glided swiftly away down carpeted steps, the man in the dark green jacket managed to sufficiently suppress a shudder that neither of the overly plump Amnian ladies noticed.

"Who *is* that delectable man?" Simylra Lavartil inquired of the world at large, ruffling the furs that supported her bosom with an enthusiasm that threatened to shred them.

"That, madam," a servant murmured, as he bent to offer her a fresh drink of manycherries wine from a tray of full tallglasses, "is Dumathchess Ilchoas, as yet bereft of any noble title . . . though I believe the ladies have given him one; they've taken to calling him 'Dauntless.' "

Simylra thanked him profusely, and proved the fervor of her gratitude by seizing not one but three glasses from his tray, draining them in rapid succession before hurling herself back in her chair to stare at her cousin with a gasp of mingled satiation, longing, and delight.

"Dauntless!" she cried. "Oh, can the world *hold* such pleasures?"

"Evidently, madam, not for long," the servant murmured disapprovingly, as he surveyed the wreckage of his tray and glided away without giving Cathlona an opportunity to work similar havoc upon it.

She stared sourly after the dwindling form of the servant, and asked, "So just what did our Dauntless see over that rail to make him abandon us—nay, *spurn* us—in such unseemly haste?"

Simylra gathered her strength with a visible effort and leaned forward again to gasp anew. "Why, it's the most daring costume yet!"

"Some lord's come naked?" Cathlona asked, raising her delicately plucked brows questioningly.

"No, cuz . . . not a lord, but a lady, and not *quite* naked. She's wearing some black leather straps"—

and Simylra giggled and colored prettily, waving a few fingers before her mouth—"here and there, you know. They must bear some powerful spells; her disguise is nearly perfect."

"Her disguise as *what?*" Cathlona asked, not quite daring to lean forward again after her previous experience.

"A drow princess," Simylra breathed, her eyes glittering with envy as she watched the new arrival sweep across the entry hall with catlike grace and every male eye below turn toward her.

The lady was daring indeed to come as an outlawed, evil being, wearing little more than a pair of gleaming black buttock-high boots with silver heel spikes, and elbow length gloves of the same material. Her breasts and loins seemed to be covered by nothing more than crisscrossing leather straps hung with spindle-shaped rock crystal stones, and a black ribbon encircled her throat. Her hair reached to the backs of her knees in a magnificent raven dark sweep that was bound in a cage of silver chain ending in two delicate chains, little larger than glittering threads that hung in loops attached to the spurs of her boots. Two tiny bells hung from pointed silver medallions glued to her nipples, and she wore a calm, crooked smile that broadened as the man known as Dauntless swept up to her and proffered his arm. As she turned to display herself to him, the two gaping cousins saw that a walnut-sized diamond bulged glitteringly from her navel—and that a tiny sculpted dagger hung point-downward from the cluster of diamonds and silver scrollwork at her loins.

"Gods," Simylra murmured, and swallowed noisily. "How can anyone compete with *that?*"

"Simmy," her cousin said grimly, "either get me a drink—a very *large* drink—or let me go home."

* * * * *

"May I say, my lady, what a splendid costume you chose to grace our eyes with, this night?" Dauntless offered gallantly, keeping his eyes carefully on hers.

Qilué laughed, low and musically. "You may indeed say so, Lord Dauntless. I find your own appearance very pleasing on the eyes."

Dauntless chuckled. "As I've said, good lady, I'm hardly a lord—but I am, I must confess, a man smitten. I would know your name."

In reply he got a light laugh and the murmured comment, as the devastatingly lovely lady leaned into his grasp, "I'd much rather remain a woman of mystery this night, if you don't mind."

"Ah, but I do," Dauntless said smoothly, handing her forward into a curtained alcove where a waiter was holding a tray of drinks ready. "A *woman*, did you say? You mean you're not really a drow princess?"

"A drow princess? No," Qilué replied, curling long fingers around a glass. "Magic can work wonders for the outward appearance, if deftly applied."

"Your own spellcraft," Dauntless asked, leading her on into a shadowed bower, "or did someone else transform you?"

"Dauntless," the lips so close to his breathed, "that would be telling, now, wouldn't it?"

The Harper moved in close, until their noses were almost touching, and said, "I appreciate both your choice of such a daring disguise and the skill with which it has been spun."

Her response was a low purr of laughter and the huskily whispered words, "Go ahead, my lord, test it."

Dauntless looked into her eyes, found a welcome there, and extended his head forward until their lips met . . . and clung, tongues darting a soft duel . . . then tightened, mouth to mouth, bodies melting together.

When at last they broke apart to breathe, Qilué spun deftly out of his arms and asked, "So, Dauntless, do I pass your test?"

"Several tests, and more, Lady of Mystery. Are you free for the rest of this evening—or any part of it?"

"Regretfully, no, my lord. Business brings me hither, and business must be my master this night. Had I freedom to pursue pleasure, good Dauntless, rest assured that I'd be at your heels, and nowhere else, until dawn—and as long after as you might desire."

"Forgive my forwardness, lady," the Harper murmured, "but tell me, if your true shape returned to you at any time during such a pursuit as you've suggested, would I be aghast? Or disappointed?"

"That, my lord Dauntless, would depend entirely on your own tastes and inclinations," the dark elf said gently. "Not, I believe, on whom I turned out to be. I'm not one of the well-known and well-wrinkled noble matrons of the city, gone out to play in a disguise. It is my fond hope that my true shape would not offend you overmuch. Now, if you'll excuse me? That business I mentioned, you understand."

"Of course," the handsome young man agreed, bowing deeply. "The pleasure has been mine."

"Well, someday perhaps 'twill be," she purred in reply. She unhurriedly stroked the back of one of his hands. then put her emptied wine glass into the other before she stepped away.

Dauntless watched her lilt away across the room beyond the bower, through an envious and watchful crowd, and his eyes slowly narrowed. Business here, now, would be what exactly?

What would a drow pretending to be a human wearing the spell-shape of a drow be doing here at a revel for nobles and would-be nobles?

She'd left suddenly, as if catching sight of someone she wanted to meet. Who?

Dauntless faded in behind a potted fern as the Lady of Mystery turned at the far end of the room to look back, almost challengingly. Gods, but her lips had been inviting. . . .

He was doomed to spend most of the next hour acting innocent and unobtrusive, trying to stay in the background but within sight of the drow princess as she glided enthusiastically around the revel, letting many men and women test the efficacy of her costume. Often, Dauntless was sure—though she never once looked in his direction—she did so just to silently tease him.

It wasn't until the end of the second hour, after frequent subterfuges of being either drunk or about to be sick to escape the clutches of enthusiastic matron after smitten matron, that Dauntless thought he saw the guest his drow princess was shadowing. He wasn't sure until that person—a buxom lady in a plain-fronted mauve gown with shoulder ruffles—suddenly moved to a spiral stair masquerading as a large spiral plant stand in one corner of the room she was in, and began to climb it.

The Lady of Mystery moved purposefully, too—to a dark alcove where a beaded curtain hid her from public view for, it seemed, just long enough. By the time Dauntless drifted up to it, it was empty—but the casements of its lone window stood open to the night.

He peered out and up once, quick and quiet, and was rewarded by the sight of a shapely body the hue of glossy jet climbing up through the shadows of the wall to a stone gargoyle-shaped waterspout protruding from the overhanging balcony on the floor above. The same balcony the spiral stair led to. In another instant, his Lady of Mystery was going to be hanging upside down from that gargoyle, just under one end of the balcony.

He'd have to move like silent lightning, but there was another window—and another gargoyle—at the other end of the balcony, hidden from the Lady of Mystery's perch by the curving buttresses that supported the balcony. Fortunately Dauntless could move like silent lightning, and he did so.

Out and up, thus, and he was there. A pleasant night outside, to be sure. He'd just hang around for a while in the cool night air to catch whatever words the lady in purple was going to whisper over the balcony rail. He hoped—before all the gods, he hoped—they wouldn't be something that would force him to have to kill his Lady of Mystery.

The voices began, then, and Dauntless got another surprise. The first voice was unfamiliar to him, but he could see from purple ruffles and a moving chin, just visible over the edge of the balcony, that the speaker was the lady in purple. The second belonged to someone who must have been already on the balcony, waiting. It was a distinctive, harsh croak that belonged to only one woman in all Waterdeep: Mrilla Malsander, one of the most ambitious of the rich merchants currently trying to become noble by any means possible. Their words were sinister but too cryptic to force him to kill anyone.

Qilué clung to the crumbling curves of the snarling gargoyle, and listened intently as the slaver Brelma—who made a very fetching lady in purple, she had to admit—said without any preamble or greeting, "The trouble was a spy, but she's dead now. The project is still unfolding nicely."

"Good," the other lady replied, her voice like the croak of a raven. "See that it continues to do so. If not, you know whom to speak with." With that she turned away and started down the stair, leaving Brelma to look innocently—perhaps wonderingly— out at the lamplit night skyline of Waterdeep.

* * * * *

As Qilué swung herself back in through the window, she felt another twinge of the nausea that had plagued her recently, and it strengthened her resolve. Duty to Dove was one thing, and blundering around in Waterdeep making matters worse was another. The time for an expert on drow was past; the time for an expert on the City of Splendors had come . . . and her sister Laeral dwelt not a dozen streets away, in the brooding city landmark of Blackstaff Tower.

She must now enlist Laeral in taking over the unfolding investigation of the dark elven invasion of Scornubel, and whatever lay behind it, just as Dove had enlisted her. A drow priestess is a little out of her depth in the interwoven, bloodied velvet politics of Waterdhavian nobility—and can't help but be just a mite obvious, too.

Leaving the revel swiftly was simplicity itself. Every Waterdhavian mansion has servants' stairs, and in the shadowed candlelight, concealing gloom was everywhere. If her handsome pursuer wanted to come along, he was quite welcome. Whether he was part of those she was investigating or some nosy Waterdhavian watchwolf, Blackstaff Tower should give him something to think about.

One of her own covert contacts in the city had told her that the endless renovations to the tower interior had recently reached a pace she described as "enthusiastic," but hopefully the back entrance Qilué remembered still existed. She strolled unconcernedly thence through the streets of the city, acting as if she had every right to be there. The three watch patrols she encountered gave her hard stares, seemed about to challenge her, then thought better of it. She must be a noble matron wealthy enough to squander spells on a party disguise. After all, didn't real drow creep and skulk about, maniacally attacking any human they saw?

With that sarcastic thought still twisting her lips, Qilué came to a certain spot along the curving tower wall, turned to face the dark stone, and with her fingertips traced a line to a certain spot. Her fingers dipped into an almost invisible seam, then emerged, moving diagonally a little way down to touch a junction of stone blocks, before—she knelt smoothly—darting into a gap right at ground level. The wall receded silently into itself, magic lending a velvet silence to what should have been a grating of weighty stone, and Qilué slipped into a dark embrasure.

It would remain open for only a few seconds before the wall shifted forward again to expel her straight back out onto the street, but if she reached *thus* in the darkness, a side way should open. . . .

It did, and Qilué stepped forward through some space of magical darkness into a dimly lit, curving passage whose inside wall was seamed with many closed cupboard doors, warning radiances flickering around their locks and catches. What she sought was just ahead: a tall, narrow cupboard or closet door.

There it was. A touch here should open it, and—

The moment she touched the panel, a sickening, tingling feeling told Qilué that something was wrong. The lock spells must have been changed. She stepped hastily back and away from the panel—but the flock of guardian hands bursting out of the outer wall of the passage swerved unerringly toward her, snatching and grabbing with their usual icy accuracy.

With three quick slaps the drow priestess kept them clear of her face and throat, then Qilué simply hunched down, gasping at the pain, and endured their cruel grasps all over the rest of her body. Oh, would she have bruises.

She could try to pry off each of the flying obsidian hands and shatter them before they began their numbing, ultimately paralyzing washes of electricity, but she needed to see Laeral anyway, and a little lockpicking would attract immediate attention from the duty apprentice seeing to the wards.

Struggling against the rigid holds of the gripping hands, Qilué plucked the dangling dagger ornament from her crotch, twisted it to its full length, and shielded it in her palm from any guardian hand strikes or clawings. Khelben's one failing was to purchase all of his locks, before he laid spells upon them, from the same dwarven crafter whose work, sold in Skullport to the few who could afford it, was familiar to Qilué. Their maker had shown her the one way to force them open. It required a lockpick of just the right angle . . . like this one.

A sudden movement, a twist, a click, and the panel sighed open. Qilué got her nails under the edge, hauled it open with a strength that surprised the being who was watching her by then, and sprang onward, straight to the next door.

The duty apprentice was attentive. As Qilué moved, the hands began to crawl up her body with bruising force, seeking joints to jam themselves in, and her throat to strangle. Qilué snarled her defiance at them as she picked the next door, rushed up a short flight of steps, then threw herself out of the way of the huge iron fist that slammed down across the passage.

The iron golem it belonged to emerged into the narrow way with ponderous care, and by then she was through the door beyond and into a room where spheres of flickering radiance drifted toward her from all sides in menacing, purposeful silence.

"Khelben!" she snapped to the empty air, as magic missiles burst from her hands to destroy these guardians, "Laeral! Call off your watchwolves! I've no wish to destroy them!"

Numbing lightnings were leaping from the hands on her body, now, playing across her skin until she hissed at the pain and stumbled like a drunken dockhand under their punishment. The next door was there, but could she reach it?

Grimly Qilué staggered on, gesturing rudely at a crystal sphere that descended from the dimness near the ceiling. Its depths held a voice that said, "She called on the lord and lady master. We'd best open the doors."

It also held the frightened face of a young man sitting at a glowing table, who stared out of the sphere at the struggling intruder and gasped, "But she's a drow!"

"Get Laeral!" Qilué roared. "Bring her to me, or I'll start *really* destroying things." In sudden fury she tore a crawling guardian hand from her breast, waved it at the sphere, and hurled it to the floor, bounding onto it with all her strength and ignoring the lightnings it spat around her boots as it died. "Are you deaf, duty apprentice?"

"You hear? She knows our duties. She must be—"

"Half Waterdeep has heard of the defenses of Blackstaff Tower," the young man said scornfully. "She's a dark elf, and *I'm* not letting any dark elf into this room with us."

"But—"

"But nothing. You've always been too soft, Araeralee! You'd let Szass Tam of Thay in here, if he put on the body of a beautiful maid and whimpered at the door. How do we know that isn't him now? Or Manshoon of the Zhentarim, up to another of his tricks?"

"Well, I'm rousing Lady Laeral to decide for herself."

"Araeralee, don't you *dare*! This is my duty watch, and—dark gods take you, wench! You've done it! You've burning well gone and done it! It'll be the lash of spells for you, once I tell Khelben. Now I'm going to have to rouse all the apprentices . . . don't you know we're supposed to do that first, before bothering the masters? *Drown* you!"

"Drown you, enthusiastic young idiot," Qilué snarled at the sphere as she forced the lock of the next door and came out into a large, many-pillared chamber that by rights shouldn't have fit within the tower walls, but which was probably on some other plane or fold of spellspace . . . a chamber rapidly filling with barefoot, sleepy-eyed apprentices.

"A drow!" one of them gasped, and others quickly took up the cry. Young faces frowned in fear and determination, and young hands moved in a weaver's nightmare of complicated gestures.

* * * * *

In the chamber whose domed ceiling winked with glimmering stars, Laeral stirred, lifting her head from Khelben's bare, hairy shoulder. The chiming came again, and the Lord Mage of Waterdeep answered it with a louder, barking snore. Laeral's lips twisted in wry amusement. Of course.

She sat up, her silvery hair stirring around her bare shoulders, and sighed. The books they'd been studying lay spread open around them on the bed, abandoned for slumber, and Laeral carefully lifted her long legs over them as she rolled off the bed, plucked up a robe, and went to see what was wrong.

She was still padding down the tower stairs with a crystal sphere of stored spells winking ready in her hand when she heard shouts from below, the whoosh of released magic, then a blast that shook the entire tower.

She lurched against the wall, cradling the sphere to keep it from a shattering fall—and was promptly flung across the stair by another, even more powerful blast.

"*True* trouble," she murmured to the world at large and launched herself down the stairs in a long glide that called on the stairway enchantments to let her fly—and not crash on her face.

The tower shuddered and shook under another blast before she hit the bottom, and a long, racing crack opened in the wall beside her. Laeral lifted her eyebrows at it as she plunged through an archway where dust was drifting down, headlong into the battle raging below.

* * * * *

"Gods above!" Dauntless murmured, as the door he'd seen the drow slip through banged open in front of his nose, and dust swirled out. There was a dull, rolling boom, and doors and windows creaked and slammed all over the tower. "I must be crazed to leap into this," he murmured, touched the silver harp badge pinned to the inside throat of his jacket for luck—and trotted into the booming darkness. Not far away, in the shadow of another building, a cloaked and hooded figure the Harper hadn't noticed nodded to itself and turned away.

The passages inside were an inferno of whirling spell energies, swirling dust, and shouts—but he could follow their fury up and on, stumbling in the gloom, until he came out into a room whose floor was cracked and tilted crazily, where dust-cloaked figures knelt and scrambled and waved their arms in spellcasting.

In their midst, standing alone in a ring of fires in the center of the room, was his beautiful Lady of Mystery, shards of black glass all around her, something that looked like silver smoke boiling away from her sweat-bedewed body, and fury blazing out of her dark face. He almost cowered back at the sight of it—and in his moment of hesitation, a white-faced young man in flapping robes

17

bounded out from behind a pillar with a long, bared sword in his hand, green-glowing runes shimmering up and down its heavy blade, and charged at the drow.

Spells slammed into her from three sides as he ran, almost tripping over the embroidered edge of his robe, but she was staggering helplessly in their grip when he skidded to a halt, grimly aimed his blade—and with both hands thrust it through her flat belly.

The Lady of Mystery coughed silver fire almost into the duty apprentice's face, and he reeled back as the sword shattered with a wild shrieking, spat bright shards away in all directions, and slumped into dust around the convulsed dark elf. The young wizard hurled himself away in real horror as silver fire scorched his cheek and he realized who—or rather, *what*—this intruder must be. A cold, bright golden glow cracked across the chamber, Dauntless found himself slammed back against its wall in the company of all of the dusty robed figures, and a furious Lady Mage of Waterdeep strode barefooted into the center of the room, snarling, "Is *this* the hospitality of Blackstaff Tower?"

In the utter silence that followed her shout, Laeral set down a crystal sphere she'd been carrying and strode toward the drow who was standing upright again, silver fire blazing up around her in an unearthly nimbus of glowing smoke.

Laeral's unbound hair swirled around her as she stretched forth her hands, like a mother desiring a daughter's embrace, and asked in a voice not far from tears, "Sister—too long unseen—what troubles you?"

"My own ineptitude," Qilué replied, and burst into tears. She swayed amid silver flames, weeping, for a long moment, then, with a sob, rushed into Laeral's waiting arms.

August 1999!

Lost Empires

The series that uncovers the hidden secrets of the
FORGOTTEN REALMS® world's most ancient, and most dangerous civilizations. Explore the ruins of Faerûn in:

The Lost Library of Cormanthyr
Mel Odom

To avenge the murder of his mentor, the ranger-
archeologist Baylee must battle the Waterdeep Watch, a lich
and his drow henchman, and the spirit of a centuries-dead
elf, and find a storehouse of ancient knowledge lost for six
hundred years.

Faces of Deception
Troy Denning

Atreus wants nothing more than to be beautiful again,
and will travel to a hidden valley in the faraway Utter East
for even the slimmest hope of success. Will the price of
acceptance be too high?

Star of Cursrah
Clayton Emery

The sands of the Calim Desert hide many secrets, and
powerful forces willing to do anything to keep it that way.

And coming in 2000 . . .

The Nether Scroll
Lynn Abbey

What lurks in the darkest corners of the haunted Weath-
ercote Wood? A race for the possession of one of Faerûn's
greatest artifacts is on, and the Beast Lord himself is in the
running!

From under the waves of the FORGOTTEN REALMS® world's mightiest oceans comes a rising tide of war, hatred, and death—and the face of Faerûn will never be the same again.

The beginning of the first must-read series since Avatar—*Rising Tide* begins the epic story of the Threat from the Sea, a story that continues in:

And coming in 2000:

Featuring stories set against the backdrop of the sea invasion by R.A. Salvatore, Ed Greenwood, Elaine Cunningham, Troy Denning, Lynn Abbey, Mel Odom, and a host of your favorite FORGOTTEN REALMS authors!

The epic tale concludes in:

October, 1999

You'll never look at the blue spaces on your maps the same way again. . . .

R.A. Salvatore

The Spine of the World

The New York Times best-selling author returns with the sequel to last year's hardcover sensation *The Silent Blade*.

Wulfgar's life is at a crossroads and he finds the path to redemption to be the most dangerous, most treacherous, and most important journey of his life.

Available in hardcover
September, 1999

The Silent Blade

"Salvatore shows here . . . intelligence in using the classic elements, a pleasant dry wit and a narrative gift that make this book certain to keep FORGOTTEN REALMS readers turning pages."

—*Publisher's Weekly*

The Silent Blade reunites Drizzt, Wulfgar, Cattie-brie, Bruenor, and Regis in a quest to destroy the hated Crystal Shard once and for all.

Now available in hardcover.
Available in paperback June, 1999